THE ROOTS OF FURY

A World of Fury: Book 2

By Jacob Alan Richmond

◇◇◇◇◇◇◇◇◇
PREFACE

March 2019

Hello, reader. First, thanks for being a fan of my first book, *The Love of Fury*.

Second, I think prefacing is generally uncool, indulgent, and unnecessary. And if that's true, imagine the adjectives you'd need to describe this preface to the preface. Despite that, I decided to write this preface because I care about *you*.

It's amazing to me that so many people loved my debut novel. I'm not sure that will ever fully dawn on me. I'm humbled. I'm indebted. I'm honored. It also makes me beholden. More to the point, as I finished writing Book 2, I realized it was making me pretty scared. Why? Because *this* book is not like *that* book.

Basically, I want you to feel surprised, but not tricked.

The Love of Fury was pretty traditional in a lot of ways. It had a beginning, middle, and end. It followed a couple of main characters through a journey of tension, growth, and ultimate realization. I tried to stick to what works, but make it better, faster, sharper.

The Roots of Fury is a little more sprawling. You'll get to know more characters, but not quite as well as you got to know Percy and Rafiq. There's plenty of action, I think, but not compared its predecessor.

Specifically, I want to warn you that there are several email exchanges between Maggie and Nabaa, and those email exchanges are purposefully heady and meandering. I feel like I know those characters pretty well by now, so I believe that the emails are also realistic — the way they'd be written if the two characters were actually corresponding. But do lengthy, realistically written emails belong in a novel that's in the thriller category? That was a question I got from a couple of people who read early versions of this book.

So I considered deleting them altogether. I considered shortening them so they appeared as excerpts that ended with ellipses, encouraging the reader to explore the topics externally. I considered adding all the emails, in sequence, as bonus material after the epilogue. Of course, I also considered leaving them as-is and saying, "Fuck it — they'll get it or they won't."

In the end, I trimmed them as much as I could, left them within the novel's timeline … and wrote this lame preface. That means you can feel free to skip right over the email chapters, if you want. Read them all as they're placed, read them at the end — or don't. Your call. Either way, I don't think it'll get in the way of your understanding of the story.

Just one more thought before you jump in: Book 1 was a rocket ship ride, and it did its job — it brought you into the orbit of this *World of Fury*. But this trilogy is not a series of three rocket rides; it's one long expedition. Along the way, I hope it'll inspire you to think more about our deepest human flaws and how they get in the way of our highest potential. I'm eternally grateful that you decided to follow me on the trip, and I promise I'm doing my best to reward your investment. All I ask is that you don't expect it to be something familiar.

There. See? I've self-deprecated, I've complimented you, I've thanked you, and I've warned you. And thus I've successfully abdicated my responsibility to entertain you. Prefaces are great.

PROLOGUE

August 2010

In the distance, Percy Mackenzie could see thermal waves rising from the vast, flat, concrete flight line of Luke Air Force Base, Arizona. They'd been sitting in air-conditioned buildings all morning, so his skin welcomed the dry, 105-degree air.

The last time I was here, he thought, *this airfield was on fire.*

He closed his eyes, opened them again, and took a deep, quiet breath.

He noticed motion in his left periphery, and he straightened himself a little. Lined up on his right were his wife, Maggie, his adopted daughter, Nabaa, and his father, retired Air Force Colonel Michael Mackenzie. On his left, immediately next to the red-carpeted steps attached to the stair truck, were Lieutenant Colonel Paul Wooters, the commander of Luke's security forces squadron, and Tom Tulloch, the commander of the entire installation.

A huge armored sedan slowed to a stop to Percy's right. A few men in dark suits stood loosely around it. Other men in dark suits approached from the rest of the motorcade and gathered in the shade next to the stairs.

United States President Christopher Brennan emerged from the open door of Air Force One and descended the steps. At the bottom, he returned salutes from both military officers and shook their hands quickly but warmly. Then he turned to Percy and beamed.

"Good to see you, man," Brennan said, grabbing Percy's outstretched hand.

"You, too, sir," Percy said.

Brennan let go and locked eyes with Maggie. "And you as well, Mrs. Mackenzie." He held out an upturned hand in a gentlemanly fashion.

"Oh no, sir," Maggie said. She outstretched her arms, leaned in and forcefully embraced Brennan, who laughed and squeezed her back. "It's my policy," she said into his ear. "Anybody involved with my daughter's rescue gets a hug." Maggie released the president and, still holding his shoulders, showed him her most thankful smile.

He beamed back, then took another step and turned to Nabaa. "And it's a sincere pleasure to finally see you again, young lady."

Nabaa glanced at Maggie, then held out her hand.

Brennan shook it and let go, still smiling. "Not quite the hugger your mom is, huh?"

1

"Percy has a rule," Nabaa said. She clasped her hands behind her waist. "He and Grandpa Mike are the only guys I hug until I am 16."

"Pretty good policy," Brennan said, glancing over at Percy.

"You can consider the President of the United States an exception to that rule," Percy said to Nabaa. "But always err on the side of caution, right?"

She nodded politely. *There's no rule against smiling,* Percy thought. But he knew she was still uncertain about all of this, despite all his pleas and explanations. She had no interest in coming back here. She didn't understand why he wanted to. Why he had to give the speech after all this time. So he had tried to persuade her. Fear can't be our guide, he'd said, many times in many forms. You'll feel better afterward. I'll feel better afterward. We'll close a book that needs to be closed. She told him he was being prideful, that fear was smart sometimes. She always let him have the last word, but he knew he hadn't convinced her. He'd barely convinced himself.

Nabaa was here because Maggie asked her to relent. But she wouldn't pretend to be happy about it.

Percy couldn't blame her. It was a lot for him to ask of her, coming back here just a few months after the attack. And Maggie, too. *This better go well.*

Brennan turned to the elder Mackenzie. "Colonel Mackenzie, I'm so glad we finally get to meet. Heard a lot about you."

"Is that right?" Michael said, shaking the president's hand.

"Yeah, it sure is," Brennan said. "When I heard this boy of yours was basically raised by a single dad, I had to learn a little about the hero behind the hero. Well done, Mike."

"Oh, I just tried to survive the teenage years mostly," he said. "His mother did a pretty damn great job before she died."

"I don't doubt it." They both glanced at Percy, who smiled and nodded.

"Excuse me, Mr. President," Colonel Tulloch said. "I believe this is where we say farewell for now. But we'll be here to see you off later on."

"Of course, Colonel," Brennan said. "And Paul —" He turned to Wooters. "We'll chat then, ok?"

Wooters said, "Absolutely, sir." He and Tulloch rendered a departing salute and headed toward the nearby building.

As they left, the president's eyes scanned the expansive airfield, and his mood visibly changed. Dozens of F-16s were parked next to and underneath what looked like jet-sized carports. In the distance, a few airmen busied themselves with routine maintenance activities.

"It's a little weird being back here now," Brennan said. "Air Force life looking like it's all back to normal."

"Yeah," Percy agreed. "Definitely weird. But … good, you know?" They shared a moment of silence. "When were you here last? A week after the attack?"

Brennan nodded. "Four days," he said. "You?"

"First time since the day of," Percy said. "It definitely took some mental effort to walk through the door onto the flight line. But I got over it pretty quickly. I've got a damned good therapist."

Brennan smiled sincerely. "You better." An unidentified member of his entourage approached from Brennan's right side. The president turned and nodded, then looked back at Percy. "Shall we?"

"Yes, sir." Percy took Maggie's hand, and his dad took Nabaa's. The four of them followed President Brennan toward the black sedan 10 yards away. Just under the left wing of the aircraft was another presidential limousine with two black SUVs behind it. Parked ahead and off the nose were two more black SUVs and two military police cruisers at the front of the line. "Not much of a motorcade today, sir," Percy said. "I thought I was a bigger deal than this."

"The Full Monty is right over there," Brennan said. He nodded his head to the left and waited for Percy follow his gaze. "They'll catch up once we start moving."

About 50 yards farther down the flight line, Percy counted eight other vehicles. Four large passenger vans, two white SUVs, an ambulance, and one vehicle that looked like a U-Haul truck painted all black and with sirens on top of the cab.

"That looks about right, sir," Percy told Brennan. They shared a smile.

"Good. And I hear we'll have plenty of local cruisers guiding the way once we leave the base. Your popularity is not in question, at least in these few square miles."

The president saw Nabaa glancing back and forth between the Cadillac in front of them and the one under the wing. "You look like you've got some questions, Nabaa," Brennan said. "Fire away."

She looked at the president blandly. "What is the difference?"

"I'm not the best person to answer that, actually," Brennan said. He turned to the secret service agent holding the back passenger door. "Jeff, can you answer the young lady's question?"

"Yes, sir. This one," the agent said, tapping the door, "has rocket-propelled grenades, multi-spectrum infrared smoke grenades, and pump-action shotguns. And that one," he said, swinging his pointing finger to the other limo, "has bulletproof windows, night vision optics, onboard oxygen tanks, and a tear gas cannon."

Brennan smiled widely as Maggie's eyes opened in surprise. Nabaa furrowed her brow. "What Jeff failed to mention, is that they *both* have all that stuff, and plenty more. They're identical. I think Jeff here just

3

flips a coin every time to decide which one I ride in. Speaking of coins …"

He pulled an official presidential challenge coin from his pocket and handed it to Nabaa. She briefly inspected both sides, then pocketed it.

"I'd rather just choose myself," she said. Then she strode under the arm of the secret service agent and stepped into the limousine.

"Your charm works on most people," Percy said, smiling. "Nabaa is immune."

"Yeah," Brennan said, motioning to Maggie to go ahead. "My only problem is that I'm really, really aware of how charming I am, which occasionally ruins the charm. The curse of an accomplished politician."

Percy, and then Brennan himself, entered the limousine, and the doors closed with a heavy, but quiet thud.

The motorcade slowly made its way through the flight line entry-control point. Then they felt the vehicle speed up significantly. At the exit gate for the base itself, they were joined by a half-dozen motorcycles. A few of them accelerated and pulled ahead to stop intersecting traffic.

"So, what exactly are all these vehicles for?" Maggie asked, looking out the back window. "Do they all have an actual function?"

"One is to keep me connected to the internet at all times," Brennan said. "One is to send out jamming signals to block the communication of other people nearby who might try to spy on me. A couple are carrying my staff. A couple are carrying the journalists who follow me around and write about everything I do. And the other limo is just a decoy, so you don't know which one I'm riding in. But in case someone attacks us anyway, one of those SUVs is carrying my Secret Service protective team, who will whisk me away from danger at a moment's notice. And another one is carrying a group of guys who will ignore me and focus on eliminating the threat. Am I forgetting something?" He cocked his head in thought. "Probably," he said, shrugging. "Either way, it's all for me," he said, pointing a thumb at his chest and sending a wink at Nabaa. "Because, as you all know, I am very, very important. The world cannot afford to lose me."

She almost smiled, Percy noticed. Then she turned her gaze back out the window.

"And yet, you probably have the third-highest national approval rating in this vehicle alone," Maggie said, executing a perfectly dramatized wink of her own.

Brennan and Percy both laughed.

"Not a fair fight," the president said. "Mine would be better, too, if I went into hiding for several months."

"I'll continue enjoying the anonymity as long as I can," Percy said.

4

"Oh yeah?" Brennan said. "I think that'll change. You're not the kind of dude who can sit on the sidelines forever. Which reminds me — I've got something to discuss with you on the way back."

Percy nodded. He slid closer to Nabaa, put his arm around her, and kissed the top of her head. They rode in silence for a few minutes until they arrived at Glendale High School.

The motorcade began funneling into the parking lot. They exited the limo, met the principal and vice principal, and someone named Natasha Wilkinson. The latter introduced herself as the "President's communications advance lead." She then turned to Brennan and confirmed the media and communication mandates had all been met.

"Looks like the press embargo stayed solid, Mr. President," she said. "No local media is here, not a single query to the school office or the district. Our pool cameras should be in place within two minutes. Entrance is this way."

She turned, and they followed her and the school administrators along a fifty-foot sidewalk to the side of the gymnasium, where they stopped at a door. Wilkinson nodded at the principal, who walked through the door alone and let it close behind him. Then, Wilkinson pushed her ear against the crack where the door met the threshold and waited. After a few silent seconds, they all heard the principal say, "Students and staff!" A few moments of pause. "It's my pleasure to introduce The President of the United States of America!"

Wilkinson opened the door, and they all followed her in — Secret Service first, then Brennan, Percy, Maggie, Nabaa, Mike Mackenzie, followed by two more agents. The expanse of the gym opened to their left. Chairs covered most of the basketball court floor, each occupied by a teenager. On either side, cascades of bleachers seated hundreds more students. The students maintained a strange silence, probably for the first time in the history of GHS assemblies. The primary industrial air conditioning system labored against Arizona's tireless August heat, edging the silence with its low hum.

The students and staff hadn't been informed about the nature of today's gathering, Percy knew. They probably had assumed it was some routine, start-of-the-school-year pleasantry coordinated by the administrators. He smiled.

Wilkinson motioned to a row of plastic classroom chairs against the near wall. Taking the cue, Percy and his three family members sat down. A half-dozen of Brennan's straggling staff members arrived and gathered at the side of the bleachers, whispering and checking their cell phones. Brennan himself didn't break stride; he walked directly to the lectern that stood just shy of the free-throw line.

Gripping the sides of the lectern, he craned his head over his shoulder in the direction of the principal and said into the microphone,

5

"Tough crowd you've got here, sir. I see you get these young republicans trained early."

The ensuing laugh was tepid, probably from the handful of teachers in the gym, but it was enough to break the tension of the students' surprise at suddenly being in the presence of The President.

"Good morning Glendale!" Brennan's voice bounced off the 100-foot-high ceiling.

The response was fast and loud, if not perfect unison. He had the room.

"I hope you understand why we had to keep this visit as quiet as possible," Brennan said. "This town has been through enough, and I'm certainly not here to bring attention to myself. I brought a few folks with me today who I'm sure you'll be happy to hear from." He half-turned and extended his left hand toward Percy and family. "Percy, Maggie, Nabaa — please say hello."

The three of them stood and waved. A couple of people in the crowd made the connection instantly and began shouting "Woooooooo!" The applause began sporadically, with students leaning toward each other and whispering. Then the shouts and claps snowballed, and within 10 seconds, the entire student body was on their feet clapping, waving, yelling, and high-fiving.

So many wide eyes, Percy thought. So many smiles. Nabaa was squeezing his hand. Brennan was clapping along with them.

Maggie touched his shoulder, lightly tugging him down so she could whisper in his ear. "Some of these kids know you as the person who saved their friend or their brother or sister."

He just took it in. He couldn't name the feeling. He felt a surreal combination of humility and pride and discomfort. But he recognized it. *Just like when I got the Medal of Honor.*

"I want to say a few words …" Brennan paused and let the applause taper. That was the Mackenzies' cue to sit back down. "I want to say a few words before it's Percy's turn, mostly because he's too humble for his own good. You're all familiar with the famous video Fadi Itani made in the moments before his suicide. Now, just a few months later, that video is actually making a huge impact around the world. At this very moment, protesters are gathering in Egypt, Syria, Jordan and Iraq, clamoring for an end to the violence of jihad and the corrupt governments that sponsor it. And it's not because of something we did. It's because the enemy went too far, even for himself. Those who vehemently disagree with American culture and religion still recognize this conflict has gone too far. We have all seen ugliness in this world. The people of Glendale have seen the absolute worst." He took a moment and scanned the faces of the students. "All we can do when we experience something ugly and senseless is reflect on everything in our

6

lives that's beautiful and meaningful. And that's what thousands of people are doing right now, in many other corners of our world."

Or if you're like me, Percy thought, *when you experience something ugly and senseless, you could go overseas and do some ugly and senseless things to a prisoner.* The thought jarred him. He realized with dismay, if his guilt touched him even in this moment, it would be with him forever. His hand went to his upper thigh. He squeezed, simulating his self-punishment of choice: a combat application tourniquet applied with enough force to temporarily stop blood flow, but only briefly. He had gotten good at it over the years.

Maggie noticed, and she placed her hand on his, slowly drawing it over to the middle of her own thigh.

Brennan continued, "You know the Percy Mackenzie who saved a dozen American lives during an ambush in Iraq and prevented countless other deaths by denying our enemies access to an MRAP, our most effective tool against roadside bombs. And, of course, you know the Percy Mackenzie who saved 17 more lives — all children — in the aftermath of the worst terrorist attack in American history, just a few miles from where we are now.

"But you don't know the Percy Mackenzie I know," President Brennan said. "The man who is a shining example of how to respond to adversity. As a 10-year-old boy, he lost his mother in a tragic accident on a hike. He couldn't save her, so he responded with an immutable determination to save others. He resolved to join the Air Force and learn to be an elite pararescue trooper. When that dream was crushed by a devastating ankle injury in training, he responded by choosing a new Air Force job: public affairs and journalism. He chose it because that job would get him on a deployment as soon as possible. When he was on a patrol mission to take photos and write a story about the security forces, his convoy was hit by an IED. They were surrounded by enemies on rooftops, raining down accurate rifle fire. The security forces on the patrol were injured, killed, or pinned in place. Percy responded by single-handedly eliminating the surrounding enemies with rifle fire of his own.

"He and his wife, Maggie, adopted the 12-year-old girl who found herself in the middle of that deadly ambush and later found herself without a family. And we all know that wasn't nearly the end of the horror Nabaa would have to endure." He paused. The gymnasium's silence was reverential.

"Imagine being Nabaa's adoptive father and mother. Imagine that your only daughter went through a living hell at the hands of two men. First, at the hands of Rafiq Itani and his ambush team, and then his father, Fadi Itani. Could you forgive them?" The words echoed through the rafters. Brennan stared out over the sea of teenage faces, waiting.

7

"Percy Mackenzie did," Brennan said. "I don't know about you, but when I first saw Fadi Itani's video — his last act on this earth — it moved me. When he spoke of the futility of vengeance, he sounded like a reformed man who had learned the worst human cost of the worst human obsession. When he spoke to his son, Rafiq, and begged him to 'fight for peace from where you are,' I saw a man of contrition who wished to pay for his sins and stop the cycle of violence.

"I'm a Christian," Brennan said. "I believe in understanding and forgiveness." His eyes fell down to the lectern. After a breath, he picked his head up again. "I'll admit — even now, that's difficult for me. But Percy Mackenzie? You don't know what he did, so I'll tell you. He got Fadi Itani's video on an iPad, traveled down to Naval Base Guantanamo, and paid a visit to Fadi's son, Rafiq." Brennan scanned the room, watching student reactions. The students were at their most rapt now. "Rafiq Itani, the man whose perverse plan to impress his father and steal an American MRAP resulted in the death of two American soldiers, along with Nabaa's own mother. It also set into motion the elder Itani's plan to abduct Maggie and Nabaa, senselessly kill thousands of civilians in front of Percy's own eyes, and then brutally murder Nabaa's siblings for the purposes of propaganda and negotiating leverage.

"But Percy is not a regular man. He understands people. His heart is not only strong enough to ruthlessly defend what he loves, but it's big enough to forgive his enemies. He took Fadi Itani's video to Guantanamo so a son could hear his father's last words."

Brennan paused and shook his head twice. "He's a better man than I am. He's the kind of human being we should all *try* to be. Ladies and gentlemen, I'm honored to introduce Glendale's favorite son, Percival Mackenzie."

A moment passed, then the gym erupted. The sound of applause and whoops and shouts was excruciatingly loud for a solid ten seconds. Then, it either quieted slightly, or Percy went deaf. He wasn't sure.

He stood and walked toward the lectern.

This is crazy, he thought. *How long do I wait to start talking?* He glanced back at Maggie and saw her, Nabaa, and his dad all on their feet, adding their voices and banging hands to the cacophony. Maggie was smiling and gently shooing him forward. Percy realized that he had stopped halfway to the lectern. *Keep walking, dummy.* He turned to President Brennan and got his feet moving again. *Clear out the damned cobwebs and your guilty bullshit, too. You will never forgive yourself if you screw this up.*

Brennan shook Percy's hand and then strode away to take his own seat next to Percy's dad.

Percy looked down at the lectern. There was one primary microphone on a flexible metal shaft. He lifted and stretched it upward to get it closer to his face. He noticed four other lavalier mics resting on the lectern's flat surface. He carefully pushed two of them to the side to make room for his single page of bulleted notes. The applause finally died down. The gym was quiet again.

"The President makes it sound like I'm the bravest person on the planet. But I'm not even the bravest in this room." *Deep breath.* "And that's why I'm here to tell you about my adopted daughter, Nabaa.

"When I first met her outside the gate of Joint Base Balad in Iraq, it was during a donation giveaway. Hundreds of charitable Americans had sent toys to Iraq, and a bunch of military members were handing them out to the poor Iraqi children in the neighboring village. Nabaa was 12 at the time, and she made it her mission to ensure every child got a toy. She lined up everyone by age, assessed the toys, and explained them to the kids who had never seen some of these things before. She even mediated the many disputes among the jumping, clamoring kids. I watched her in awe. She's a natural leader. I even quoted her in the story I wrote about the event. I still remember that quote: 'My parents taught me to be helpful, not selfish. I like toys, but I like helping more.'

"I didn't forget her face, either," Percy continued. "So, a few months later, when I saw that face running toward our convoy, I recognized her instantly. She knew there was a bomb buried under the ground and that there were bad guys with guns nearby, but she still ran from her home to warn us. With her mother chasing her and screaming at her to stop, this little girl did what she thought was right. Unfortunately, her mother was shot and killed that day, right in front of Nabaa. And while Nabaa made it out of that awful situation alive, the world witnessed the horror she had to endure months later, when she was abducted by Fadi Itani's people right after the March 20th air show attack."

Percy paused. "And yet here she is. She was part of a large Iraqi family, and now she's the only one left. She's been through more trauma than any human should endure in a lifetime. But she still smiles. She still finds the good in situations. She's kind. We adopted her because she captured our hearts, and I think we found a way to eventually capture hers, too."

He turned his head and looked at her for a few moments, then turned back to the crowd. "Sometimes, I still hear her crying at night, when she's trying to get to sleep. She loves us, but she misses her family. How could she not?

"So, let me ask all of you a question," Percy said. "Why do we go to war?" No hands went up immediately. He waited, and then he saw one, and then another, then a few more. He pointed at the owner of the first raised hand and said, "Say it so everyone can hear."

9

"To prevent more terrorist attacks," the boy said loudly and forcefully.

"Yes, that's part of it," Percy said. Then he pointed at a girl raising her hand to his right. "What do you think?"

"To protect democracy and spread it throughout the world," she yelled.

"Good. That's also true," Percy said. "What about you?" he said, pointing directly in front of him, at a boy who appeared to be the smallest kid in the gym.

"To protect people in other countries who are getting killed and abused!" he shouted.

Percy nodded. "True again. Those are all part of the answer. But these reasons all come from one thing, one deep-down reason. We go to war," he said, slowing his pace, "because we fear for the safety and security of our loved ones." He let the sentence hang for an extra second. "It's why Palestinians shoot rockets at Israel. It's why Israel orders air strikes against Palestinians. You might say that's *off*ensive, not *de*fensive. I would tell you neither side feels like it started the conflict. Both sides feel like they're taking necessary measures to provide security of their people and their home. It's even why we overthrow countries and reinvent their governments for them. At the source, it's even why al-Qaida believes its jihad is righteous." He stopped to let the students absorb the idea. "It's basically what Fadi Itani communicated in his dying video, right?

"Does that mean all of our enemies are righteous, noble men? Of course not. Many of them are ignorant, brainwashed fools, motivated by manufactured hate. And guess what? So are a lot of Americans who hate them."

Percy brought his hands to the edges of the lectern. "That's why I came back here. Some of you might remember. I was supposed to come give a speech here on the night of 3/20. *This* speech. It's bothered me ever since. The irony of it." He shook his head.

"That awful day took a lot from us. It took a lot from me, too. But I didn't want to let it take this one last thing: the moment I was supposed to have here, with you, talking about my daughter's courage. So here I am." He turned and smiled at Nabaa. She smiled back. It warmed his heart and gave him a shot of confidence. *Maybe this is going all right,* he thought. He looked back at his notes.

"William Faulkner once wrote, 'The past isn't dead and buried. In fact, it isn't even past.' For me, that echoes in all the violence I've seen in my life. So many hateful people in this world are just living out the anger of their trauma, or their father's trauma or their great-great-grandfather's trauma. Why not break that chain? Now. *Today.* It's your choice. Each of you has that power. You're young. You all have hopes and dreams and maybe even some realistic goals. Maybe some of you want to make world a better place. There are lots of ways to do that. But there's one *easy* way: Don't be ignorant on the sidelines. Don't let yourself be brainwashed, even by your own tribe — *especially* by your own tribe."

He raised his arm and pointed toward Nabaa. "Remember this girl's spirit! I hope your courage and resilience is never put to the test like hers has been. But if it is, *never fight for anything with hate in your heart*. If you have to fight, fight for what you love, and believe your enemy is doing the same."

He paused to take a breath, and the audience thought he was finished. Applause erupted again. He spoke loudly into the microphone.

"With that in mind — you know what ... Nabaa, please join me up here for a minute." After a brief hesitation and a prod from Maggie, Nabaa stood and walked toward him. He grabbed her hand and held it in his.

"I'm happy to announce that today, with the help of President Brennan and some generous anonymous donors, we're starting the Nabaa Mackenzie Peacemaker Scholarship. Every year, two students from Glendale High School will be awarded a four-year scholarship, with all expenses paid, to any university that accepts them. You are eligible if you fight for peace from where you are.

"If you work in a hospice, bringing peace to the elderly in their last moments on Earth, you're eligible. If you babysit a kid every week while his dad goes to grief counseling because he lost his wife in the attack, you're eligible. If you create a rehab program for people in the community with PTSD, you're eligible. If you write peacemaking poetry and get it published in a kids' magazine, you're eligible. The three of us, Nabaa, Maggie and I, will look at all applications. All we need is an essay and a letter of recommendation from anyone who's familiar with your work."

He looked down and smiled at Nabaa, who was turning her head slowly to take in the sea of students filling her field of vision.

"I sincerely appreciate the opportunity to be here, talking to all of you," Percy said. "Thanks for listening, and God bless."

Nabaa reached up and pulled the microphone down to her level. "*As-salamu alaykum*," she said, clearly and calmly. Then, in accented English, "Peace be upon you."

The applause started again softly. Within a few seconds, it had raised to its previous crescendo. The student body was standing again, but nobody was whooping or hollering this time.

Percy and Nabaa walked back to where the seats were, and a teary-eyed Maggie pulled them in for a group hug. Brennan waited patiently for her to release them.

A few seconds later, Secret Service agents were ushering them back out the door and into the limousine.

"Well, this is it, Perce," the president said as they pulled out of the parking lot. "You ready to go underground for a while?"

"Sounds pretty good, sir," Percy replied. Then he remembered what Brennan had said before. "What did you want to talk to me about?"

"Right," Brennan said. "Are you familiar with Senator John Banusiewicz? Maryland, where you'll soon be living. I happen to know he's serving out this last term and retiring. But that term just started, which means his spot will go up for general election at the end of 2016." He paused, staring at Percy. "Are you interested?"

"What? Me?" Percy laughed reflexively. "A U.S. senator? I'm not even old enough, am I?"

"Minimum age is 30," Brennan said. "You'd turn 30 about seven months before the election. Perfect timing. And I happen to think you would win."

"That might be the best reason not to try."

"You say that now," Brennan said. "But you're a *doer*, Percy. You *do* things. Five years from now? I have a feeling you'll be itching to get out of the shadows and serve your country again."

"Wait." The idea swirled in Percy's mind. He wanted to reject it immediately, but he found himself trying to imagine it. He glanced at Nabaa, who was staring at him. *Oh shit,* he thought.

"2016?" Maggie said. "So, you'll hopefully be wrapping up your second term, right?"

"Yep," the president said dourly. "I don't want to count chickens, but 2012 is looking pretty good for me right now. According to my political people, at least."

"You do not sound excited about that," Nabaa said sharply.

"That's because I'm not," Brennan said. "Another two years of this might be enough for me, to be honest. It's a huge honor, but also the hardest thing I've ever done. But either way, even if I'm no longer in office, I've got enough favors saved up that I could help Percy no matter what. Some of it would actually be easier if I'm just a former president and not the current president."

"Respectfully, sir, this isn't even something I can imagine right now," Percy said.

"I get it, Perce," Brennan said. "I know the timing of this conversation sucks. But this just came up, and I wanted to broach the topic with all three of you at once. It's a family decision, of course. And on that note, even if you decide to do it, Maggie and Nabaa could remain in WITSEC as long as they want. Maggie's presence next to you on the campaign trail might help, but if not, you'll be seen as a guy who wants to keep serving but doesn't want to put his wife in harm's way again. I think voters would forgive a lady for staying out of the public eye after being abducted and nearly killed by terrorists."

Percy didn't know whether to be impressed or horrified. "Wow. Mr. President, I think you just managed to successfully turn my wife's terror into a political benefit — all before I gave any indication I might be interested in this. I'm starting to understand how you rose to power."

Brennan's face lost some color. "I'm sorry, Percy." He looked at Maggie and then Nabaa. "I'm sorry to you ladies, too. Sometimes I think I'm immune to the political disease, and then I find myself acting like an asshole." He took a deep breath and exhaled. "Too much, too soon. Copy that. Forget about it. And in five years or so, when you're looking for a job, we can talk about it then."

"Apology accepted," Maggie said, nodding and lightly smiling.

"Thanks, Mr. President," Percy said. "Please know I'm honored that you asked."

Brennan nodded, and then the three of them all looked at Nabaa. She looked at them one at a time, then turned back to the window.

Brennan made a wincing face at Percy, which served as another apology. Percy shrugged and shook his head.

Finally, the motorcade arrived back on the Davis-Monthan flight line. The limo door opened, and Nabaa exited immediately without a word. Percy and Maggie shook Brennan's hand and said their goodbyes, hurrying to catch up with Nabaa.

They found her 50 yards away, sitting on a bench under a mesquite tree near the base operations building entrance.

"Nabaa —" Percy began.

"*WHY DIDN'T YOU SAY NO?*" she yelled.

"What?" He was confused. "I did!"

"No you did not! You said other words, but you never said no!" Tears tumbled down her cheeks. "It wasn't enough to become a Thunderbird, it wasn't enough to come to Glendale in March. It wasn't enough to come back here again, to this awful place, where the blood has barely dried! I know you! Not today, not next week, but eventually — you will find a way to say yes to the president and become a senator. And we will go along with it … because you are Percy, hero on his path to glory. Who can stand in the way?" She wiped her eyes in frustration. "You talk about *me* overcoming *my* fear. *You* are afraid, too, Percy! You are afraid of fear itself! You are afraid of not doing enough, and so you always do too much!"

She buried her head in her hands and cried.

"Nabaa …" Maggie said. She sat down wrapped her arms around the girl's shoulders.

13

Percy stood, silent, shaken, and shaking. Her words, stolen from his own heart, had woken his rage. *No,* he ordered his mind. *Not her. Never her.*

He walked away.

CHAPTER 1

September 2014

Rafiq Itani recognized the inbound autumn by its unmistakable smell. Although sunny and about 70 degrees, a faint gust of cool crispness foreshadowed the inevitable reduction of outdoor recreation time. Sitting on his usual chair against the sidewall of the caged rooftop recreational yard, he wondered if the brief fall breeze delivered its message only to higher altitudes, or if the free people down on the streets had detected it, too.

He turned another page of *The Godfather,* a thick paperback Percy had mailed to him a week ago. Rafiq loved reading books in the sunshine. The winters here were hard, rarely seeing the sun, feeling fresh air a few times per month. It was the only time he felt the faint touch of despair.

Overall, though, his last few years of confinement at the Metropolitan Correctional Center in Manhattan had actually been more tolerable than he would've guessed. But he constantly missed the sun. He had spent the first 25 years of his life seeing the sun every day; now, he was thankful that the guards allowed him to bring books up to the roof for an hour at a time.

His idle gaze settled on the handful of inmates playing basketball — poorly, it appeared — on the unlined, single-hoop half court. It was odd to think this would probably be his last winter at the MCC.

"Itani!" A guard's voice yelled from the threshold leading to the interior stairwell. "Your lawyers are here!"

Rafiq felt his brow furrow; he wasn't expecting a visit till next week. Would this be good news or bad? He glanced at the page number, closed the book and stood. Tilting his face skyward, he took a deep breath and walked to the guard — a stocky man named Ramirez. He was one of half a dozen who Rafiq didn't despise.

"You know where IR3 is, right?" Ramirez asked.

Rafiq nodded and headed down the stairs slowly, hearing the guard's heavy footsteps following closely behind. After a winding five-minute walk, they reached Interview Room 3. Ramirez opened the door.

Two men and a woman sat at the six-person table, and they all stood when Rafiq entered. Ramirez closed the door behind them and stayed in the hallway. "Hello, Mr. Itani," said one of Rafiq's two lawyers, a lanky, bald man named David Dennard. The other lawyer — an unconventionally but arrestingly attractive, Mediterranean-looking blonde — was Becky Whitfield. She only smiled.

Rafiq didn't recognize the second man. He was pale, dark-haired, skinny, and appeared to be in his late 20s. His direct gaze implied intelligence; his fiddling hands betrayed his nervousness. Rafiq turned to his lawyers and nodded. "Hello, David. Becky."

"Sit with us, Rafiq," Whitfield said. She placed a digital voice recorder on the table and pressed a button. Rafiq heard the familiar beep that announced it was recording.

He sat, then decided to address the unfamiliar man. "Who are you?"

The man glanced at Whitfield, and then back to Rafiq. "I'm Chad Sorenson. I'm a legal researcher for the ACLU. I've worked with David and Becky a few times, and they asked me to give your case one comprehensive scrub."

"It's something I like to do right before pre-trial motions," Dennard said. "Usually, there are no surprises at this stage. But not this time. Chad found a whopper, and it might change our approach."

Rafiq immediately felt the unease that had become familiar whenever he met with his lawyers. But this sounded like something more than the usual legal pirouette they often had to explain to him in layman's terms. *Did they find out about Percy's arrangement?* It was a fear he'd harbored all along, but he was prepared to deal with it. If it came to that, he figured Dennard and Whitfield could handle it.

Of course, part of Rafiq's trust in Dennard and Whitfield came from Percy's initial vetting. The lawyers didn't know that, of course, but when Rafiq was first transferred to MCC, Percy himself had visited off-the-books and without escort. He'd brought a folder full of printed pages for them to review together —biographical information, case histories, and transcribed oral arguments. Rafiq went along with it, of course. He trusted Percy, but he also didn't have any other options. It took him a while to believe the trial was even possible, much less winnable.

Counting the first visit at Guantanamo, Percy had visited Rafiq three times. He explained how the American Civil Liberties Union provided legal services for people whose rights might be in jeopardy and showed Rafiq portraits and biographies for both attorneys. He made it clear that the arrangement had been somewhat orchestrated — not just serendipitously taken on by the organization — but that it would be handled with extreme diligence. Percy assured Rafiq that Dennard and Whitfield were the top choices from among 50 experienced ACLU lawyers whose records he'd thoroughly reviewed. Percy described them as excellent trial lawyers who also had the rare quality of uncompromising integrity. They would have Rafiq's best interests at heart, but wouldn't play with the truth for the benefit of the outcome.

16

"I am not particularly interested in changing our approach, David," Rafiq said. "I thought we were all clear on the goals."

"We get that, Rafiq," Whitfield said. "But this isn't the kind of thing we could just ignore."

Rafiq turned to her for a silent moment. "Ok. What is it?"

Sorenson began to explain. "Well, I initially focused all my efforts on events that occurred before you were detained," Sorenson said. "And, as we've known all along, the case is pretty strong there — I found no trace of evidence you actually committed violence. Just conspiracy. But David mentioned that one potential positive outcome would be a guilty verdict with a sentence of time served. You're aware of that?"

"Yes," Rafiq said. "We discussed it several months ago, I believe. Becky and David agreed that the assigned judge might be sympathetic."

"Exactly," Sorenson said, nodding. "District Judge James Greene. He's tough on violent criminals, but he's also tough on law enforcement overreach. So, I decided to explore your long detention to see if we could paint a picture of a punishment that fits the crime. I quickly found myself in a rabbit hole."

"Rabbit hole?" Rafiq didn't recognize the expression. "You mean you got stuck?"

"Sorry. It's a reference to … an old British book. I mean, I started down a path that seemed straightforward at first. But, pretty soon, I saw so many angles of research that it was dizzying. FBI and CIA detention practices, the role of special forces, responsibility of host nations, international detainee transfers, nonconfidential DOJ literature, and all kinds of other stuff that wasn't ultimately pertinent. I know I spent more time on those angles than David would've preferred, but I eventually found something."

Rafiq remained expressionless and silent.

"As you know, the government won't reveal the specifics of which agencies were responsible for your interrogations, much less the individuals who conducted them," Sorenson said. "But you described some pretty horrific things at Bagram. And we know it occurred shortly after the 3/20 air show attack. I figured if I could find out who performed that particular interrogation, we could light a fire under that agency's public information office. At a minimum, it would show the judge there's probably something being hidden."

Sorenson paused until he got another nod from Rafiq.

"Anyway, David and Becky gave me the notes from your interviews with them. I noticed that you said the last interrogator at Bagram was someone you had never seen before, and that the familiar men spoke to him like he was a visitor. That gave me a hunch that the government sent in one of their best, probably someone who wasn't in theater — I imagined it was some hotshot interrogator with a long record in the field, but who had been promoted to a desk job or something. It made sense. I mean, first of all, the stakes were as high as they could be, so they would want to send in a ringer. Plus, the kind of guy who would break a detainee's shins, tase him into unconsciousness and fish-hook his eyelids open —"

"Chad," Whitfield broke in. "Please. I'm fairly sure Rafiq remembers the details of his interrogation."

Sorenson looked at her, ashamed, then said to Rafiq, "Right. I'm sorry."

"I do not need an apology or a varnished version of events. I made peace with the torture the instant it was happening. Continue, please."

"Ok. So, I was hopeful. The kind of guy who would do those things probably isn't an average interrogator who still has his career ahead of him. And if the interrogator wasn't just some run-of-the-mill agent in a deployment rotation, I figured it would improve our chances of getting someone to admit to what they did to you. So I decided check the military air traffic records in the couple of days after the 3/20 attack and see if anything stood out. I submitted FOIA requests to all the Air Force bases on the Eastern seaboard ..."

"Wait — 'foya'?" It was a word Rafiq didn't recognize.

"Oh, right. It's an acronym that stands for 'Freedom of Information Act'. It's a law that says upon official request, federal government agencies must release any nonconfidential information about its communications and activities."

Rafiq nodded thoughtfully, both impressed and amused at all the ways America convinced itself it was a free country.

Sorenson continued. "Anyway, I was fairly certain that a C-17 was the only type of aircraft they would use for a short-notice urgent mission like that. So I sent a FOIA request to all the bases on the East Coast that could support C-17 missions. Not surprisingly, I found no record of eastbound C-17 departures at all. I figured they had been scrubbed. However, I then requested all the jet fuel logs for the same bases, then I did some research and calculations. Sure enough, at Charleston, an unknown aircraft had received roughly the amount of fuel needed to top off a C-17 tank if it had been filled up and then flown about 2,000 miles."

"Chad, this is a lot of information," Dennard said. "Maybe we should just cut to the chase."

"No," Whitfield said. "Let him finish. If we don't, Rafiq will just ask all the questions until he gets the whole story."

Sorenson looked back and forth between them, then at Rafiq, who was smiling ever so slightly.

"So," Sorenson said, "I expanded my search to all C-17 bases to see if anything stood out. I found two things: a C-17 flight from Travis Air

Force Base in California to Davis-Monthan Air Force Base in Tucson, Arizona. And then another from Davis-Monthan to Charleston."

The skin on Rafiq's forearms tingled. *They know it was Percy.*

"I'm pretty certain neither the CIA or FBI has counterterrorism assets in Southern Arizona — or at least not before 3/20. At first, I wondered if our guy might have been stationed at the Customs and Border Protection unit there. But it didn't feel right. Then I remembered something I read a long time ago, a few weeks after the 3/20 attack. In one of the hundred stories on the news, I remember hearing someone talking about the dramatic moment when Percy Mackenzie and his wife had hurriedly flown from Davis-Monthan to greet their rescued daughter on the flight line at Nellis Air Force Base. Apparently, they had been holed up at Davis-Monthan in the days right after the air show attack at Luke. That's when it hit me." Chad stared intently at Rafiq. "Percy Mackenzie was your interrogator."

Silence. Rafiq kept his face unreadable. Sorenson looked to Dennard and Whitfield.

"If we're wrong, this probably sounds crazy to you," Dennard said. "But when we discussed it, we realized it does make some sense. He had high motive for being willing — you held the information that could save his newly adopted daughter. And the Feds presumably had motive for sending him. He was the guy who captured you 15 months prior. We know you hadn't given anybody a shred of intel until those last days when you were tortured. Maybe they thought he could get you to break. And the torture itself makes more sense then, too, right? He's a father in desperation mode. Doesn't know the rules, and doesn't care about them anyway."

"Of course," Whitfield added, "that's when we realized that if it *was* Percy Mackenzie, you would've either recognized him instantly or he would've identified himself to you. So we're either wrong …" She paused and held Rafiq's gaze for three long seconds. "Or you failed to mention to us that you knew all along who your torturer was."

More silence.

"Of course, you did tell us about Mackenzie's visit to your cell in Guantanamo," Whitfield said, smiling. "You told us that what he said and did during that visit meant a lot to you. So I've got a theory. I think, during that visit, you made a deal with Percy. He gave you a priceless gift — your father's last words before he killed himself on camera. In exchange, he made you promise to never name him."

"Your theory is not accurate, Becky," Rafiq said calmly. "The man who visited me in Guantanamo is not the same man who interrogated me."

"Rafiq, please think about this," Dennard said, measuring his words. "We all agree Percy is not the kind of person who would lie under oath.

All we have to do is surprise him with the questions, and he'll give us what we need to get the sentence we want. The jury might actually grant you some empathy."

"I am not aiming for empathy, David."

"Ok," Whitfield said. "Then think about the effect his admission could have on the treatment of future detainees."

Glaring at Whitfield, Rafiq reached across the table and grabbed the digital voice recorder. He turned it over in his hand, found the off switch and flipped it. He set it back down on the table.

"There was a single promise," Rafiq said. "Percy promised to fight for my trial in America. And he has kept that promise. As I said, he was a different man in Bagram than he was when he came to visit me in that hellhole in Cuba."

Rafiq paused, surveying the lawyers. They were glancing at each other. *Already, they plan to defy me.*

"Listen closely," he said. "I appreciate your intentions, but this trial will follow my plan — not yours. I do consider the treatment of future detainees, Becky — in all countries. In all conflicts. That is the only reason I agreed to this trial and the testimony. I didn't do it simply for the hope of moving from a terrible prison to a slightly less terrible prison. But I have my limits. I have made peace with myself and with Percy Mackenzie. That means a lot to me. If you try to break that peace, I will recant my entire testimony and claim it was an ACLU fabrication."

Dennard's eyebrows raised. Whitfield's furrowed. *Good,* Rafiq thought.

"Thank you for your time," he said, and stood. "I would like to return to my reading now."

CHAPTER 2

October 2014

Nabaa stared at the screen, checking her charts and captions for the third time. The whole report was due to the research associate tomorrow, and she didn't think it was going to get any better.

I might be making it worse with every edit, she thought.

She erased the last two sentences and typed, "Lab stimulations cause photonic reactions in somata of astrocytes and neurons (see Figure 3). More stimulations generate higher amplitude of reactions (Figure 4)."

She stopped and reread what she typed. *Ew. Too jargony,* she thought. *Or maybe that's what they want?*

She knew a layperson would have no clue what she had just typed, but she had to hope it would make enough sense to her lead researcher. She was too close to the data; she was becoming so familiar with the experiments and results that she sensed she was losing the ability to translate it to someone less initiated. And she needed a break anyway.

She folded the laptop closed and set it next to her on the bed. *Reread it in an hour. Relax first.*

She closed her eyes and began to regulate her breathing. She was still a novice meditator; when she first tried it, the experience felt to her like she was trying to build a dam in a flooding river. From then on, every time she meditated, she visualized the same river. She imagined herself placing large rocks in a shallow section of the strong current, telling herself that every time she returned to her mindful place, the river would be a tiny bit slower. Someday, she would find the river of consciousness slowly trickling through the little hand-built dam, and she would be pleased.

Her reverie broke after only a few minutes, and she couldn't retrieve her peace. She kept her eyes closed and tried willing her thoughts to return to her studies. *Live in this moment,* her therapy voice said. *Obsessing about the future is no better than dwelling on the past.*

She loved and hated her therapy voice — it was like a vending machine of mindful wisdom and positivity, stocked by her years in counseling. *Own the thoughts. Flank your fears. Don't let them ambush you.*

Often, it helped her. But it always annoyed her, including now.

She turned her head and stared at the medicine cabinet above her sink. The bottle of clonazepam still had, what, four or five left?

No, not now. Nabaa didn't want to dampen her neural activity when she needed it most. Whatever thoughts she was trying to keep at bay probably just needed to be freed. She turned her head forward again, closed her eyes, and convinced herself to keep meditating.

She couldn't. She felt her anxiety slowly building. Her blood felt warmer. A static electricity charged her skin.

She knew what was actually happening — chemicals were passing through her neural network in increasingly wrong proportions. Norepinephrine was outpacing serotonin, which was causing her heart rate to speed up.

And because I recognize what's happening, it will of course make me more anxious, not less. Nabaa got up and began pacing. She knew if she couldn't reverse the course soon, it would become a full-force panic attack.

How did this start? If she could figure out the trigger of the anxiety, she had a chance to stop it. But she didn't know. She was just finishing a project — one that she enjoyed. Was that the difference? She was too invested in the project?

I haven't been sleeping enough, she thought. *Or eating well.* Those realizations clarified the problem. She was both intellectually and emotionally invested in a project. She was on a deadline. *And* she hadn't been disciplined about sleeping or eating habits for the past week.

Fuck! Fuck fuck fuck. Her heart suddenly felt like a combustion chamber.

Isolating the issues didn't help. It only made her realize she couldn't think her way out of this particular anxiety attack. If she had slept or eaten well the last couple of days, she knew her brain would have the resources it needed to naturally balance serotonin and norepinephrine levels and allow her to function.

But now? It was too late. Her synapses drowned in the misproportioned chemical bath. Soon, she would feel like she was in cardiac arrest.

And then the memories will break down the dam.

She went to the medicine cabinet and grabbed the bottle of clonazepam. Hands shaking, she opened it and looked inside. Three circular, high-dose 2-milligram pills, and one last half-pill from the several she had split months ago. She reminded herself that the higher dose wouldn't hit her system any faster, and when it did, it would put her in a stupor. She tapped the bottle against her open left palm until the half-pill fell out.

Nabaa used her front teeth to bite off a corner of the half-pill and then maneuvered it under her tongue, a faster-absorption trick she had read about in an internet forum. She grabbed her water bottle and swallowed the rest of the pill.

And now it was a waiting game. She continued pacing, thinking through what the clonazepam was on its way to do.

The benzene and diazepine ring will travel to the synapses of my neurons. She visualized the tiny chemicals dissolving into her saliva and stomach acid, then merging into her blood, then riding the river all the way up to her brain. *It will find the gamma-Aminobutyric acid where it is bound to its receptor. It will increase the electrical conduction of chlorine ions through the neurons' membranes. And the resulting hyperpolarization will help the GABA do its job — the blasts of imbalanced chemicals across the synapse will slow down.*

And that's all she could hope for — slowing the flood. Fixing the imbalance itself was a problem for tomorrow. Right now, pacing. Breathing.

It wasn't working. The familiar thoughts started ratcheting the rollercoaster up the track. *How did I get here? I used to be a normal, happy girl living in a small village in Iraq. How did I get here? Now I'm a teenage college student in America on crazy pills. How did I get here? My family is all dead. How did I get here? I made one choice on one dusty road when I was 12. How did I get here?* She screamed at her brain with her brain. *HOW DID I GET HERE?*

After all these years, she still couldn't make sense of it: how her brain was processing information in that fateful moment. How Fadi Itani's brain could convince him to do what he did. How so many people can decide, in their right mind, to do such crazy or dangerous or evil things.

She was almost 14 when she had made the connection — that all her troubles stemmed from that fateful decision — and that's when she realized she didn't understand her own brain. And then she realized she couldn't exactly trust something she didn't understand. *And that's when I started going crazy.*

Her therapist at the time — the second one — had suggested that she start studying neuroscience to help bridge the gap. He was right, in a way. It kept the crazy at bay. But she also realized quickly that everything she learned about the brain also revealed a new mystery. Sometimes two or three mysteries.

And so the question persisted. *How did I get here?*

The only thing she could do, the only thing that helped a little, was stretching out her story. If she tried to jump from the 12-year-old Iraqi village girl to the 18-year-old American neuroscience researcher, the rollercoaster sped right up. But if she focused on each little step along the way … maybe the pill would get its chance to work.

She forced her thoughts back to their first year in the federal Witness Security Program.

Percy and Maggie were legally named Charlie and Elizabeth Hamilton. Nabaa was a refugee from India. She was given the Indian surname Khatri and was allowed to choose her fake first name, as long as it was also one in the Hindu lexicon. She chose Aahna, because it meant "exist." She thought it was an appropriate reminder of her status as the only survivor of her family.

Percy grew a full beard, and he was hired — quickly, of course — by the State Department to be a liaison to the dozens of think tanks around D.C. Maggie, with a straight auburn bob where her long, curly blond hair had been, became Nabaa's homeschool teacher, focusing heavily on learning English. With her characteristic blend of patience, intelligence and determination, she helped Nabaa achieve a college-level fluency in just under a year.

Nabaa remembered being mostly happy, but often missing the company of other children. After a while, Maggie, too, started to struggle with a dearth of peer interaction. So they became each other's best friend.

Percy focused on creating an entirely new professional persona, which didn't seem difficult for him. He would come home after a long commute, drained but content. On the weekends, Percy would usually want to relax and enjoy the refuge of their home, while Maggie and Nabaa were always anxious to go somewhere after being cooped up all week.

The WITSEC officials told them to keep their social interactions to a minimum, since their manufactured biographical story was initially pretty thin. On the few occasions when a neighbor or friendly stranger had asked innocent questions about her background, Percy or Maggie would say something vague about violence in Kashmir and then add an ominous head tilt or raised eyebrow to silently say, "We don't like to talk about that around her." They were allowed to say they were in the process of adoption, but it was anyone's guess how long the process would take.

Finally, almost a year later, WITSEC had drummed up paperwork to show that Aahna had been legally adopted by the Hamiltons, and soon after become a U.S. citizen. That was when they were told to move from Sykesville to Crofton, Maryland, where they could start living a more normal American family life. Maggie got a job at the Johns Hopkins Children's Center, and they enrolled Nabaa in high school.

By then, Nabaa was 14. She approached American school like a racehorse hearing a starting gun. Her teachers — and Percy and Maggie — were awestruck at every turn. They knew she was smart, and Maggie had prepared her well, but they couldn't have predicted her appetite for knowledge.

Nabaa didn't understand why it was supposed to be difficult. Or why other students seemed bored and inattentive. Just about everything they taught in school was fascinating. Fun, even.

She convinced Percy and Maggie to let her take a couple of night classes at the community college, then a few summer courses, too. She signed up for all the CLEP tests and AP tests she could find and earned credit from all but one — calculus. She wanted to graduate as soon as she could.

In retrospect, Nabaa recognized that part of it was avoidance. She had been keeping her brain busy enough to avoid the hard question lurking below her consciousness. *How did I get here?*

Of course, she remembered the moment when she went from well-adjusted student to mental health patient.

Second year in high school, middle of a Friday AP Psychology class. The question strode forward, broke through her cortex, and announced itself.

Her teacher, Mr. Dusick, was leading the class through the world of behavioral conditioning and Freud's psychoanalysis theory. The lesson was about nature and nurture, and how they combine to form a person's destiny. Suddenly, Nabaa was dizzy. She felt like she was falling down a black hole. She sat at her desk, half-listening, half-obsessing about the chain of events that had led her to the present moment, and the body count along the way. The question was emblazoned on her inner canvas.

How did I get here?

First her mother, then the airmen on patrol, and later, her father and sister and brother. And then the 3/20 attacks. So many dead people. Thousands of deaths. People with futures were now either buried with bullet holes or heads sewn back on posthumously. Others had been vaporized into the air, never to be seen in human form again.

And it wasn't exactly the grisliness that bothered her — perhaps that was a demon in a different cage, still locked for later haunting. But the *number* of deaths. The sheer quantity of human energy just *gone* ... and all of it was connected to *her*.

She remembered that thousands more were paralyzed or missing limbs or missing brain function or simply living in depression after losing their loved ones. She wondered how many had committed suicide in the months and years after 3/20. Dozens? Hundreds?

She skipped the rest of her classes that day, went home and opened her laptop, then typed all the questions in her mind as they appeared. Then she started searching for answers — about the American military's tactics in Iraq, about the overall strategy, about al-Qaida, about the 3/20 attack, and then about cognition and free will and everything in between.

The more she learned, the more it became indisputable to her: All of the thousands of dead people and braindead people and maimed people were dominoes that fell because of a single choice she made as a 12-year-old on a dirt road in front of her home.

And, oh by the way, the same choice had rendered her a brotherless, sisterless orphan.

That night, she had her first real breakdown.

She remembered the feeling so clearly. Nothing could solve the problem. Nothing mattered anymore. In her single life, however long it may be, how could she ever make up for the loss she had caused?

Even then, the timing seemed so strange. It was a random Friday in early December, almost exactly three years after the seminal event. Why then? Another unanswerable question.

She had stayed in bed the next day. She declined to eat breakfast. She refused the Saturday grocery store trip with Percy and Maggie. They thought she was sick until they both entered her room to ask her about lunch. She declined again, this time angrily.

Percy insisted she tell them what was wrong. Percy, always trying to help and always believing he *can* help.

"Why should I tell you?" she screamed at him, tears suddenly bursting the dam of her eyelids. "Because you can make it go away? There are some problems you can't solve, Percy! What are you going to do? Bring all the people back from the dead? They're *DEAD!* And all because of *me!"*

The memory brought goosebumps to Nabaa's forearms.

How did I get here? She forced herself to change the question in her mind. *What happened next?*

Therapy. Prescriptions. Titrating. Stop. Withdraw. Try something new. Over and over again. All the while, attending school, doing extracurriculars, trying to live a normal life. A *pretend* normal life. Only as normal as she deserved, she figured.

At first, she was seen by two psychiatrists — sometime separately, sometimes simultaneously — and each had to be vetted, read in, cleared, and threatened by the FBI WITSEC people. The doctors said she had developed a unique mix of depression, anxiety, and borderline psychosis, all stemming from late-onset PTSD.

They were both nice enough. Professional. But her symptoms didn't quite fit their normal protocol. So they tried a lot of things. After a while, Nabaa felt like an experiment.

Especially in the first few weeks of trying a new pill, she would feel — and act — crazy. Then her physiology would adjust to the new chemicals, and then she could tell whether it would make her feel worse or nothing at all. She was constantly perplexed by how doctors could prescribe medicine that they so clearly didn't understand.

26

Eventually, they all came to the conclusion to stop trying the daily pills. None of them had benefits that outweighed the side effects. Finally, they prescribed clonazepam, for treating symptoms as they arose. The next time she felt The Guilt rising, she took one. The relief was quick and wonderful. The side effects weren't debilitating. At first, she found occasion to take a pill at least once weekly. These days, she only needed her meds a few times per month.

More often, she needed her regular email chats with Maggie.

A few years ago, she started seeing a cognitive behavioral therapist. A lot of his suggestions were helpful, but none more so than his idea to conduct what he called "intimate written communication" as a tool to combat her PTSD.

After a lot of prodding, Nabaa had told the therapist her real feelings about Percy: that she loved him dearly, but that his approach to mental health often made her more anxious, not less. Strangely, his approach had worked perfectly well for quite a while — all the way until her breakdown. From then on, when he tried to help, it felt like her brain was allergic to him. She often snapped at him or withdrew, which wounded him, which increased her guilt, and then her anxiety. Maggie was always there to pick up the pieces.

The therapist told her that it made a kind of sense. She was a different person before her breakdown. Back then, her brain was trying to keep a lid on her trauma. Apparently, Percy's "way" was conducive to that. But after the breakdown, the lid was off. She was an open wound, which required new tools, new routines for healing. So he told her to open a private world with Maggie, one that only existed in emails. He explained that thoughts grew deeper roots when they were written down, so if she could have a safe space — and a guide — for transcribing her mental journey, it could have a lasting positive effect.

So they tried it, and Nabaa started feeling better immediately. Even in the beginning, despite seeing each other in person every day, she and Maggie quickly realized they could discuss deeper issues over email than they ever would in person. Years later, that hadn't changed.

Through all of that, her brain could never quite stop occupying itself, and soaking up knowledge was still her best inner refuge. She became obsessed with cognition, with behavioral conditioning, with neural function, with free will. She exhausted her biology and psychology teachers' knowledge and started spending free time reading scholarly articles about all types of neuroscience. She soon realized that some of the best research was coming from a university nearby, and she immediately wanted to be a part of it.

So, she set the record at her high school by earning her diploma in 27 months. She spent a month prepping for the ACT, scored a 32, and got accepted into Johns Hopkins. She enrolled there in the fall of 2013.

How did I get here? That's *how I got here. The pieces fit,* she told herself. *Let them.*

It wasn't easy to keep the question at bay. She lived her life in a constant battle for her mental health. Like a good commander, she deployed every advantage she could. She steadfastly ate a clean diet, exercised daily, meditated, wrote to Maggie often, and got at least seven hours of sleep every night.

When she failed to give her body and brain what it needed, she was not only less healthy, she also became an average academic performer. But when she kept to her routine, she held to her excellence. She knew several students who kept up with her while eating terrible food, binge drinking multiple nights per week, averaging five hours of sleep. She didn't know how. *Probably because their brains don't have 20 percent constantly fighting with the past.* She was happy for them.

Plenty of other students were struggling even more than she was. She saw them, and they seemed to be swimming upstream in a river. For Nabaa, it was more like swimming in an ocean. It was hard work, but beneath and around her, she felt the tidal force of tens of thousands of students and staff, all forming a rising wave of scientific progress.

She recalled the first time she truly felt like she was a part of that wave. Her favorite professor, Dr. William Kaiser, had stopped her in the hallway one morning and said, "Ms. Khatri, you have the mind of a great scientist. Keep it up, and you'll discover the answers you seek."

Just two sentences. But they had rooted her in her resolve.

The memory of those words broke her reverie. She realized the anxiety had passed, and she was feeling the characteristic peaceful detachment that followed the medicine hitting her system.

Her mobile phone chattered. Maggie's picture appeared on the screen. She was video calling. *Why not?* Nabaa thought. *I'm not getting any work done for the next hour or so anyway.* She knew her mental acuity would take some time to rebound. She swiped left to answer the call.

"Hey, stranger!" Maggie said, smiling through the initial pixelation.

Percy's thickly bearded face popped in at an angle from the side, then Maggie's face disappeared entirely as he snatched the phone from her. He smiled and said, "Nabaa! How's my favorite stuuuu …" His visage froze as the sound trailed off.

"Oh, you're such a moron," Maggie said. "He's pretending the video froze," she said loudly. "Sooo hilarious."

Percy held his face frozen another two seconds, then he closed his eyes with disappointment, looking off screen at his wife. It was that look that made Nabaa laugh out loud, despite her best efforts not to. Percy's eyes darted back to the phone, capturing Nabaa with a triumphant grin.

He handed the phone back to Maggie, who was smiling, rolling her eyes, and shaking her head.

"Aaaaanyway," she said, "we're just calling because we miss you and we figured you needed a break from studying."

"You are so right, and I miss you both, too," Nabaa said. "Disclaimer: I just took half a pill, and it hit me right before you called." She took a breath, knowing they would both be worried about her. "I was going over some charts for a big project due tomorrow, and I guess the pressure got to me a little bit. "

"Aw, honey," Maggie said. "Are you ok?"

"Yeah, I think so. It's been about a month since the last time, so I guess I'm due, right?" She smiled. "Anyway, I've been thinking about calling you all week, so I'm happy you did."

"Me too," Percy said, entering the frame again, behind Maggie. "Now tell me about these charts that are making my daughter anxious."

Nabaa raised an eyebrow. "So you can beat them up?"

"Of course," he said, unironically. "Do I have any other valuable purpose?"

He was trying to make light of it, but Nabaa could tell her joke wasn't funny. She regretted it and tried again.

"Well, you do make a pretty good jester, especially when you don't understand my science talk."

"What?" He smiled, then feigned incredulity. "I always understand. Try me."

Nabaa laughed. "Hmmm … now that you mention it, there's not much I enjoy more than the feeling of superiority over the Great Percival Mackenzie. But I was actually hoping to hear the latest about the trial — and the, uh, political stuff, too. Shall we agree to a trade of information?"

"Fair enough," Percy said. "I'll go first, since it'll be quick. The trial is still on the docket at the Eastern District of New York. Pre-trial arguments are next month, and the trial itself should start in January. I'm told I'll be one of the first, if not the first witness called by the prosecution. After that, my name will be back in the mainstream media, and some of Brennan's political savants start gauging the public reaction to everything. He says by May or June, we will know enough to make a decision on whether I'll actually run."

Nabaa took a deep breath. Part of her instantly hoped that Percy would bomb his appearance on the witness stand, so he would become a toxic political candidate. Her next thought was shame for hoping such a thing. Then she realized it didn't matter. Percy would never fail in a moment like that. She knew he would be great. And he'll have even more reason to run for office. *You're going to run, Percy. I've known it since the moment Brennan put the idea in your head.*

"So do you know yet whether the trial be televised?" Nabaa asked.

"Not 100 percent sure, but highly likely," Percy said. "Both sides are in favor of it."

"So, it won't just be his name, but also his face all over the media," Maggie said, knowing where Nabaa's mind was.

"That's true," he said. "So I already scheduled 30 days off of work, starting right around the time I'm supposed to testify. I'll shave clean right before, mercifully cut a few inches of this ridiculous hair, and probably put on a little spray tan, too — let people think we've been in hiding somewhere tropical."

"I'm sure it will be an improvement on what you are currently seeing in the mirror every day," Nabaa said. She made no secret of her disapproval of Percy's facial hair and occasional hair bun. Maggie agreed.

"Enjoy it while it lasts, young lady," he said. "A month later, I'll appear back at work with this lovely beard, long hair, prescriptionless glasses, and pale, Maryland-winter skin."

"I used to wonder what Jesus would look like if he were a pasty hipster," Maggie said. "Not anymore."

Nabaa laughed heartily. She realized she was suddenly in legitimately good mood. *God bless you, Maggie. And you, too, clonazepam.*

"Yeah," Percy said, stroking his chin. "Solid comparison. Educated, spiritual, with a streak of badass."

"Oh, stop," Maggie said. "Get struck by lightning when I'm *not* nearby, please."

"Your turn now," Percy said to Nabaa. "Tell us about these charts or whatever."

Nabaa checked her watch. "Ok," she said. "But I'm going to go fast. Pay close attention and try not to interrupt me with a bunch of questions."

"I never have questions when something is explained clearly," he said. Then he cocked his head and raised an eyebrow in a way that always foreshadowed pontification. "That's what separates the great scientists from the dime-a-dozen geniuses, you know. Ability to communicate to dummies like me."

She smiled. "I would argue your skull is denser than most. But anyway, you're already wasting time." She cleared her throat dramatically. "So, this is all part of the consciousness puzzle we've been slowly working on for months. I've told you a little about that. Until very recently, the best tool in neuroscience was fMRI. You've seen the results of that tool — those colorful maps of brain activity?"

"Yes," Percy said.

"So, that's an amazing technology, but it only measures blood flow in the brain as a response to certain stimuli. But blood flow is nowhere near the level we need to reach to understand cognition. If the brain is outer space, fMRI is like binoculars. We need the Hubble telescope. And I actually think we're almost there — like, in the next couple of years — because of these things called 'fluorescent reporters.' They are tiny cells that ... How can I explain this?" She paused, staring off screen.

"Like you're talking to a 4th-grader," Maggie said.

"I know, but Dr. Kaiser always tells us not to use simple analogies, since they're usually not very accurate, and ... " She switched to her best Kaiser impression. "Therefore, you risk increasing confusion while trying to decrease it."

"Sounds like that professor is one of those dime-a-dozen geniuses I was talking about," Percy said. "I mean, of course it won't be perfectly accurate. So, what?"

"Ok. Fine. But if you ever meet him, I will deny saying this." She smiled. "Let's say a fluorescent reporter is a hitchhiker. It's a tiny implanted cell that attaches itself to natural neurochemicals in the brain. And before you implant the reporter cells, you can sort of chemically train them to react when they're in contact with a specific neurochemical."

"React?" Percy asked.

"Well, yes. They are fluorescent and they report."

"So, they light up?"

"Basically, yes. They light up. And they will react relative to how much of the natural neurochemical is present around them. And then the reporter cells follow that chemical from origin to endpoint."

"Wait — so you or your team discovered these reporter chemicals?" Percy asked.

"Fluorescent reporter cells," she corrected. "No, we didn't discover or engineer them. Other neuroscientists did last year. And, um, it's definitely not 'my team' we're talking about. I probably make it sound like I'm a bigger part of the process than I actually am. Some of them like to remind me that I'm just an undergrad assistant who's only around because the professor likes me."

"Ah, yes, the time-honored practice of academic insecurity," Percy said.

Nabaa smiled. "You said it, not me. Anyway, the tech is in the very early stages, and the reporters are, by nature, genetically engineered cells, so it's problematic for human trials. But it's really promising in animal trials. So, our project — well, my *compulsion* mostly — was to forecast the field study limitations of the technology and do a sort of troubleshooting thought experiment."

31

"Uh, what?" Percy's brow furrowed intensely. "That last sentence just microwaved my neurochemicals."

Nabaa laughed. "Sorry. Right. Field study limitations. A lot of technologies sound really promising in the early stages, but *sooooo many* go unfunded. Dr. Kaiser used to do a lot of grant writing, so he's very keen to explore the factors that impact which research projects get money and which don't. It's actually a pretty fascinating sub-field by itself. It's crazy to think about what kind of advancements we could've made if some researchers simply had better grant writers."

"Hey ... that sounds similar to something I said a few minutes ago." Percy smiled smugly.

"Ugh," Maggie said, elbowing Percy. "Please forgive and ignore the obnoxious one, sweetie. I'm trying to follow along with this, and I know you don't have all day to talk. Please continue."

Percy frowned, appearing properly chastised.

"It's ok," Nabaa said. "So, in my exploration of this issue, it became clear to me that the project probably *would* get funded because there's a big pharmaceutical impact expected. Basically, if we know more about the behavior of neurochemicals in the synapses, it could make a big difference in the treatment of poorly understood brain diseases like Alzheimer's or Huntington's. And that could be great, but it kind of bothered me. It meant the research would be redirected toward breadth instead of depth."

"I see," Maggie said, then turned to face Percy and spoke very slowly. "She means ... the pharmaceutical goals ... would hijack ... the design ... of the experiments."

"Exactly!" Nabaa beamed at her phone screen. "And while that would definitely help a lot of people, I'm more interested in the *deep* potential of the research. I kept thinking about how mapping neurotransmitters in real time could have infinitely important ramifications on our understanding of normal, everyday cognition. *Consciousness.* And I'm not the only one who makes that connection, of course, but this entire industry is busy trying to get its share of limited grant money. Cognition itself isn't a disease, so there's no immediate medical impact to drive funding. But I went ahead with my thought experiment and realized, even if the goal was depth and not breadth, the technology ..."

"Wait — when you say 'depth,' what exactly do you mean?" Maggie asked. "Are you thinking what I'm thinking?"

"Yes," Nabaa said.

"Thought so," Maggie said, smiling. "Ok. Go on."

"Wait. What?" Percy looked from Nabaa to Maggie. "Don't play that secret girl knowledge game right now."

"You know Nabaa and I have some pretty fascinating discussions over email," Maggie said matter-of-factly. "Free will and other heady stuff like that. Definitely above your level."

Percy's eyebrows rose in a combination of mock offense and admiration. He turned back to the phone to look at Nabaa.

"Listen, ladies," he said. "There is no 'above my level.' I'm operating at the highest of levels. I think we can all agree on that, right?" He looked to Maggie. "I mean, did you honestly forget the last time you two tried to match wits with me?" Eyes back to Nabaa. "No? Professor Mustard, conservatory, revolver. Four turns. How quickly we forget."

"Colonel Mustard," Nabaa and Maggie said simultaneously, both trying to stifle laughter.

"Whatever," Percy said. "I'm just saying, maybe I should be added to these secret emails. I could probably add some illuminating insight."

"Not gonna happen," Maggie said.

Nabaa smiled sheepishly and made a show of staring up at the ceiling.

Percy smiled, too. "Ok. Fine. But tell me how these fluorescent reporter things are related to free will. I mean, aren't neurochemicals more related to our moods and feelings?"

"Well, first of all, modern science doesn't really know what neurochemicals actually do," Nabaa said. "We are far beyond where we were a few decades ago, but we're still not close. All we have are correlated observations. People who tend toward depression often show elevated reuptake of serotonin. So, antidepressants are created and dubbed 'SSRIs' — selective serotonin reuptake inhibitors. But, as we all know too well, they don't work for all depressed people. And with certain patients, one SSRI works great, but a different one might make them feel even *more* depressed. Or homicidal or suicidal or lethargic. Huge range of outcomes. And there's only one way to find out whether one works or not."

"Ingest it repeatedly for weeks and then report back to your doctor," Maggie said, glowering.

"Right," Nabaa said. "Rough stuff. And that's just one example. But it illustrates how science has not been able to show much *causal* evidence of neurochemicals as they relate to cognition."

Percy nodded. "And when you say cognition, you're not separating emotions from thoughts, right?"

"Correct," Nabaa said. "There's no head-heart disparity in the science. Feelings give rise to thoughts and vice versa. It's all happening in the brain. And since most scientists are materialists, most agree that all cognition is just an orchestrated mix of neurochemicals that creates the perfect illusion of free will. We are walking around, holding up this head-shaped cauldron of chemicals and electricity, and we think we are deciding whether to turn left or turn right. In reality — or in theory, I guess I should say — the chemical cauldron decided it for you."

"But what controls the chemical ... wait," Percy stopped and furrowed his brow. "If it's all chemistry, then it started with conception." His eyes got wide. "Whoa."

"Yeah," Nabaa said, smiling at him. "It's pretty hard to think about, right? But if the theory is true, then we were all slaves to our biology from the moment we were conceived. And that means *all* of biology has been on a completely determined trajectory for billions of years, from the moment the first single-cell organism split into two."

"Geez," Maggie said. "That's depressing."

"Need an SSRI?" Percy asked.

"Will it work if I was destined to feel depressed right now?" Maggie answered.

Nabaa laughed. "Well, it does make a kind of sense if you think about it. We don't control our biology — that's from our parents. They give us our set of DNA in the womb. So before the fetus has its first thought, all it has is its genetic biology. Then, at some point, it becomes conscious." She held up both fists and suddenly extended all ten fingers, the universal sign for two light bulbs coming on. "Then, suddenly, the fetus is getting sensory input. It's just simple things like warmth, a little light, maybe pressure on an elbow. But that input, also, is nothing the fetus controlled. It's just the environment that was put there. So now the fetus has added to its bucket of cognition factors. The first few seconds of sensory input goes in and fuses with the genetic biology, but still, everything in that bucket was out of the baby's control. Then the mom gets up from the couch, and her womb sloshes around a little bit, and the fetus spins slightly, which relieves that pressure on its elbow. Ahhh ... no more elbow pressure. That's nice. It creates a memory of how a slight spin can relieve pressure. And so the next time it feels that pressure, it decides to spin on its own. But that decision was destined. And on and on it goes, more inputs, more experiences, more memories, all into the cognition bucket. But at what point did the human being interject something purely of its own free will?"

Maggie and Percy looked at each other in horror, then back to Nabaa, who laughed.

"I know! I'm sorry! I remember when I first thought about it." Her smile was contagious, spreading to the faces of her adoptive parents. "If it makes you feel better, it's just a theory."

"Doesn't feel like it right now," Percy said. "But anyway. Let me see if I can summarize." He cast an upturned eyebrow at Maggie. "So, these neurotransmitter reporters. The idea is basically that if you can get down to the level of individual neurochemical behavior, eventually you'll be able to map out all that activity in the cauldron, and at the end, you'll have a big map of consciousness. Aaaand … that will prove free will is an illusion?""

"Pretty much," Nabaa said.

Maggie golf-clapped.

"Good. Glad we could settle that," Percy said. "So, you said you'd been obsessing about this for a while. What triggered that?"

Maggie turned to Percy suddenly, head cocked, eyes stern. The message on her face was obvious: *Are you that dense?*

"Oh," Percy said, glancing at Maggie and then back to the phone. "Right. Sorry. I guess that's obvious."

Nabaa was silent for a long moment. *Do I want to discuss this?* She knew the root of her pain also was extremely pertinent to their current discussion. And, so yes — buttressed by the medicine in her blood at the moment — she felt like talking about it now.

"It's okay, Percy," she said. "I do still go to those dark places in my memory, sometimes when I want to, sometimes when I don't. But it's been a little different since I started learning about all this stuff. At first, it was a simple deduction: Because my choice happened before the terrible things, then it is my fault that they happened. But eventually I had to ask myself, 'What exactly is a *choice*? I mean, I saw the American vehicles coming, and I remembered someone had been digging in the road early that morning. And I knew *where* they were digging. It seemed to be too late — the first truck was already right over that spot. But my mind ignored that. Suddenly, my feet were carrying me down the road. My voice was screaming. My hands were waving. But I don't remember *choosing* to do any of those things."

Percy and Maggie were listening, nodding.

"It was that action — subconscious or otherwise — that basically kicked off the violence that grew later," Nabaa continued. "My mother. The men Percy killed immediately after that. The 3/20 attack. The kidnapping. My brother and sisters. And it began to bother me in a different way from before. It wasn't about making the wrong choice. It became, 'How was I not in control of my brain enough to actually make a *conscious* choice?'"

She had more to say, but didn't know how to say it.

Percy broke the silence. "Are you any closer to answering the old question? Whether you would've chosen differently?"

I have never liked that question, Nabaa thought. She knew Percy had wondered it many times, but hadn't actually asked till now.

"I don't know," she said sincerely. "I know what Rafiq's plan was trying to accomplish. If he had succeeded, al-Qaida would've possibly been able to develop IEDs that could defeat MRAPs. Let's say that's all true. Thousands of casualties. But does that equate? The casualties would be armed combatants who came to Iraq to fight people like Rafiq. And even if it *did* equate on that level, what about pure quantity of deaths and injuries? Would those roadside bombs have killed 4,000 like the 3/20 attack? Would they have injured another 6,000? Probably not."

Percy and Maggie just stared back at her. Then Maggie just shook her head, a gesture that seemed to both validate and disapprove of Nabaa's line of thinking. Percy glanced at his wife, not quite following.

"I'll present a better question," Nabaa said. "A question Maggie posed to me once in an email, back when I was first getting interested in all this free will stuff. She asked me, if I could choose, after all my studying of brain function, would I rather find out I *was* responsible for making that choice or whether I'd rather learn it was all destined." She saw Maggie take a deep breath. "I've asked myself that question a thousand times since. I still don't know. Yes, that moment is my driving force in this research. But I don't think this is just *guilt* motivating me. I can't even say I regret what I did. I do not. In that moment, every fiber of my being felt like it was the right thing to do. And yet I can't help feeling like science has been simply inadequate when it comes to this subject. We barely understand how choices get made. And if *one* subconscious decision by a 12-year-old Iraqi village girl can have *that* kind of impact, imagine the kind of consequences that are caused by people who are *actually* powerful. How many of their decisions are thoughtful? How many are simply unconscious? Is there a difference? Or just a perceived difference? What if every human being knew how to stop a bad decision in its tracks? What if we learned how to recognize when the subconscious thought process was trying to hijack our decision-making and how to stop it?"

Maggie glanced at Percy, who kept his gaze on Nabaa.

"I get it," he said. "Sounds like a better world."

"Yeah, maybe," Nabaa said. "I just know I need to keep going."

CHAPTER 3

November 2014

from: Liza Hamilton <lizachucksgirl@gmail.com>
to: Aahna Khatri <aktheexister@gmail.com>
date: Fri, Nov 14, 2014 at 4:11 AM
subject: Gravity = ?

First, a minor update, since I know you're as curious as we are. You know, the big job we're hoping Charlie doesn't take? Well, odds are increasing that we don't get our way. An important "source" called yesterday and told him it's looking good so far. Informal surveys of "the DC regulars" — whoever they are — are very encouraging. Off the record, of course. But I'll do my best to keep convincing him it's not a great idea … while making him think it's *his* will being done. Ha!

Anyway, so my turn for philosophy topic. I've got a good one: gravity. My theory is that gravity is … (drum roll) … GOD.

I think it's fun to imagine. I mean, what does gravity do? It pulls things toward a center — kinda like what God does to us. And didn't gravity kind of create the universe? If the Big Bang happened, it was gravity that was at the core of it (literally) and was the organizing force that allowed stars and planets and moons to form and move around each other.

Think about it. Tell me your thoughts. I'll see if yours align with mine. Love you, Aahna. So glad you're existing. :)

Elizabeth

from: Aahna Khatri <aktheexister@gmail.com>
to: Liza Hamilton <lizachucksgirl@gmail.com>
date: Fri, Nov 14, 2014 at 1:22 PM
subject: RE: Gravity = ?

Whoa. That is wonderfully mind-blowing! I've found myself thinking about it all day.

Gravity is also like God in the sense that nobody has a theory about what it actually *is.* Like Prof Kaiser always says: "If a good scientist can't explain how something works, he must simply give it a name and move on."

The coolest part of your theory is how gravity seems to be necessary for life! I'm still sitting here thinking about how gravity is necessary for oceans to form, for rain to fall, for plants to take root ... basically for anything to make any sense at all.

Thanks for the Charlie update. I'm not getting any closer to liking the idea, Lizzie. I still get an anxiety spike every time I think about it, even though I feel like it's inevitable. Please keep talking sense into him.

Love you! - AK

CHAPTER 4

January 2015

"The United States calls Percival Mackenzie."

Percy stood and walked from the back row of the courtroom to the witness stand. He placed his left hand on the Bible held before him and raised his right.

"You do affirm that all the testimony you are about to give in the case now before the court will be the truth, the whole truth, and nothing but the truth," the bailiff said in a husky voice. "This you do affirm under the pains and penalties of perjury?"

"I do," Percy said. The bailiff nodded, took the Bible, and stepped away.

"You may be seated, Mr. Mackenzie," Judge Greene said from the bench above. "It's rare for me to address a witness before testimony, but it's even rarer that I have a Medal of Honor recipient in my courtroom. Before we begin, I'd like to say that the court thanks you for your time and for your exceptional service to our country."

"Thank you very much, your honor," Percy said. "And thanks for your service, too."

Greene smiled, then nodded to the U.S. attorney, a middle-aged black woman named Andria Jackson. She wore her thick hair pulled tightly back in a bun. Slender and pretty, she had the piercing eyes of a prosecutor.

"Good morning, Mr. Mackenzie," Jackson said. "I realize this isn't pleasant for you, but I think we should begin with you taking us step by step through the events leading up to the first time you saw the defendant, Mr. Itani."

"Sure," Percy said. He cleared his throat. Strangely enough, he could count on one hand the number of times he'd had to tell this story from start to finish. Once during the intelligence debrief in Iraq, once to his boss, once to Maggie, and once to Jackson and her team two days prior. *Maybe this will be the last time.* "So, back in 2008, I was deployed to Joint Base Balad, Iraq. I was a public affairs NCO. My job was to write and edit articles for the base website, and tell stories about what was happening on and around the base. I wanted to write a story about the security forces and how they went about preventing indirect fire attacks, so I asked to go out on a patrol with them."

"Excuse me," Jackson interjected. "Indirect fire?"

"Right," Percy said. "Mortars, basically. Insurgents get improvised explosives, put them in a tube pointed up from the ground, and shoot them over the fence and onto the base. Attacks are pretty constant around Balad, although they're extremely inaccurate. Hardly ever cause any casualties."

"Thank you," Jackson said, smiling politely. "So, you went on patrol with the security forces team. Was that kind of thing common for military journalists to do?"

"No," Percy said. "At least, that was my impression. The senior NCO in charge only allowed it because of my former training as a pararescueman."

"Pararescue. That's special forces, right?"

"Yes, ma'am," Percy said. "I joined the Air Force to become a PJ — sorry, that's short for pararescue jumper. But I badly injured my ankle right before graduating the last course. So I retrained into public affairs. In pararescue, I had been through a lot of the same training as the security forces guys, plus a lot more. So Senior Master Sergeant Almazan got it approved, and I went on patrol with them. At first, everything was routine. Our convoy was three vehicles. Two MRAPs, and one Humvee. Each had a gunner sitting in a special sling kind of seat in the middle, with his head and torso sticking out the top of the vehicle, manning a large machine gun, looking for threats. I was in the Humvee —"

"Sorry," Jackson interrupted again. "You said 'emm-rap.' That's M-R-A-P, correct? Can you describe what that is, for those unfamiliar?"

"Sure. Mine-Resistant, Ambush-Protected vehicle. It's a name for several kinds of large troop transport trucks that have a couple of things in common. They are very heavy by design, they have a secure compartment in the back where the security personnel travel, and they have a V-shaped hull below the undercarriage." He paused. *Shit.* He couldn't remember if he was supposed to explain in more detail how the MRAPs played into the ambush. The first interview with Jackson had been a rush. Jackson was still staring at him. "All of that was part of the design, so they're much less vulnerable to IEDs — or, uh, IEDs are Improvised Explosive Devices — bombs buried under the dirt roads all over the combat zone." He proceeded gingerly. "Obviously, the MRAPs themselves are pretty important to the whole purpose of the attack … do you want me to explain that part?"

"That's ok," Jackson said, holding up a hand. Her voice remained congenial. "Other witnesses will speak to that, actually. Thank you. Please just tell us what transpired that day, from your vantage point."

"Of course. So, I was in the Humvee, riding shotgun, taking photos through the windshield. Turns out it wasn't a routine patrol. As we were reaching the farthest point of the patrol route, which went through a local village, we saw a young girl running from a residence toward the lead MRAP. She was waving her hands and pointing down at the ground under the vehicle. Then we heard a rifle shot, and the girl went down, clutching her leg. Then a woman ran from the home, following the same path. Another shot, and the woman went down, hit in the shoulder, I believe. I broke protocol at that point and tried to get out of the vehicle, but the driver, a cop —"

"In this case, a cop is what you call a security forces airman, right?"

"Right. The driver grabbed my flak vest and held me there for a second. Then we heard a big boom, and turned to see the lead MRAP bounce on its wheels, with smoke and dust all around it. The gunner was partially ejected from his seat, and he fell to the ground next to the MRAP. That's when I heard the AK-47 start firing, and I could see the little tufts of dust erupting all around him, and then I saw several bullets hit the gunner in the head and body. Then he was still." *Dammit.* He felt himself starting to shake. That had been the moment he first felt the rage. *They shot that poor kid while he was lying on the ground.* He took a deep breath. These were old feelings. They were *done* feelings.

"Take as much time as you need, Mr. Mackenzie," Jackson said gently.

"It's ok," he said. *Remember why you're here, Percy.* "His name, I found out later, was Chad Williams. He was an E-3. Enlisted in the Air Force about a year before that day."

She waited a moment and then said, "Did you see who shot Airman Williams?"

He instinctively looked at Rafiq for the first time. They locked eyes, and Percy saw the familiar lack of expression.

"No, ma'am. At that point, I hadn't seen a single insurgent. But I think the gunfire came from my left."

"What about the mother or the girl?"

"My initial instinct told me those first two shots were from an elevated position on the right side of the road," he said. "And they were not AK-47 shots. Some kind of higher-powered rifle."

"Thank you," Jackson said. "Please continue."

"Yeah, so Williams was down. I could tell he was dead, even from a distance. The second MRAP pulled ahead and to the left, then angled its front end toward the front of the first one, so there was a wedge of space in between, where Williams was lying. I got out of the vehicle and ran forward."

"Go on," Jackson said.

"It was just plain dumb on my part. In that kind of ambush situation, with an MRAP that won't move for whatever reason, the cops were staying protected in their vehicles for good reason. They were waiting for air support, which would've been on scene within two minutes. So, after I got out, I heard the Humvee peel out in reverse, getting out of the kill zone. The gunner in the second MRAP, Ben Cox was his name, was screaming for everybody to stay put, spraying the rooftops with his .50-cal. I don't think he hit anybody, but it gave me cover to reach the girl and drag her into the wedge of space between the two MRAPs. Right as I set her down, Cox was hit. The guys below immediately pulled him down into the vehicle."

He took two long, deliberate breaths, focusing on keeping his shoulders flat. He didn't want to appear dramatic to the jurors, but he needed a moment. He looked at Jackson, then at Rafiq. Both were pictures of silent patience.

"Did you see who shot Mr. Cox?" Jackson asked. "Or where the shot came from?"

"I didn't see the shooter, no," Percy said. "But again, my instinct told me it was elevated sniper fire."

"Was it fatal?"

"I had no idea at the time, but yeah, Cox died later that day in the hospital. Bullet went through his flak vest and ruptured both lungs."

Jackson nodded.

"So, I started to put a tourniquet around Nabaa's leg," Percy continued.

"Nabaa? You mean the Iraqi girl?"

"Yes," he said. "Nabaa is her name. Her leg was bleeding pretty badly. Then, all of a sudden, she screamed like crazy. I looked up and saw she was staring sideways under the MRAP's undercarriage, eyes wide. I dipped my head down to see what she was seeing, and right as I did, I saw the woman from before trying to get up, but as soon as I saw her, I heard another gunshot and saw her head drop to the ground. That time, I did sort of see the shooter — or, at least the shooter's boots. Immediately after the shot, those boots were making a beeline back toward cover."

"Where was cover?"

"The row of brick and clay homes on that side of the road, on the north side — so, left side of the route we were traveling. I watched for a moment as he ran, but then I focused on Nabaa. I secured the tourniquet, readied my M4, and then went to the front of the two MRAPs, scanning the rooftops, looking for the sniper or snipers. I didn't see one immediately, so I got up on the metal step under the driver's door of the bombed vehicle and looked inside the cab. I saw both airmen inside were unconscious. Not uncommon after a direct IED blast in an MRAP. Then I stretched out a little closer to the front of the vehicle, still scanning the rooftop on the right. That's when I saw the sniper. Thankfully, he didn't see me. I took a breath and shot him in the head." He paused, didn't get a question. *Good.* "I hopped back down to the ground and heard voices coming from the street, about 30 yards behind the MRAPs. I turned and saw three insurgents. One was pointing toward me, and the other two were raising their AKs in my direction. They started firing, I got hit in the top of my shoulder. Hurt like hell. I dropped to a knee and shot all three of them in the head."

"Mr. Mackenzie, to clarify, up to that point, had you seen the defendant?"

"No," Percy said, directing a brief glance at Rafiq. "But a few seconds later, I did. I was scanning the road behind the vehicles when I heard shouting behind me. I immediately dropped and low-crawled under the MRAP on the left and kept crawling till I could see up ahead. There were four more armed men about 50 yards away, near the corner of a building. One was giving commands to the other three, who then started jogging across the street in front of me."

"That insurgent who was relaying the commands," Jackson began. "Do you see him here in this courtroom?"

"Well, at that moment, I was too far away to make out his face, but yes. A few minutes later, I was much closer."

"Apologies," Jackson said. "What happened next?"

"I decided to shoot the leader in the knee, which I figured would turn the other three into non-moving targets. I was right. Mr. Itani screamed, pretty much like anybody with a shattered knee would do, and the three other men immediately stopped and turned to look. Within a couple of seconds, I took each of them down with headshots."

Percy's outer voice was doing its job, relating the sequence of events. His inner voices were busy, too. One was trying to meditate, like he practiced. *It was self-defense. I was defending Nabaa. It was what I was trained to do.*

And there was always the other voice. *Stop pretending you're wounded. Stop pretending you're not proud of what you did. Seven shots, seven hits. Who else could do that in an ambush situation? You weren't trained to kill. You were BORN to kill. That's what you wanted, right? To avenge your mother?*

No, he thought. He thought of Maggie and instantly wished she were there in the courtroom, so he could look at her for support. But he knew better, and they had talked about it. He didn't *actually* want to see her face as he talked about the day he killed seven men and maimed another.

And don't forget, Percy — that wasn't even your worst day as a human. Maybe bottom-five, but nowhere near the top.

"Mr. Mackenzie?" Jackson asked, cocking her head slightly. "You can continue."

"Right. Sorry." *Wake up, Percy.* "At that moment, alarm bells started going off in my head, telling me there was another enemy unaccounted

43

for. I realized it was the one who executed Nabaa's mother. I crawled from under the MRAP, into the space between the two vehicles. As I stood up, I saw the Humvee barreling down the road toward me — angled toward the disabled vehicle. It was coming fast. Then the last insurgent appeared from behind the MRAP. He knew I was there, and he was raising his AK toward me. But then he must've processed the sound of the hummer's engine behind him. He turned his head toward it just before the Humvee slammed into him and sent him flying. He landed in the dirt a few feet past me."

"Dead?" Jackson asked.

"Probably. I walked over and shot him twice just to be sure." Percy glanced at the jury members, a few of whom were in the middle of a deep, calming breath. A few others were shaking their heads. "Listen, I'm not proud of it. Any of it. In that moment, I was thinking we had casualties to attend to. The last thing we needed was some asshole regaining consciousness and firing at us." The jurors started looking at each other awkwardly.

"Mr. Mackenzie," Judge Greene interjected. "You're not on trial here. Just answer Ms. Jackson's questions."

"Sorry, your honor," Percy said, then stared at Jackson.

"Just a few more, Mr. Mackenzie, and I will skip ahead a little." She checked her notes. "I understand you and Sergeant Watson — correct?" She got a nod from Percy. "You both got the two casualties into the MRAPs?"

"Yes," Percy said.

"Then what did you do?"

"I commandeered the functioning MRAP from the airmen inside the cab. I started driving forward. I was going to pull up in front of the disabled MRAP and connect it to back of the functioning one with a tow rope. But I saw the insurgent with the shot knee dragging himself toward a weapon on the ground. I turned toward him, and as I drove, he looked up at me. We had a few seconds of solid eye contact. Then I rode slowly over both his legs. He screamed."

"To clarify again," Jackson said, "can you point to the man you saw in that moment?"

Percy pointed to Rafiq. "That man right there. The defendant. Rafiq Itani."

"And you decided to drive a 15-ton vehicle over his legs, shortly after you shot him in the knee?"

"Yes," Percy said.

"Why?"

"I wanted to incapacitate him. But I'll admit I was also angry and full of adrenaline, so the primal part of me also found the scream of pain somewhat satisfying."

44

Jackson continued without expression. "Did you notice anything else pertinent?"

"Yes. Ahead, on the corner of the intersecting street, there was an old tractor rig. On the ground, I saw what looked like a tow rope and some chains. The rig drove away right after the defendant started screaming."

"Do you know what the purpose of the chains and tow rope were?"

Percy nodded. "I was briefed later that the insurgents' plan was to steal the disabled MRAP and study it. The chains were to secure the doors of both MRAPs and prevent any soldiers from exiting."

"Thank you," Jackson said. She turned toward the defense table. "That's all from me."

Becky Whitfield stood. "Mr. Mackenzie, good morning. And I'd like to echo Judge Greene's sentiments about your service to our country. Thank you sincerely."

Percy nodded. "I appreciate that."

"I'll try to keep this brief," Whitfield said. "How many times did you see the defendant fire a weapon that day?"

"Zero," Percy said.

"To your direct knowledge, has the defendant ever hurt anyone at any time by his own hand?"

"No, not to my knowledge."

"You said Mr. Itani was giving instructions to the other insurgents that day," Whitfield continued rapidly. "Do you believe he was in charge? That it was his plan?"

"I do," Percy said.

"Do you believe the plan was," she paused dramatically, "evil?"

"No," Percy answered immediately. "Militarily, it was a good plan. Strategic and operational impacts were obvious, and the tactics were pretty sound. If a couple of my bullets had missed, or if the shoulder shot had got me in the head, it probably would've been successful."

"So, you don't believe it was an act of terrorism?"

"I do not."

"Interesting." Whitfield paused. "The girl, Nabaa. She is now your adopted daughter, correct?"

"She is," Percy said. "The rest of her family fled immediately after that attack, and she had nobody. I stayed with her in the hospital for a while after and spent a lot of time with her during her long recovery."

"So, I would assume you harbor some pretty intense hatred for the defendant on her behalf."

Percy waited for a question, enduring the awkward silence. It would be best if he didn't make it too easy for the defense.

"Sorry," Whitfield continued. She was slightly flustered, but recovered quickly. "Would that assumption be correct?"

"No, ma'am," he said. "I try not to have hatred for anybody. But even if I did, like I mentioned before, I don't believe what the defendant did was evil. To be honest, I think it's just as likely the defendant is an honorable man."

Murmuring began in the seated area of the courtroom. Brows furrowing, several jurors began looking at each other quizzically.

"An honorable man?" Whitfield said. "Why would you come to that conclusion?"

"It wasn't a conclusion, ma'am," Percy said. "I said it was just as likely he is honorable as it is that he is evil. I don't know the man. But from the limited information I have, he strikes me as somebody with honor. He certainly has values and political beliefs that conflict with the defense policy of the United States. But over the centuries, we've fought plenty of wars against honorable enemies. This war we've been in since 2001 has been different, for sure. And a lot of our enemies in that war are simply terrorists. Misguided young men who willfully kill innocent civilians to terrorize other innocent civilians. But I've got no evidence that the defendant is one of them. He planned a military operation to achieve a military goal. The fact that his fighting force doesn't represent a specific country's government does not automatically make it terrorism to me."

Percy ignored an urge to glance at the jurors. The courtroom felt like someone had pressed pause in a movie. Only Whitfield was in motion.

She stared silently at Percy for three long seconds. "Is it true you visited the defendant when he was detained in Guantanamo?"

That wasn't in the script. What are you playing at? "Yes," he said. More murmurs all around.

"Why?"

"That's a long story." Percy stared back at Whitfield, proceeding with caution. "But since you asked … After the 3/20 attacks, my wife and Nabaa were both captured by men working for Fadi Itani, the defendant's father. My wife escaped, but the men were able to flee the country with Nabaa. Fadi Itani had found and also abducted her two siblings, and was demanding his son's release. When his demand wasn't met, he killed her siblings live on the internet. He threatened that Nabaa would be next." His brain was involuntarily replaying the grisly images of the children being beheaded. Then the image of Fadi shoving a huge knife into his own neck. *Done feelings, Percy. Let the images play. Breathe. They have to play.* He tried to clear his head, the traumatic memories shifting into anger. *What the fuck. No. Not now."* Those were the darkest few days of my life. As you might imagine. I was—" He tried to think of what to say. "I was out of my mind. I was convinced Fadi would kill Nabaa just like her brother and sister. But with literally seconds to spare, a special forces team was able to rescue her."

46

Percy was visibly disturbed. Whitfield noticed. "Take your time, Mr. Mackenzie."

"What was the question again?" He remembered the question, but the "whole truth" would be breaking the law, and possibly putting an even bigger target on Rafiq's back. He visited Rafiq mostly to pay him back for finally giving up Fadi's location. But that one piece of information was classified.

"You were getting to why you visited the defendant at Gitmo."

"Right. Sorry. So, even before 3/20, I had already been dealing with some … I wouldn't say guilt. I don't have regrets, per se. But, there was some mental or spiritual conflict, if you will. Maybe a kind of PTSD in modern vernacular, I don't know. Anyway, after I had my daughter back, obviously I was relieved. God, it was just indescribable relief. But after seeing Fadi's video, I couldn't stop thinking about Rafiq. It was like there was a big shining light on that old 'conflict' I'd been chewing on for years." He took a few slow breaths, gathering his thoughts, purposely looking pensive. He did want to tell as much of the truth as he could. "I had an idea of what Rafiq had endured and my role in sealing that fate. I just kept imagining him alone in a cell, probably hearing his father had died, probably that he committed suicide. The shame of that, for a proud son— it just stuck in my head as wrong, somehow. Fadi's last words were directed specifically at Rafiq, and I wanted to make sure he saw the video unfiltered. I was the guy who put him in there, and I doubted anyone else would set the record straight. It was like some kind of unfinished karmic business I had to attend."

The steady gaze between Whitfield and Percy was a charged cable in the air. "How did you get approval for that visit, by the way?"

"I've met lots of powerful people in my career, ma'am. I found the right ones and asked nicely."

To Percy's surprise, she smiled. "How did the visit go?"

"As planned, I guess. He didn't say much. But he communicated his appreciation."

"His father, Fadi Itani. Do you view him the same way you view Rafiq? Just a man who has different ideals but otherwise honorable?"

"No," Percy said. "We have indisputable evidence that he committed gross acts of terrorism against innocent people. To be fair, though, he seemed to realize that about himself before the end of his life. And the video he recorded right before his suicide has become one of the most powerful anti-violence messages in history. That's another reason why I wanted the defendant to see it. He wanted his son to hear that message, and to hear his apology along with it."

He waited a moment for another question, but Whitfield seemed to be contemplating whether she was finished or not. Knowing his time was almost up, he decided to elaborate a little more.

"Many of us do awful things we regret," Percy said. "We can't go back and undo them. But if we acknowledge our mistakes, we can hope for understanding and forgiveness. I believe that applies to sins big and small."

"Interesting perspective," Whitfield said.

"Thanks," Percy shot back at her.

"Almost done. I'd like your perspective on one more thing." She turned and stared at Rafiq for a few moments. He was staring back at her icily. She turned back to Percy. "The day you incapacitated and detained the defendant — that was December of 2008, correct?"

"Yes."

"And the rescue of Nabaa was the end of March 2010?"

"Yes."

"Is it fair to say he was being intensely interrogated for 16 months in order to discern his father's location?"

The judge looked to the U.S. attorney's table. It was the kind of question that should have elicited an objection, but Percy had told Jackson not to object under any circumstances. And now he understood what was happening.

Whitfield wanted to tell the jury about Rafiq's torture — paint him as a man who had been punished plenty for his crimes already — but her client clearly had not given her permission. Now she was going rogue. Percy glanced at Rafiq, who basically confirmed the suspicion by making a half-second of eye contact and then casting his gaze downward to his lap. *It's ok, man. I can handle myself.* He suddenly felt much more at ease.

"Yes, that's probably a fair assumption," Percy said.

"So that's just an assumption, then?"

The prosecutors were busy whispering into each other's ears.

"No, ma'am. I suppose not. It's a little more than that. I hope you realize that I might have some general information that's classified, and therefore it's not appropriate to discuss openly in a public trial. But I'll do my best to answer your question in a very general way, since it's one I've wrestled with for a long time. And I've done quite a bit of research into our detention and interrogation methods, and the legal bases for all of it. I'm an American. And I'm not somebody who dismisses patriotism as quaint. I care about our ideals and how we apply them in tough times. Also, obviously, this is an issue close to my heart. So I learned about it, and I wasn't proud of what I learned. We routinely find ways to torture the people we think have information we want. And the interrogation policy makers tend to stay one step ahead of legal definitions."

"And interrogators tend to also stay a step ahead of subpoenas," Whitfield said, a tiny, caustic grin aimed at Percy.

"True enough," he replied.

"Can you elaborate on what you learned so the jury might have a sense of what Rafiq might have endured? I'll ask him the same questions, but they might only believe him if they hear it from a true patriot first."

The words *true patriot* were enunciated with just a touch of derisive irony. *You are an ACLU lawyer through and through,* Percy thought as he eyed her. *Good for you.* He found himself suddenly enjoying the experience of being cross-examined. Rafiq actually had a true advocate in the U.S. justice system. He was getting the fair trial he deserved. Ironically, this exact line of questioning and the prosecutors' refusal to object was helping Percy deliver on his promise.

"I understand, ma'am," Percy said. "Here's what I would tell you. We define torture pretty traditionally. You know, anything that causes physical pain is off the table. So, interrogators have gotten creative over the years. We've heard about waterboarding for a while now, and that's a good example of what I'm talking about. It's controversial because there's disagreement among intellectuals. The hawks tell you it's not physically painful, and there's no risk of death or injury beyond what is normal for detention. Human rights advocates explain the mental trauma it induces. I'd bet just about every detainee who's suffered through waterboarding would easily prefer a traditional beating.

"But that's just one example," Percy continued. "There's also extended isolation, playing loud anticultural music for hours on end, interrupting sleep, interrupting prayer, frigid water exposure, and all the nudity-related indignities that are against the rules but impossible to enforce unless people are dumb enough to take photos. And if none of that works — you know, if we don't get the information we want — it's perfectly legal to temporarily transfer detainees into the custody of other countries that have no rules at all."

Whitfield nodded lightly. Her eyes betrayed mild curiosity. "As a former member of the armed forces, how do you feel about all of that, Mr. Mackenzie?"

"I think it's wrong," Percy said. "And it's even more wrong because we have plenty of evidence that shows torture in any form doesn't actually work. I think we can all *assume* interrogators were creatively trying to get Rafiq to reveal Fadi's location for 16 months, and obviously 3/20 still happened."

"Thank you for your time and your candor, Mr. Mackenzie." Whitfield, finally seeming satisfied, looked at Judge Greene. "I have no more questions."

49

◇◇◇◇◇◇◇◇◇
CHAPTER 5

January 2015

Maggie grabbed her keys from the hook. "I'm leaving, honey!"

Percy hurried from the kitchen to the foyer and wrapped her in a bear hug, crumpling her purse and insulated lunch bag against her body. She groaned in mock suffering. He let go, closed his eyes, bent forward slightly, and puckered his lips.

Maggie sighed and kissed him on the cheek. "Yeah, I'd be in a good mood, too, if I had a month off to sit around and do nothing."

"You have no idea how much energy it takes to grow a beard," he said.

"You've mentioned that," she said. "And I know about the couch that might float away without your vigilance and the eyelids that need to be inspected for cracks. I got it." She pulled his shirt toward her and gave him a quick kiss on the lips. "Love you. Dinner better be hot and ready when I get back."

"Always," he said. "Drive safely, babe."

She left. Percy headed back to the kitchen, where he'd left a spoonful of honey sitting in his big, black mug full of hot coffee. He stirred it twice and took his coffee to the living room, where the TV was tuned to Fox News on mute.

His phone buzzed, and he wondered what Maggie forgot to take with her. He pulled it out of his pocket and read the screen, which said "Handyman Chris." It was the president calling.

"Good morning, sir," Percy said.

"Good morning to you," President Brennan said. "And good news."

"Oh yeah? Lay it on me."

"Broad support, man. People on both sides of the aisle. I'm told it's around 80 percent favorable among left-leaning people, but even among conservatives, you're around 65."

"Whoa," Percy said.

"You sound surprised," Brennan said. "I'm not."

"Just a pretty high number, sir. I mean, I've been watching the news coverage for the past two days, and it's been pretty fair. But the talking heads they pit against each other tend to polarize everything, so I guess I wasn't sure what most people actually thought."

"Well, I don't think you could've handled yourself any better," Brennan said. "Even if you never serve in public office, it was the kind of message that has a positive and lasting effect on the national consciousness. I admire you all the more for that, Percy."

"Thank you, sir."

"You're welcome. So, are you still on board with joining the good guys in blue?"

"Well, sir, I don't think I can commit 100 percent quite yet. Maggie and I still haven't quite come to consensus. Hoping we will soon."

"Oh," Brennan said. "I was just referring to whether you're going to change your party registration."

Percy laughed. "Oh. That. Yeah, I don't see why not. I've been feeling more blue than red for a while anyway. And 80 is a lot higher than 65."

"Agreed," Brennan said. "You know, you never did tell me how you ended up a registered Republican."

"I registered when I was 18," Percy said, "I was walking around Mill Avenue in Tempe, and some college activist put a registration form in my face. I checked the box my dad would want me to check. I've since realized I'm not much of a joiner. And I'm definitely not a fan of either party these days."

"I know what you mean. I'm more independent than democrat. That part has always been hard for me, and it will be for you. But as much as I hate to admit it, there have been plenty of times in my career when I've been glad I've had a party affiliation. I'm not independently wealthy enough to make the money factor irrelevant. And hey, neither are you. Right?"

"You are correct, sir," Percy said.

"Not to mention Maryland is one of the bluest states in the country. As I've told you, I think you could win either way, but I believe the last 12 Senate elections in Maryland have gone to democrats — most of them incumbents, of course."

"Wow. That's a little bluer than I thought."

"Yeah. Of course, I carried the state both times," Brennan said with a smile in his voice. "But Maryland also voted for far less charismatic democrats in the two or three presidential elections before me, too."

"Ok. So, if I want to ensure victory, I need to change my registration from one den of thieves to the other. And if *I'm* not trying to ensure victory, then someone else is. Right?"

"Wow," Brennan said. "You've mastered the first 99 percent of American politics. You might be better at this than I thought. Good thing you can't come for *my job.*"

Percy laughed. "Yeah. But first I guess I have to decide whether I'm going to do it at all." Silence hung over the line for a couple of seconds. "I know you've put in a lot of time on my behalf, sir, and I appreciate it."

"Don't mention it, Percy."

"It's true what you said, back in 2010," Percy said. "I've had enough of the sidelines. Living this anonymous life, working in a cubicle, writing reports — it was a nice break for the first couple of years. Now it's driving me crazy."

"I can imagine," Brennan said. "And that will be me in a couple of years. Scares the shit out of me."

"So how long do I have to make up my mind?"

"How 'bout I have somebody from the DNC send you the paperwork? Just sign it and send it in. In the meantime, talk to Maggie — and your daughter, too — and get back to me in a couple of weeks."

"Give me a couple weeks, please, sir," Percy said. "I can't have that showing up in the mail before I talk to Maggie. It wouldn't go well."

"Roger that, Perce," Brennan said. "And I want to be very clear about something, since you might be starting to think my approach is a little too aggressive. You would be right. It's not really in my nature to be pushy, but on this topic, I have to remind myself that I am only one force in the equation. Your wife and daughter are the opposite force. They will convincingly pull you in the opposite direction I want you to go, as they should. I don't blame you. Nobody wants you doing this without family support. There aren't many ways to make politics less fun, but that's one of them. But in the meantime, I care deeply about this country, and I know all too well how easy it is for the wrong people to find their way into powerful positions. So when I see someone who would actually do good, I have to be the other force, pulling you into this world. It's a world that spawns bad guys and therefore needs a few good guys. I hope you understand that."

"I do, sir," Percy said.

"For what it's worth, I think you'll mostly love it — especially all the times you'll get to piss off the establishment."

"You might be right, sir. Talk to you soon." Percy ended the call, briefly relishing that he beat the leader of the free world in the age-old, unspoken race to hang up first. He took a long swig of his coffee, which had cooled to the perfect temperature. The caffeine felt like an army of urgency racing to his extremities and flanking his entire consciousness.

The phone call made it all so real. For the first time, seeing himself as a U.S. senator didn't feel like a fantasy, but like foretelling. For a moment, it was the height of quiet excitement.

Then, like a falling icicle, fear for his family pierced him deep in the belly. With just as much certainty as he felt for his eventual victory, he reminded himself what an excellent target he would be for hostility, and not just in the media.

This is what Maggie and Nabaa feel every time they think about this.

There were plenty of other moments in his life when things seemed so good, so promising. When he was sitting in a gazebo on Luke Air Force Base, smoking a cigarette with his friend and colleague, Master Sgt. Ryan Wains, talking about the speech he was going to deliver at his high school alma mater later that night. Fifteen minutes later, thousands of people were blown to bits before his eyes.

When he was dominating the pararescue program for 62 weeks, with only two weeks to go before earning his maroon beret. Everything felt like it was in place. Everything was easy. He was doing what he was meant to do. Then one casual jump from a helo rope ladder, and his ankle was shattered.

When Maggie announced she was pregnant — those shimmering, happy, watery eyes. That kiss. That hug. That warm feeling in his belly. A few months later, the fetus was gone and so was Maggie's fertility.

And, of course, his 10th birthday, when he was standing on a mountaintop staring down at the East Valley. It was the last on his list of local peaks to conquer and his mother, his favorite human being on Earth, was by his side. Two hours later she was dead.

You're not meant to have nice things, Percy.

This run for Senate was starting to feel too ... what? Destined? No. Too hopeful. It was starting to feel like some kind of redemption.

Is this what I'm supposed to do? Is it in service to others, like I've convinced myself? Or is it just the usual Percy Mackenzie with something to prove?

Without thinking, he set down his coffee, clasped his hands together and brought them to his forehead.

Dear God, I have a simple request. Please keep them safe. Please, please, please keep them safe.

He suddenly thought of Nabaa's fateful choice on the village road. *And if this decision of mine is going to cause more violence than it prevents, remove it from my future.*

It was a simple request, submitted to a God who showed little sign of simplicity.

He wanted to leave it there. To have faith. To trust that his fear was nothing more than a product of shitty luck, repeated too often.

But what if you're wrong? You think that prayer is enough? No, he didn't. He never did.

Percy reached in the cargo pocket of his pants and retrieved his combat application tourniquet. He unfastened it, opened it into its widest circle, carefully brought it down and around his right foot, raised it up to his lower thigh, then pulled the strap tight and pushed down hard on the Velcro. He turned the lever once. Twice. The third twist was difficult, but he made it work.

The blood flow stopped instantly. Soon, he knew, would come the near-numbness, and then he would meditate — two minutes. Maybe three. He would feel the panic in the moments before it went too long. And then he would release the pressure, and his heartbeat would respond in force. The dammed blood would collide with the sequestered blood below the tourniquet, and he would feel all the ensuing friction on his nerves. And the indescribable tingling pain would go on for minutes. It would remind him that he was alive. And why.

Not because you *should be, but because* they *should be. That others may live, so do you.*

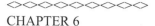

CHAPTER 6

January 2015

"As promised, today you'll get to hear your own voices a lot more than mine," Professor Horatio Kibbe said. Brow furrowed, he was bent over slightly, trying to get the desktop computer to project its image onto the huge white canvas hanging behind him. "And I know you all enjoy class a little more when we can relate our Islamic studies to a current event right here in the U. S. of A."

Chatter in the lecture hall had quieted, but then the mellow din of hushed voices returned as the projector too-slowly warmed itself up. Nabaa was pretty sure she heard the word "Mackenzie" whispered a couple of times. *Of course,* she thought. She should've guessed Percy's testimony would come up in this class.

And then, there he was. Her adopted father and American hero of heroes, raising his right hand and facing the federal court bailiff.

The professor paused the video. "Raise your hands if you know who this is." Almost everyone raised a hand. "Keep them up if you watched this testimony, live or sometime in the last few days." About half the students dropped their hand. "OK. A quick recap for those who are unfamiliar."

Kibbe spent the next minute summarizing the situation preceding the trial. Then, he bent forward at the waist again and used his mouse to slide ahead in the timeline. "So, the U.S. attorney, woman by the name of Andria Jackson, started by getting Mackenzie to describe the entire ambush sequence. If you want to hear that part from his perspective, you'll have to do it on your own time. I found it pretty fascinating, but it has nothing to do with Islam. All right. Here we go." He stood up straight and gestured toward the huge image on the projection screen. "This woman is Becky Whitfield, an ACLU lawyer and the lead attorney for Rafiq Itani."

He pressed play, and the class watched Whitfield's entire cross-examination. Several minutes later, he paused it again.

"OK. Heavy stuff, right?" He buried his hands in his pants pockets and surveyed the lecture hall. "Who can tell me the first moment you thought to yourself, 'That thing he just said has some bearing on world religion'?" He waited a moment as several hands went up, then pointed up to his right. "Russ. Go 'head."

"Right away, when he said the ambush wasn't evil." Nabaa turned and looked toward the voice. It came from a tall, sandy blond-haired male student. *Definitely a frat boy,* she thought. "It was surprising to hear at first, but when he explained himself, it made a lot of sense. It made me immediately question my preconceptions."

"Interesting," Kibbe said. "And you think those preconceptions are religious? Or might they be cultural?" The frat boy only nodded introspectively and turned to see other hands going up. Kibbe pointed in Nabaa's direction.

"You've said before that it's almost impossible to separate those two forces in most countries," said a young woman two seats away. "The founders tried to do it in America, but Judeo-Christian ideas still shape our culture, and even the policies of our government."

"Good," Kibbe said. He pointed to another raised hand, this time to a female student in the second row who wore her dyed red hair in a ponytail. "Stacie?"

"What he said about honor really struck me." *This girl loves to sound smart,* Nabaa thought for the hundredth time. "I mean, even if you believe church and state should be separated — and I do — religion is still mostly a force for good in the world, right? So, if you're judging actions by their motivations, it seems honorable to me that someone would choose to fight — or, you know, defend their homeland — on the basis of their religious beliefs. It's better than some of our other motivations for violence."

"Oh really?" Based on the speaker's appearance, Nabaa had always assumed he was one of the few Muslims in the class.

He smiled and shook his head a few times, apparently not willing to elaborate.

"Ibrahim, I gather you're not the talkative type, but it seems you have more to say." Kibbe's expression was more serious than Nabaa was used to. Ibrahim stared back at him for a few tense moments, then relented.

"I just object to the premise," Ibrahim said. "I mean, religion can be great, but it's one of the *worst* motivations for any kind of violence. Just look at history. It's the ultimate ends-justify-the-means rationale. So many young Muslim men are fucking *lost* ... Sorry." Ibrahim shook his head again.

"It's fine. Continue." Kibbe smiled. Hands back in pockets, he was still staring intently at Ibrahim.

"I'm a young Muslim man," Ibrahim said. "And, you know, that part of my life is hard. Any religion is a struggle to understand and follow, right? Faith asks a lot, especially of young people who are counterbalanced by a lack of experience in life. And these jihadi leaders *know* that. These radical clerics *know* that. So they're helping raise an entire generation of young Muslims who at best are wondering if violence should be part of their life's work, and at worst are strapping on suicide vests."

"Fair enough," Kibbe said. "But do you feel like that relates to Mackenzie's testimony? Or to Rafiq Itani's case?"

"I was mostly just disagreeing with her," he said, gesturing to the redhead. He looked at her. "And sorry for my tone. I sounded condescending."

"That's all you have to say?" Kibbe asked.

Ibrahim exhaled. Nabaa saw virtually every head in the room was turned toward him, interested.

"OK," he said. "I respect what Mackenzie did. He seems like a genuinely good dude, a guy who clearly has some anger or guilt he's wrestling with, but a good dude. I just don't necessarily agree with him that Rafiq is honorable. Or *might* be honorable. Rafiq isn't the worst, but he's still responsible for the death of one innocent civilian in this *military operation* he planned. Almost two." He looked at Sara, who was shaking her head gently. "Even if he didn't pull the trigger, he either didn't properly prepare his men for the possibility of civilian interference, or he sanctioned it in the planning phase."

Kibbe was nodding, brow furrowed. "Ibrahim, thank you. Your perspective is an important one here, obviously. So, if you don't mind, I've got one more question for you." Ibrahim nodded, so Kibbe continued. "True or false: Native people have the right to mount an insurgency against in invading force. In other words, do they have the ethical standing to use nontraditional warfare tactics? For example, the kind of tactics we westerners might associate with terrorism."

"True. Of course. You mean ambushes and hidden bombs — that kind of thing?"

"Right. What about suicide bombs?"

"Sure. That's their prerogative."

"OK. So, we've covered the ethical part," Kibbe said. "Maybe there's a leap there from ethical to honorable. Do you believe engaging in ethical insurgency operations *can* be honorable?"

Ibrahim thought for a moment, then nodded. "Yes. I don't see why not."

"And do you agree that some civilian casualties are inherent to all wartime operations?"

"Yeah, I agree," Ibrahim said. "I mean, there's certainly a point where there are so many dead civilians that it's no longer possible to call a military operation ethical, much less honorable."

"So, is that your main objection with the operation Rafiq Itani planned and led? That one civilian was killed and another was hurt? Is that beyond your threshold for that particular operation?"

Ibrahim's eyes were intense, but aimlessly searching the walls of the lecture hall. "That's a good question. I don't know," he said. "Honestly, it *feels* wrong, but I'm trying to articulate why. I mean, it's probably evidence of my bias. I don't like the image of a sniper putting a little girl his sights and pulling the trigger. I don't like an insurgent standing over an injured mother and executing her. That just feels like it's inherently evil."

He paused, but seemed to have more to say. Kibbe and the rest of the class waited.

"But thinking of it in the context of war, it's more complex," he continued. "If I grant that the combatants, Americans and insurgents, are ethically engaged, then I guess that little village road is fair game for a battle. That means the girl, Nabaa, and then her mother became combatants by entering that specific battle zone. So, I guess that means it was ethical to target them." He paused and made a pained face. "Whoa. Gross. That feels awful to say."

Wow. That is one honest boy, Nabaa thought. *And smart, too.*

"War is an ugly thing," Kibbe said. He spoke to the entire class. "These distinctions are really, really difficult to define. And even harder when religious beliefs are in play. I don't know about you all, but I'd absolutely rather be here analyzing the morality of combat years later than trying to make those life-and-death decisions in the moment. "

"That's all true, Professor," Nabaa said suddenly. "And I understand why you're alluding to religion as the basis for moral intent. Most people agree that intent is a big part of any moral determination." She waited for his assent, but Kibbe was only waiting her for to continue. "I mention that because we don't know Rafiq's actual intent, do we? We can't assume all insurgents in the Middle East are operating with a heart full of righteous Islam."

Kibbe smiled. "Very good, Aahna. Did you see my lesson notes?"

Nabaa smiled back. She caught Ibrahim staring at her. He started shifting his gaze back to the professor, but she noticed that his head moved before his eyes. *Just a second too long, young man,* she thought. *Now I might have to get to know you.*

"That's not the only generalization we're making here," Ibrahim said. "We also can't lump all Arabs into the group 'natives,' for the purposes of this discussion. Rafiq and Fadi Itani are Lebanese, right? And of the men he had with him that day, I think seven or eight in total, I believe I read only two were Iraqis."

"We also shouldn't assume that foreign fighters have different motivations," Kibbe said, smiling. "Isn't it more honorable to fight for the freedom of others? But your point is well made."

"Yours too, Professor," Ibrahim said. "In this case, though, we have evidence to the contrary. Fadi Itani's famous video told us that his son's

58

capture had changed his motivation to revenge. And you probably know about how his wife died 20 years ago in an Israeli air strike. Are we sure Rafiq wasn't motivated by revenge, too? Maybe, maybe not. Maybe he was able to find the peace of Allah and not carry vengeance in his heart. Maybe he missed his dad growing up and wanted to impress him by planning an insurgent ambush. That's not really honorable, either."

"Fair enough," Kibbe said. "We don't know his motivation. But why do you suppose Percy Mackenzie — who's actually spoken to Rafiq down at Gitmo — would be willing to give him the benefit of the doubt? Why is he sympathetic, even when Rafiq directly caused him pain?"

Nabaa stared down at Ibrahim. With him facing mostly forward, she could only see a partial profile. But her eyes were riveted to his face. She was momentarily aware of how much she cared about how he answered the question. *This is your test,* she silently told him.

"I guess that's because I believe him to be a good man," Ibrahim said. "He understands that our job as humans is to speak uncomfortable truths to our own tribe while trying to understand the plight of others. For him, the ultimate 'Other' is Rafiq Itani, so he's sympathetic to his suffering. For me, Itani and his father feel like part of my own tribe, since we share a faith. I see their actions as dangerous to our shared faith. So, from within that tribe I need to call out what I see as wrong. And that's what I see as the difference between my faction of our tribe and their faction. It's actually the most common difference in any tribe. One subgroup sees danger from outside and wants to violently close ranks. Another subgroup is looking at the people outside the tribe and trying to find a way to make peace. Obviously, I think we should almost always make sure we're in that second subgroup. It's only by *listening* to The Other that we stop fearing him and start to see ways we can coexist, compromise, maybe even collaborate. That's how progress is made. The world only gets better, and humanity only evolves, when people start to see through their enemy's eyes so much that they cease being enemies."

Nabaa realized she was smiling. Her stomach felt warm and strange. The thought in her head was both alarming and exciting. *I want to be near this boy as he becomes a man.*

◇◇◇◇◇◇◇◇◇
CHAPTER 7

January 2015

from: Aahna Khatri <aktheexister@gmail.com>
to: Liza Hamilton <lizachucksgirl@gmail.com>
date: Tue, Jan 27, 2014 at 4:55 AM
Subject: Why sleep?

There's a boy.

from: Liza Hamilton <lizachucksgirl@gmail.com>
to: Aahna Khatri <aktheexister@gmail.com>
date: Tue, Jan 27, 2014 at 5:34 AM
Subject: RE: Why sleep?

WHAAAAAT???!!? There's a boy? Where? Who is he?
Don't forget: Most boys, especially college boys, are dumb.
They might sound smart once in a while, but it's really just their
brain overcorrecting for all the dumbness the other 99% of the
time.
And now you can't sleep? Call me if you want. Love you.

from: Aahna Khatri <aktheexister@gmail.com>
to: Liza Hamilton <lizachucksgirl@gmail.com>
date: Tue, Jan 27, 2014 at 5:48 AM
Subject: RE: Why sleep?

I can't call you now, but probably will later. I don't know. I'm
probably still too nervous to say it out loud. I've never felt this
before. I don't like it! I couldn't study very well last night. And then
I woke up three hours before my alarm and couldn't sleep again.
I'm sure he's just a dumb boy. But he sounded sooo smart in
my Intro to Islam class yesterday. And somehow his smartness
made him look very handsome. If you heard what he said, you
would understand. I'll explain on the phone. *Definitely* not serious
enough yet to warrant a discussion over email.
Love you too! But you still haven't answered the question in
the subject line. And you better make it good. I've had hours to
ponder this morning, probably while you were sleeping. ;)

Ugh. I've only casually wondered about this, but never quite put brain power into it. Now it's already hurting my brain! Here are my interesting thoughts. Brace yourself.

We can reject sleep for a long time, if we have enough reason. And if we succeed, our brains and bodies will run on food fuel, fat fuel, etc. Conversely, if food and body fuel are no longer available, our bodies will need more sleep to "provide" energy.

But ... where is this energy coming from? How are we getting energy by sleeping? There's no fuel there. You can say that we're always burning kilocalories from our physiological sources, even when we're in starvation mode, but it doesn't explain why we would need more sleep. And if we can compensate for lost sleep energy by eating more, why is that compensation limited? Why does it max out at a certain point? Perfectly healthy people with plenty of food fuel will still die without sleep.

I also just did some Googling, and it turns out NOBODY knows why animals need sleep to function properly.

It's actually counterintuitive. What is the biological advantage we attain by evolving this need for sleep? It makes all animals super vulnerable for about a third of our lives. Just lying there, like a gift for predators.

Wow. Sleep is way weirder than I thought. And that's without mentioning dreams!

Thank you!

I got sent down this rabbit hole because of my research and related obsession into free will. There's this thing called the "deterministic consciousness model." It basically says everything is predestined, because genes plus experiences = all choices, and both genes and experiences are outside our control. But I realized *that only works during waking hours.* But it seems quite separate from sleep. The macro version of that model ... wait.

I just had an idea as I type.

BRAINS ARE BATTERIES!

61

Think of a car. Or any type of vehicle, I guess. What powers it? The engine. What powers the engine? Fuel. OK, but what power source ignites the fuel and keeps the rest of the car in synchronous order?

A battery.

Humans have an engine: the heartbeat. Humans have fuel: food. But what energy source keeps the heart beating and the fuel burning constantly to maintain a living being? By process of elimination: The brain is the battery. Of course it is! It has to be charged every night!

This means something. I have to go to class, but I will check email again right after. Tell me what you think!

from: Liza Hamilton <lizachucksgirl@gmail.com>
to: Aahna Khatri <aktheexister@gmail.com>
date: Tue, Jan 27, 2014 at 8:02 AM
Subject: RE: Why sleep?

!!!

That makes so much sense.

I have ruminated. I have contemplated. What if brains are the batteries of our *soul?* What if the "consciousness" energy that is so hard for science to pin down is actually the mystical energy that animates each human being … which, in essence, is our body.

If that's true, is it any surprise that our batteries only get charged while we are unconscious? During the very time when we are no longer interacting with the living world and all its distractions? Our brains are always full of stupid stress and ambitions and desires and all kinds of irrational worries. So we literally have to turn ourselves off.

Only then does divinity get access to us. Dreams you say? Easy. Clearly our brains are constantly trying to reconcile the spiritual and physical worlds, so we have dreams.

Boom. Next question!

CHAPTER 8

January 2015

Smiling, Nabaa walked into R. House — a chic, food-court-style lunch destination in a renovated warehouse on the south side of campus. Local chefs rotated in and out of the stations, and the food was always fresh, healthy, and delicious. It was expensive, but she treasured the couple of times a month she could justify splurging here.

She saw Ibrahim a few moments later, standing in line at the falafel place. Before she could properly strategize, her feet were carrying her toward the same line. Her mouth was opening to say something to him.

She stopped. *What do I say? How do people do this?*

Sensing her presence, Ibrahim turned and looked at her. He smiled.

"Hey! Intro to Islam, right?" He held out his hand.

Nabaa shook it, smiling back. She was about to introduce herself, but Ibrahim held up a finger.

"No, don't tell me. I remember …" His eyes narrowed playfully, piercing hers. "Anna?"

The American pronunciation of her alias jarred her briefly. In that moment, she realized it was actually her real name she expected to come out of his mouth. For the first time in a long time, her veil of identity had lapsed in front of a relative stranger.

Be careful, she told herself. She recovered and put her smile back on her face.

"Close," she said. "AH-na. Ahna Khatri."

"Ibrahim Khan," he said. "It's a pleasure to meet you."

It was a common name on the Asian subcontinent, so she learned nothing from it.

"You as well," Nabaa said. "So where are you from? Your family, I mean?"

He smiled. "I assume you mean my Muslim heritage? Pakistan, but -- it's complicated."

She smiled and nodded. "Maybe we could start a campus club called 'Complicated Muslim Heritage,'" she said. "I feel it might be popular." She feigned playfulness, but was wary of the direction of the conversation. She could fool most Americans with her basic understanding of the conflicts in Kashmir, but if Ibrahim was familiar at all with Northern Pakistan, she might have a hard time keeping up. She changed the subject. "What are you planning to order?"

"I honestly don't know," Ibrahim said. "I've never been here before. Have you?"

She nodded. "I *love* R. House. Been here about a dozen times, but this station is my favorite. You chose wisely."

"Well, even if the food's not good, the company might be." His smile was infectious. "Would you be so kind as to dine with me, Aahna Khatri?"

Her stomach did a tiny flip. *From small talk to a date in 60 seconds.* "It would be much easier to say no if I had come with friends, but I see you've boxed me in." She returned his smile and added raised eyebrows. "So, yes! I'd love to!"

Ibrahim's laugh was loud, sudden, and sincere.

"All right, fair enough," he said. "If I'm not a wildly entertaining lunch date after 10 minutes, you are dismissed. Deal?"

"That's not really a concession. It only takes me nine minutes to eat my lamb burger and falafel fries."

He paused, mouth open in mock shock. "Wow!" Now he was shaking his head and furrowing his brow dramatically. He lowered his voice to just above a whisper. "For the sake of a joke at my expense, you revealed what you intend to order. And now *I* will order a lamb burger and falafel fries, and you will bear the public shame of walking up to the cashier and copying my order." He raised his voice back to normal volume. "I didn't expect such a novice mistake by someone who claims to be a veteran hipster lunch patron." Then he smiled mischievously and turned back toward the food counter.

Nabaa tapped him on the shoulder. "I'm suddenly in a mood to negotiate," she said over his shoulder. He turned back to her, and she continued. "I propose you allow me to take your place in line and order before you."

He waited a beat. "And why might I do that?"

"First, you get to *appear* to be a gentleman, which you've just recently shown to be untrue." She paused just long enough to raise one eyebrow. "Second, I will chew more slowly than usual in order to extend your opportunity to impress me with your conversational talents."

Ibrahim looked toward the ceiling, pondering dramatically. The line moved, and he took one step toward the register.

"This is my final offer," Nabaa said. "If you choose to reject it, I will simply walk around and stand in front of you. What will you do then? Complain like a child? Force your way back in front of me? Your options will all be bad, and you will eat alone."

He smiled and nodded, then held his hand out. "Deal." They shook, and he motioned for her to take his spot in line.

When it was Nabaa's turn to approach the counter, Ibrahim smoothly slid forward and said to the cashier, "Two lamb burgers and two orders of falafel fries." Smiling triumphantly, he refused to meet Nabaa's gaze for several seconds. Once he had paid, he looked at her. "See? Everyone wins. You get a free lunch, and I don't have to feel like a rookie order thief."

"*And* I get the satisfaction of seeing the fruition of a plan that formed the moment I saw you." She smiled only with her eyes.

On his face was a respectful but smoldering look of resignation. *Here is a boy who is not used to losing,* Nabaa thought.

They got their food and sat at a four-top table near the back of the restaurant. Ibrahim took a bite of his burger immediately.

"Hmmm." He was nodding as he chewed. "Mmmmm. Wow. That is delicious." He swallowed. "Thank you. Seriously. I wouldn't have ordered this, but damn. It's so good." He took another bite.

"You're welcome," she said through her own mouthful of delicately spiced, perfectly juicy ground lamb.

"While I eat, I'd love if you told me something about yourself," Ibrahim said. "Like … Khatri. That's Indian, right? Where are you from?"

"Yes, it is," Nabaa said. "I'm from northern India. Chandigarh."

"Really? I think I know where that is. Isn't there a military base near there?"

She took another bite. *Here we go.* "Yes," she said. "Chandi Mandir. My father was in the army. He died in 1999, after being shot in the Kargil War."

Ibrahim put his burger down. "I'm sorry to hear that."

"It's OK," Nabaa said. "Not the first time I've had to share that with a fellow complicated Muslim."

"My father told me a couple of his cousins fought in Kargil. So senseless." He shook his head and returned to his burger.

Nabaa nodded. "Are you a first-gen American, then?"

"Yeah. My parents emigrated here in 1991, finished med school, and had me a few years later. Yes, they're both successful doctors. Yes, I'm a spoiled only child. Yes, they want me to be a doctor, too." He exhaled wearily. "But that's not much of a cross to bear when I'm sitting next to someone who lost her father. How old were you then? Five?"

"Two. Almost three."

"Oh no," Ibrahim said, shaking his head. "That's awful." His expression changed. "Umm, wait. You were two in 1999? So, you're … 18 now? Or 19?"

"18. How old are you?"

"Twenty. So, you graduated early?"

"I see you're good at math." She smiled at him. "By the way, I'll spare you the eventual awkwardness and just tell you that my mother is dead, too. I was an emergency cesarean, and it didn't go well. She died from a blood infection a few weeks after I was born." The familiar lie came naturally, but it made her feel more unclean than usual. *I don't want to lie to this boy.* So she added some truth. "I'm an orphan."

"Wow." Ibrahim's eyes were wide. "That's awful," he said again, clearly somewhat unsettled by where their conversation had gone.

"It's OK," Nabaa said. "I know there's not much you can say. Being an orphan sucks. But you eventually get used to it. Having good surrogate parents helps a lot." She smiled lightly and dipped a falafel fry into some green, creamy sauce. "What about you? Are you close to your parents?"

"I guess so," he said. "They're stereotypically traditional, each in their own way. So there's only so much closeness that can be achieved. And they've been slightly more distant ever since I insisted on studying neuroscience instead of medicine. I think my dad still hopes I'll eventually become a brain surgeon, and I don't have the heart to correct him."

Neuroscience? How have I only seen him in a religion class? She chalked it up to different schedules, probably different minors. "So why *are* you studying neuroscience? What do you want to be when you grow up?"

"An author." He smiled back. Then took a huge bite of his burger. "Mmm." He wiped the corners of his mouth with a napkin. "I could start by writing sonnets about this ground lamb. Unreal."

"You don't need to pay Johns Hopkins tuition for that."

"True. But I do like the idea of figuring out that kind of thing, from a brain-chemical perspective. I've always felt like more of a philosopher than a physician. Don't get me wrong — I have great admiration for my parents, and for doctors in general. But it's just not me, exactly." He took another bite and realized Nabaa was still listening, waiting for him to continue his explanation. After chewing and swallowing, he looked at her. "I do want to help people in my vocation. And since I was raised in the West, I decided I want to start by helping the Western world. I figure that helps everyone, since the West tends to lead the way in terms of social and cultural evolution. And it has come a long way in bettering itself. But I can't stop feeling unsatisfied with its rate of progress. Right here on this campus, brilliant scientists are revealing mysteries of the brain multiple times a year. And yet, when we look out into the world, people — even our leaders — are still behaving primitively."

"So, are you going to write philosophy books?"

"I don't know," Ibrahim said. "Maybe someday. But human stories, fiction or nonfiction, are usually what animates change in the world. My dream is to write stories that help people know how to think, how to feel. And maybe then a lot of other good things will happen."

Nabaa smiled. *We are going to get along just fine, Mr. Khan.* "I get it. One great idea can improve more lives than all of the world's medicine. Is that about right?"

His eyes sparkled with wonder and satisfaction. Years later, Nabaa would remember that expression as the moment Ibrahim fell in love with her.

◇◇◇◇◇◇◇◇◇

CHAPTER 9

February 2015

"The defense calls Rafiq Itani, defendant." Becky Whitfield's voice was a gale through the stale air of the courtroom.

It's finally time, Rafiq thought. He stood and made his way to the witness stand, placed his left hand on the Quran, and performed the oath. He closed his eyes briefly when he said "so help me Allah." Then, he sat down and waited for Whitfield's first question.

"Mr. Itani, have you ever hurt anyone?"

"Other than a couple of playground fights, no. I have not."

"Ever?"

"Never," Rafiq said.

"Why do you suppose that is?"

"Why have I never hurt anyone?" Rafiq was slightly confused. She had told him that not all of his testimony would be practiced beforehand. She wanted the jury to hear him at his most sincere and extemporaneous.

"Yes," Whitfield said.

"Probably because I hate violence," he said.

"But you're the son of an infamous jihadi, one of the most violent men in the history of the world. And you're telling us that you've lived a completely nonviolent life?"

"I did not say that," Rafiq said. "In many ways, violence has defined my life. But I, myself, have never hurt anyone. I don't believe my father did, either, with the exception of the last few days of his life. And his final words would seem to clarify how he felt about that. In the rare moments we had together when I was growing up, he is the one who taught me to hate violence."

"Interesting," Whitfield said. "Why were those moments rare?"

"He was hardly ever home. He was busy helping to form what would eventually become al-Qaida."

"Do you know why your father dedicated himself to that work?"

"I believe I do, yes," Rafiq said.

"You believe you do? Or you do?"

"It was a source of semantic debate between my father and those close to him," Rafiq said. "I believe, like my mother and uncle, that my father sought revenge for his father. He would say that he was simply following his father in the occupation of soldier."

"What happened to your grandfather?"

"It's a long story," Rafiq said. "Is this necessary?"

"I believe it is, yes." Whitfield's expression was serious but unassuming.

"My grandfather loved Lebanon and sympathized with the PLO. He — "

"What is the PLO?"

"Palestine Liberation Organization," Rafiq said.

"And how do you know your grandfather's opinion about it? He died before you were born, correct?"

"Yes. But my father talked about him frequently when I was a boy."

"Thank you," Whitfield said. "Can you describe the PLO a little for those who are unfamiliar?"

"It's a militant group that opposes Israeli occupation of Muslim homelands. My father said my grandfather did not like the PLO methods, but he loved the cause. And when Israel invaded Lebanon in 1982, he decided to actively help the resistance. That's how he died. An Israeli air strike in Ain al-Hilweh hit the house he was in, while he was apparently planning defensive operations with some members of PLO."

"How old was he?" Whitfield asked.

"Late 40s, I believe."

"This was a few years before you were born?"

"Yes. I was born in 1986."

"And your father would have been how old at the time of your grandfather's death?"

Rafiq thought for a moment. "17 or 18, I suppose."

"Do you have a sense of your father's reaction to the death of your grandfather?

"I only knew my father as the man who was motivated by it," Rafiq said. "My mother had known him since they were children, and she often said my father was much different — much happier — before the Israelis took his father from him."

"And you believe that's what prompted him to become a jihadi?"

"Of course."

"And how old were you when your father left you and your mother to attend to the jihad full-time?"

"I was five," Rafiq said.

"But you have memories of when he lived with you?"

"I do. Many. My mother said those were the only times he would smile. Then, one day, he was gone on Allah's business."

"So, your mother raised you?" Whitfield's eyes burned with apology.

Rafiq had successfully held his emotions in check during their practice interviews, but it was clear to him that the pain of these memories was not lost on his attorney.

"My mother raised me until I was 10 years old. Then it was mostly my uncle, my father's brother."

"If you don't mind, Mr. Itani, please tell the jury what happened to your mother when you were 10. It was your birthday, right?"

"Yes. It was very early in the morning. Still dark. I woke up early because ..." *Already, this is difficult.* Whitfield wanted him to share as many details as he could muster. He took a silent, slow breath. "We didn't celebrate birthdays like Westerners, but I was always aware of mine. I had decided that the only appropriate way to celebrate my birthday was to write my mother a letter to thank her for raising me by herself. I loved her very much, and I realized that I was a happy, healthy child because of her efforts alone. That's what I was doing when the bombs hit our building. Writing her a thank-you letter."

"What happened with the bombs hit?"

"They destroyed our building. We heard the sounds and started running down the steps, and the blast threw us into to the air, along with the pieces of our home. When everything settled, we were still holding hands, but buried in rubble. My mother was impaled through her torso by a long metal bar that was jutting from broken concrete." He closed his eyes. *Breathe.* Whitfield thankfully gave him a few moments to recalibrate.

"Was she dead?" she asked.

"No," Rafiq said, opening his eyes. "She was alive for many hours. Rescuers couldn't reach us until the sun was setting, and she had finally died about an hour before then."

"You said the attack came before dawn. And rescuers came at dusk?"

"Yes."

"And what about you?" Whitfield asked. "Were you hurt?"

"Yes. My leg was broken and trapped under a large piece of rubble. I couldn't move."

"So, you had a broken leg and were lying next to your mother, who slowly died from a traumatic stomach wound. Do I have that right?"

"Yes. I believe she technically died of hypovolemic shock, but essentially yes."

"Blood loss?"

"Yes," Rafiq said.

"How long was she conscious after the attack?"

"Until the end. Around midday, she started alternating between begging for death and apologizing to me."

"Did you learn later where the bombs came from and why they were dropped on your apartment building?"

"The bombs came from American-made Israeli fighter jets. Israel claimed later that Hezbollah terrorists were using our building for their operations."

"Do you believe them?" Whitfield asked.

Rafiq paused introspectively before answering. "I don't know," he said. "I've thought a lot about that question in my life. I believe it's most likely that my father was working with Hezbollah at the time, and Israeli intelligence found out where he kept his home. They either thought he was home or they wanted to send him a message by killing his family. I don't know. I just know it makes the most sense if my family was the sole target. Our building was the only one hit in a 50-kilometer radius."

"Interesting," Whitfield paced back to the defense table, picked up a piece of paper, then turned back to him. "Why do you mention that radius? Were there other attacks outside that area in that time?"

"Yes," Rafiq said. "The Qana massacre. It happened the same day my home was attacked, in the city of Qana, about 50 kilometers away from Nabatieh. Civilians were gathered together at a United Nations compound, specifically to avoid being caught in the fighting between Israelis and Hezbollah. Israeli forces attacked that compound with artillery shells. More than 100 innocent civilians died. It is a traumatic memory for all Lebanese people."

"A UN compound?" Whitfield was purposely incredulous. "Why on earth would Israel do that?"

"That remains unanswered." Rafiq heard an edge come into his own voice. "Two humanitarian groups and a UN investigation all concluded that Israel acted knowingly. Israeli officials were universally and globally criticized at the time, and they apologized in the press. All of this is documented and publicly known throughout the Arab world. It even has its own page on Wikipedia, if the jurors are inclined to verify my claims." As he spoke those words, he knew they carried the rare combination of passion and knowledge that translated into authority. "But, Israel never answered for their actions, partly because America came to Israel's defense. They claimed that Hezbollah was hiding out amongst civilians and putting them at risk. To me and many others, it was just another attack in a long history of malicious attacks on civilians that may or may not have some connection to Hezbollah activity."

Whitfield paused to let the courtroom absorb Rafiq's bitterness. When she spoke again, her voice was quieter than before. "Did your father return for your mother's funeral?"

"No," Rafiq said. "Islamic burials are traditionally done within 24 hours, so he didn't make it in time."

"Were you upset by that?"

"Upset?" Rafiq asked. "No. I was beyond upset by my mother's death. I felt nothing for months."

"When did you see your father next?"

"He arrived the day after the funeral and stayed with me during the three-day mourning period. We talked a lot during those days, although we were frequently interrupted by visitors with condolences." Rafiq reached for the glass of water and sipped it. "And then he was gone again."

Whitfield let silence fill the room for a long moment. "Rafiq, do you believe your father's work was motivated by revenge?"

Rafiq considered his answer. "There are many ways to parse his motivations. If he were here now and in a philosophical mood, I think he might do just that. But I think most jihadis of the last few decades are basically animated by a desire for personal or tribal vengeance. That was certainly true for me. And for my father, the jihad had been personal since his own father's death."

Whitfield strode to the defense table and retrieved a piece of paper. "Mr. Itani, can you please read the words printed here?" She walked over and handed it to him.

He read. "'The events that affected my soul in a direct way started in 1982, when America permitted the Israelis to invade Lebanon and the American Sixth Fleet helped them in that. This bombardment began and many were killed and injured and others were terrorized and displaced. I couldn't forget those moving scenes— blood and severed limbs, women and children sprawled everywhere. Houses destroyed along with their occupants and high rises demolished over their residents, rockets raining down on our home without mercy.'"

Whitfield took the printout back from Rafiq. "Do you know who spoke those words?"

"I do," Rafiq said. "Osama bin Laden."

She handed him another piece of paper. "Can you please read this quote from bin Laden as well?"

"'And as I looked at those demolished towers in Lebanon, it entered my mind that we should punish the oppressor in kind, and that we should destroy towers in America in order that they taste some of what we tasted and so that they be deterred from killing our women and children.'"

"Thank you, Mr. Itani," Whitfield said, taking the paper from his outstretched hand. "Would you say it's well known in Lebanon that the 9/11 attacks were directly motivated by the suffering of Lebanese people?"

"Yes, I would," Rafiq said. "It was certainly well known to me and the people I knew. I was just one of many children who grew up in a family still suffering the pain from the 1982 attacks. Most people I knew also had a friend or relative who died or was maimed by Israeli shelling."

"It must have been pretty awful if it inspired al-Qaida," Whitfield said.

"Objection," Andria Jackson projected lazily from the prosecutor's table. "Your honor, if the defense is going to editorialize, I might ask that it at least takes the form of a question."

"Sustained," Judge Greene said. His face was nonplussed. "Move on to your next question, Ms. Whitfield."

"Thank you, your honor. I'm almost finished," she said. "So, from your perspective, the Israelis took your grandfather's life. Then, the need to fight the Israelis took your father away from your life. Then the Israelis took your mother's life. Do I have that about right?"

Some old, knotted thing inside Rafiq began to fray. To his own surprise, tears began welling in his eyes. *Is my life that simple?* He felt his reflexive physiological protocols kick into gear, trying to re-deaden his emotions and keep the control he had worked so hard to maintain. *It does not matter. I have nothing more to lose.*

"Yes," he finally said, with only a small break in his voice. "I suppose you do."

"I have no more questions, your honor," Whitfield said. She sat down.

Jackson stood up, carrying her own piece of paper. "Since you're reading, Mr. Itani, I was wondering if you could kindly read the words printed here, too."

Rafiq took it from her hand. "'Please hear me. Vengeance is not the way. Violence — purposeful violence — is a necessity. But vengeance is purposeless. It is the path to pure evil and a loss of self. That path is where I stand now.'" He looked up and handed the paper back to Jackson. "Those were some of the last words spoken by my father, Fadi Itani, moments before he thrust a knife into his own neck."

Jackson nodded, turned, and walked back to her table. "That's all I've got, your honor."

◇◇◇◇◇◇◇◇◇

CHAPTER 10

March 2015

"Daddy, did he say Fadi Itani?"

Jerry Czarnecki swallowed the bite of oatmeal in his mouth and looked down at his 4-year-old son, Isaac. He had stopped playing with his train set and become transfixed by the image of Rafiq Itani being led away from the witness stand.

Like millions of Americans, Jerry had been following the case on TV and catching up online whenever he had the chance. He usually tried to watch the proceedings when Isaac wasn't around, since the subject matter was often unsuitable for kids. But today, Isaac had a fever, so Jerry was home from work — and he wasn't going to miss the defendant's testimony.

"Yes, buddy, he did," Jerry said.

The cameras stayed locked on Rafiq as he made his way back to the defendant's table and listened to his lawyer whisper things into his ear. Isaac kept staring.

"Why did you ask that, Isaac?"

Isaac's response was distracted. "Why did I ask what, Daddy?"

"Why did you ask if he said 'Fadi Itani'? Have you heard that name before?"

Isaac finally turned away from the TV. "Yes," he said flatly. "He was the one who made me die last time."

Goosebumps rose on Jerry's forearms.

"What? What do you mean he made you die?"

"When I was a little boy last time," Isaac said. "Fadi Itani stole me. He yelled at another man a lot. The other man didn't want to make me die, but Fadi Itani yelled at him and made him do it."

Jerry's mind raced. *Did they go over that in the trial?* No. They couldn't have. Fadi was not on trial — Rafiq was — so the lawyers were careful not to go into the gory details of what the elder Itani did. *How does he know?*

It wasn't the first time Isaac had made a reference to a past life. He would occasionally reference his "other mommy" or "daddy before" or talk about missing his sisters, though he was an only child. They'd tried to press him on the details with no luck. It got so bad once that they once took him to a pediatric psychologist, but by the time the appointment rolled around, the latest nightmare was three weeks past, and Isaac refused to talk about it.

74

And, of course, there were the nightmares. Every few months, Isaac would wake up crying and yelling for his mom and dad. He was always too distraught to explain the dream, but he would always say, "I died!"

"Isaac," Jerry said gently. "Are you talking about before? When you had a different daddy and mommy?"

"Yeah," Isaac said. He went back to playing with his trains, but his mind still seemed to be churning.

"Are you telling me about your nightmare?"

"No!" Isaac said. Then his face scrunched, like he was trying to find the right words. "Yes, Daddy. It's the same. I have a scary dream about it because I died." He raised his eyebrows and looked right at Jerry. "I really died, Daddy."

"Ok," Jerry said. "I believe you, but you've never told me about it before." Isaac turned back to his trains. Jerry picked up his phone and started a video recording, then held it inconspicuously near his knee, hoping Isaac wouldn't notice. "Can you tell me ... after Fadi Itani yelled at the other man, what did the man do?"

"He pulled my hair!" Eyes wide, Isaac sat up straight, grabbed a handful of the hair on top of his head, and pulled it straight up. "He said, 'ALLAHU AKBAR!' Then he cut my neck with a big knife!" He pointed to the three-inch-wide birthmark on the front of his own neck. "My sisters were there, but they were just scared. They were crying a lot." He looked at Jerry. "I miss them, Daddy. Do you know where they are? Did they die too?"

Oh my dear God. Jerry was shaken. "I don't know, buddy. You don't have any sisters that I know about."

"Not *this* time, Daddy! When I was alive before, I was a brother." He stared at the ceiling. "I think one sister died. Someone told me that. Before I went into Mommy's belly, someone told me my smaller sister died. I think she's an angel now." His eyes suddenly got wide again. "But my biggest sister! She's alive, right Daddy? She lives close to us! That's why I picked this mommy!" He sat up again, smiling the kind of smile that only comes with the memory of something long forgotten. "I know Mommy was close to my biggest sister! I want her to come to our house, Daddy! Can she?"

Jerry didn't know what to say. "What is her name?" *He can't know that, can he?*

Isaac thought for a moment. "Nabaa!" He grinned again.

Jerry thought back through Rafiq's testimony, which was still fresh in his mind. He didn't remember Nabaa's name being mentioned.

Maybe Isaac heard it on the news, from earlier in the trial?

Knowing his son and how successfully he could tune out adult programming that seemed less likely than ... *reincarnation?* His palms were sweating with the wildness of the possibility, but what else could explain it? All of it. The recollections of a life that didn't match the one he was living. The nightmares. And now this? Describing a scene he couldn't have learned from elsewhere. *And speaking in Arabic?*

"Isaac, do you know what allahu akbar means?"

"Yes, Daddy."

"Tell me."

"It means God is the best."

A shot of ice-cold certainty flushed through Jerry's veins. Isaac laid himself back down on his belly and started twirling a train car in his hands, legs casually moving back and forth in the air.

Jerry stopped the video and sent a text to his wife. They had some plans to make.

CHAPTER 11

February 2015

Operations Officer Rona Kavian shifted uncomfortably on the cheap love seat in her therapist's couch. She crossed her arms and her legs and tapped her right foot against the air.

"And here we are again," he said. "Work is bothering you. A few months ago, it was too stressful. Now it is not stressful enough. You tell me these things, but then you tell me basically nothing about your work."

Mehmet, the grey-haired counselor she'd been occasionally seeing during her assignment in Izmir, had grown up in America, like Rona, and that was one reason she picked him. It turned out he also was very good at his job.

Almost good enough to actually help me, she thought.

The CIA employed plenty of mental health professionals, but in most field assignments, an agent's only access to them was via remote video chat. So she decided to find someone local. Using her unique resources, Rona researched the public and private lives of 20-plus Turkish therapists in the area. She found many who spoke English and a few who had spent considerable time in the West, but her prying revealed Mehmet to be the only truly decent man of the bunch — aside from him, the rest were all hiding something from someone.

"Mehmet," she said, smiling. "I've told you. My work is confidential. I can't talk to you about it."

"Well, you *can,*" he said. "Especially since I've explained the confidentiality rules that protect you. But you're *choosing* not to. And I respect that, Azra. I really do. I even tolerate the knowledge that 'Azra' is probably not your real name. You're not the first of my patients with such concerns. I just want you to keep asking yourself what carries more risk: telling me more information about your career or *not* telling me, and failing to get the help you need?"

She cocked her head and nodded at him. "Does this mean you can't give me the help I need *unless* I tell you about what I do for a living?"

He laughed. "I didn't say that, exactly. But it does make my job more difficult."

"Hmmm," Rona said. "It sounds like you should talk to your therapist about that."

Mehmet smiled and shook his head. "Touché."

He's a good man, she thought. *And still I torture him.*

"I'm sorry," she said. "But you can't accuse me of being too guarded. I've told you a lot, haven't I? Let's do a recap." She lifted her left hand up with her thumb up. "I told you that my great-grandmother was raped in a dark Turkish alley." She stuck out her index finger. "I told you how my grandmother, the product of that rape, was given away to distant cousins in a faraway village to avoid bringing shame to the family." She stuck out her middle finger. "I told you how she grew up in an arranged marriage to an abusive husband, then raised my mother to distrust men." Her ring finger jutted out. "And then how my mother convinced my father to emigrate to the U.S., and to have a child immediately." Her pinky came out. "And how she then cheated on him so many times that he was forced to divorce her and return to Turkey in disgrace. What else?" She switched to her right hand, which was trembling. "Oh — and how my dad …" Her voice caught in her throat.

Dammit, Rona!

Mehmet picked up the tissue box next to him and held it in front of her. She shook her head. He put it back in its place.

She used her fingers to press the gathering tears out of her eyes, then she squeezed her wet fingertips into her palms. "

Finish the sentence. She took a breath and steadied her voice. She locked eyes with Mehmet again.

"How my father stopped calling and writing to me when I was five years old because he started a new family. I told you that, too, right?"

Mehmet took off his glasses and sighed. Then he looked at her and nodded. "Yes, Azra. You did. And I'm sorry. I should not have implied that you were not being open with me."

She nodded. "It's ok, Mehmet."

"Speaking of your father," he began, voice treading lightly. "Have you thought any more about trying to find him?"

"No." Rona shook her head. "I would just remind him of my mom. I'm sure he deserves better."

"I didn't ask whether you should find him," Mehmet said. "I asked if you've *thought* about it. You said no, you haven't. And that's my point. You need to go through the process — as painful as it may be — to think about, to imagine what a relationship with your father might look like. Whether it's worth pursuing. Only you can answer that, and only after you spend time thinking about it."

"Ok," she said. "I'll think about … thinking about it."

Mehmet chuckled. "I'll take what I can get," he said. "But you should really consider the effect it's having on your life. Most women with severe unresolved emotions toward their fathers can't successfully navigate any relationship with any man."

"That might matter if I wanted a relationship with a man that lasted more than a few hours," she said. "But that's about when their

78

usefulness expires anyway. And it also happens to be all the time I can spare, in my current occupation."

"Ah yes," he said, putting his palms out in surrender. "Your job. My apologies."

She smiled, then looked at the clock on the wall behind him. "It's 5:57. Time's up." She stood and slung her purse on her shoulder.

"Will I see you next week or the week after?" Mehmet asked, then waved off the question. "Nevermind. You don't know."

"Exactly. But if I can't come, you know I'll pay anyway." She gave him a hug and polite peck on the cheek. "Thank you, Mehmet. You are always helpful, despite all evidence to the contrary."

"Goodbye, Azra." He smiled and nodded.

She walked out of his building, got into her car, and looked at the dashboard clock. 6 p.m. *Is it too early?* She ignited the engine. *I guess we'll find out.* She retrieved her phone and searched for bars within a 10-mile radius. She found one she'd never visited before and pressed the button to start navigation.

At 6:15, Rona pulled into a parking garage a block away from the bar. She turned off the car and opened the visor mirror. She reapplied her mascara, added some lipstick and eyeshadow, and looked at her reflection. *Perfectly overdone.* She put the makeup back in her purse, pausing to drag her index finger across the barrel of the 9mm Glock inside.

She emerged from the parking garage a few minutes later and stood in the day's last light, which was coming in low between the buildings. She turned her head westward and closed her eyes, taking the humid, 50-degree air deep into her lungs. She felt her heart pounding with the usual anticipation, but this time it was tinged by doubt.

Focus. Get into character and stay there.

Tonight would be her 17th seduction. Number 16 — a handsome, funny man named Kenan — didn't go as planned. Well, it did for a while. But when she got back to his place and pretended to pass out on the couch, he had walked out of the room. When he returned a minute later, he simply covered her in a blanket, kissed her forehead, then ran his hand gently through her hair.

Without thinking, she had quickly grabbed his hand then pulled him down to kiss him passionately. But she was too sudden, too coordinated. When he pulled away and saw her stone-sober eyes, his face went dark and confused. He knew she'd been playing him, but didn't care to know why. Without another word, he told her to leave.

So she'd walked a half-kilometer to a gas station and then waited 40 minutes for a taxi.

One man, one mistake, she thought. She couldn't afford to believe otherwise. It would mean giving up her favorite new hobby.

Rona walked to the bar, entered, and surveyed the place. In the center of the main room was a 20-by-10-foot rectangular space for the bartenders, surrounded by a two-foot-wide marble slab and expensive-looking stools with ornate seatbacks.

The bartender was a skinny, college-aged kid with a beard that was almost filled in. He smiled at her and approached right away.

"Hello," he said. "What would you like?"

"Raki, please," she replied.

"Water, too?"

"Yes. Bottled."

He returned a minute later with the popular milky-white, anise-flavored cocktail. Then he reached down into a trough of ice below the bar and grabbed a bottle of water.

"Thanks," she said. "So are you the only bartender working tonight?"

"Yes, till about 8 p.m."

"Good." Rona slid a 200-lira note across the bar. "The rest is your tip — with only one condition."

He looked down at the bill, which equaled about $80 U.S. dollars, then back at Rona.

"I'm going to be here for a while, and I *need* to be able to drive home later," Rona said. "If anyone buys me a drink later, please do me a favor and make it extra, extra light. Then put a cherry in it so I know it's mine."

The bartender smiled and nodded, then pocketed the bill. "No problem."

She took her drink to a high, four-top table near the bar and sat down. She removed her phone, a pen, and a decorative sketch pad from her purse, then set the purse on the chair next to her.

And now I wait, she thought, fixing her eyes on the bar's entrance. She sipped her raki, then downed about a third of her water.

She sketched, doodled, and wrote musings onto the pages of her pad for 10 minutes before the first single man walked through the door. He barely made eye contact. Five minutes later, two men entered together. One smiled at her as they walked by, but he neither came over to chat. Then, a couple entered. Then a group of two couples.

Finally, after she'd been waiting almost an hour, another man came in by himself. He saw her right away, and his gaze lingered just a moment too long. They exchanged subtle smiles, and Rona sipped her drink. It was nearing the bottom. *Perfect.*

The man went to the bar, spoke to the bartender briefly, then came right over to Rona's table.

"Hello," he said. "I'm Burak."

"Azra," she said. "Nice to meet you." The shook hands.

"You as well," Burak said. "I just noticed your drink was almost empty. Can I buy you another?"

"That would be lovely," Rona said. "Thank you."

"Of course. I'll be right back." He smiled and went back to the waiting bartender.

He returned a minute later with another raki for her and a tall glass of golden beer for himself. The glass of raki had a cherry floating on top.

"He said you liked cherries," Burak said.

"I do," she said. She sipped the new drink and verified it was almost all water. Then she picked up the cherry by its stem, lifted it just above her chin, then extended her tongue to lasciviously pull it into her mouth. Burak stared.

Works every damn time, she thought. *They are all so single-minded.*

The rest of her charms worked, too. The easy laughs, the innuendos, the light touch on the shoulder as she passed him on her way to the restroom. And, of course, he seemed to appreciate how quickly she consumed her drinks.

In their conversation, she made sure to mention that she hadn't been sleeping well lately. He seemed to sympathize, but he didn't try to slow her down. Four rakis, two beers, and 90 minutes later, he was paying the bill, and they were headed back to his apartment in his red BMW 5-series sedan. A minute after they arrived, he was pressing Rona against a huge, expensive refrigerator, kissing her passionately.

She wasn't enthused about the pilsner on his breath, but he was a better kisser than most. He definitely knew what to do with his hands. As usual, Rona found herself physically responding in all the ways he wanted. She felt warmth and moisture gathering southward, and the ache that came with it.

Focus, Rona. Work tonight, play tomorrow. When they're this skilled, it just means they've had too much practice. Her mind cleared.

She kept kissing him back, but she began to show signs of fatigue. She reached down and caressed gently below his belt.

"Time to find the bed, I think," she said, slurring ever so slightly.

He nodded and took her hand in his. "This way," he said.

He led her to the back of the posh bachelor apartment, through glass double-doors and into his bedroom. Rona quickly surveyed the room. A king-sized bed filled much of it. The bed and its frame clearly cost somewhere in the upper four digits. Against the wall was a huge wooden headboard with what appeared to be a hand-carved visage of a lion's face and mane. Jutting up from the bedframe's foot corners were ornately carved wooden pillars jutting into the air, about a meter long and three centimeters in diameter.

Those might be useful later, she thought.

Rona kicked off one shoe gracelessly but accurately toward the bedroom doors. She tried to do the same with the other, but used the kicking motion to fake an awkward stumble. She almost hit the ground, but Burak caught her arm. She stood, giggling at herself, then kissed Burak hungrily on the neck. She kept his hand and led him to the edge of the bed.

She unbuttoned her blouse, removed her bra, and tossed it toward her shoes. Then she lay back on the bed, then summoned him with open arms and barely covered breasts.

He took off his shirt, climbed onto the bed and pressed himself against her, kissing her again and using a very skilled right hand under her skirt.

Rona fumbled at his belt, then let her body to go suddenly and completely limp for a few moments. Burak's lips were suddenly kissing unresponsive flesh.

"Azra?" he said, alarmed.

She opened her eyes wide, then blinked a few times. "Sorry," she said. "Where were we?" She reached behind his head and pulled him toward her again. They kissed more, and she noticed him picking up the pace. She helped him remove her skirt.

When he stood to take off his pants, she pretended to pass out again.

"Azra," he said, a little too loudly. "Stay with me, Azra."

He got back on the bed, and kissed her again. She didn't respond. He pulled away. Then he moved down to her chest, covered her right nipple with his mouth, and used his tongue to try to wake her up. She allowed herself a quiet groan of pleasure, a deep breath, then only the rhythmic breathing of someone descending into sleep.

Burak sighed with aching disappointment.

She heard his footsteps trail toward the bathroom.

Not again, she thought. *Not twice in a row. There might be one decent man in Izmir, but not two. Wait.*

A minute later, he returned. She maintained her steady breathing. She heard him set something down on the nightstand. Then his hands were up her skirt, pulling her underwear off. She let him, even shimmying her hips lazily in her feigned partial consciousness.

As soon as her underwear hit the floor, she opened her eyes and looked at the nightstand. Lube. A bottle of personal lubricant. *Of course.* She smiled for her own reasons.

Standing at the edge of the bed was a fully naked Burak.

She sat up slowly and reached for his erection with her left hand. He was surprised, but his eyes followed.

Rona's right hand shot forward and delivered a vicious chop to his Adam's apple. His eyes bulged, and both his hands went to his neck. He stumbled backward. She lunged forward off the bed and kicked him in the gut, sending him back against the wall. He doubled over.

"You disgusting fucking pig," Rona hissed. She planted her left foot in the thick carpet, then brought her right foot up in a blur that connected with his face. She felt his nose break against the hard bones in her foot. He grunted, fell sideways, and hit the ground with his left shoulder. He rolled onto his back.

"What the fuck??" he hissed through his hands, which were pressed against his nose and mouth.

Rona bent down and picked up one of the man's socks from the floor. Then she knelt next to Burak and took his scrotum in her left hand and squeezed gently.

"Put this in your mouth, or I will rip your balls off," she said softly into his ear. She pressed the sock between his hands and toward his lips.

"Please ..." he whispered, then coughed.

"Just open your mouth," she said. He did, and she pushed the sock into his mouth with her fingers. All the way into his mouth. She paused, listening to his breath. It was fast and ragged, but he was getting enough oxygen.

She stood, turned, and grabbed the top of the wooden footboard pillar with both hands and yanked it toward herself with all her weight. It snapped near the bottom.

She reached over and grabbed the lubricant. She opened it, then squeezed a little on the top of the pillar.

Burak started shaking his head. "Nnnnnuh! NNNUHHHH!"

She smiled. "Yeah, I thought not," she said, setting the lube down on the bed. "I was only kidding, Burak." Then she lifted the wooden pillar over her head and smashed it down on his left knee. The knee shattered, but the wood stayed intact.

"Aahhhhhhhhhh!!!" came his muffled, high-pitched scream. His torso lifted off the ground, hands darting toward his left leg.

Rona tossed the wooden pillar on the bed. She picked up the lube and slowly drizzled it all over his body. By the time the bottle was empty, Burak was leaning against the bed, shaking and crying.

"You are a slippery mess of a man, Burak," she said. She put her panties back on and rebuttoned her blouse. "You don't deserve anything a woman has to offer."

She pulled the sock from his mouth and waited a moment, but he didn't say anything. He just looked at her with genuine fear.

There it is, she thought. *The moment when they realize how much control they've lost.*

Every time, in those moments, Rona couldn't help but feel a pang of sympathy for the men she broke. The sympathy always came with a shot of self-doubt, too. Was it right, what she was doing?

83

All those questions would be gone soon enough, she knew. Justice always prevailed.

She took his phone from the dresser and tossed it on the carpet next to him. "Here you go," she said. "This is the part where you think long and hard about who to call."

Rona put on her shoes, grabbed her purse, and walked out of the bedroom. She retrieved Burak's keys from the kitchen counter, then walked out of his apartment and into the hallway. His door was dark grey, which wasn't a good background for her fat, black permanent marker. But the wall next to it was light grey, so that's where she wrote the word "RAPIST" in big, block letters. Then she added an arrow pointing at Burak's door.

She got into his car, turned on the navigation, and headed back to the garage where she'd parked a few hours before. Soon, she was enjoying the BMW's surplus of 8-cylinder power under her seat, and her doubts and sympathies disappeared like air over the windshield.

◇◇◇◇◇◇◇◇◇◇

CHAPTER 12

February 2015

from: Liza Hamilton <lizachucksgirl@gmail.com>
to: Aahna Khatri aktheexister@gmail.com
date: Fri, Feb 27, 2015 at 5:49 AM
subject: You ok?

Hi, honey. I tried calling yesterday, but you didn't answer. Safe to assume you watched Rafiq's testimony? I just want to see how you're doing. Please get back to me so I don't have to drive up there and shout up at the window. Love you.
   P.S. Any news on the boy?

from: Aahna Khatri <aktheexister@gmail.com>
to: Liza Hamilton <lizachucksgirl@gmail.com>
date: Fri, Feb 27, 2015 at 6:46 AM
subject: RE: You ok?

Hey, Lizzie. Yes, I'm OK. Sorry I didn't answer yesterday. I wanted to, but I wasn't quite ready to talk.
   So I haven't been keeping you updated on the boy. I keep expecting him to disappear, and he has not. His name is Ibrahim, and now I'm falling for him.
   We ran into each other a few weeks ago at a lunch place, so we decided to sit together. It went well. We have been on several dates since then, and each is better than the last. Sigh. What do I do??? I already know what you'll say. "Be smart and enjoy yourself" or something like that. But it's complicating everything. It's wonderful and awful. Ahhhhhhhh! We really need to talk on the phone again.
   Anyway, enough about that. Yes, I saw Rafiq's testimony. My Intro to Islam professor told us last week he would be willing showing Rafiq's testimony in class, and we unanimously agreed to do that. So I saw it yesterday, a day late.
   It has affected me. I prayed a lot about it before I watched, and I have prayed a lot since. I know Charlie has been empathetic for a long time, and I know he is very careful with that empathy (around me, especially). I admire him for that. I really do. But I was never sure if I could reach that place given my … history. I'm

85

still not sure. But I must admit, seeing Rafiq on a witness stand speaking about the pain in his childhood … I don't know. There were moments I forgot that he was who he was. I could relate so well to much of what he was saying that he became a kind of sympathetic character, even to me.

The part at the end where he was talking about vengeance and his father's death — it really made me think about guilt.

What IS guilt, anyway? Why are we afflicted with it? As much as my therapy has forced me to think about those last moments of Fadi's life and everything that led up to it, I've mostly focused on the vengeance and violence factors. I haven't devoted a lot of brain power to the idea of guilt.

Other animals don't seem to be afflicted with guilt (or at least not nearly to the degree of humans), so it can't be explained purely in terms of evolutionary adaptation for pack/tribe behavior. Right? I will be doing some reading on this. Or at least I intend to. But with The Ibrahim Problem, I can no longer accurately predict my work ethic. It's probably best if YOU did the research and presented it to me. I'm sure you are not as busy as I am. Your infatuation stage with Charlie is long over, I assume (?).

I love you!

from: Liza Hamilton <lizachucksgirl@gmail.com>
to: Aahna Khatri <aktheexister@gmail.com>
date: Fri, Feb 27, 2015 at 1:08 PM
subject: RE: You ok?

OK. First things first, regarding this boy, Ibrahim: Be smart and enjoy yourself! ;)

Now for my email course on guilt:

I've learned that guilt is associated with pro-community behavior. Basically, a desire to avoid guilt shapes an individual's future because it keeps behavior within accepted norms, which allows the individual to succeed within a group/tribe. On the tribe level, that manifests as cooperation, and cooperation makes each tribe stronger. Therefore, both individuals and tribes who internalize guilt are more likely to survive and pass on their genetic material.

from: Aahna Khatri <aktheexister@gmail.com>
to: Liza Hamilton <lizachucksgirl@gmail.com>
date: Fri, Feb 27, 2015 at 3:33 PM
subject: RE: You ok?

OK. That makes plenty of sense. But not ALL the sense, right? One example: A tribe (or nation) goes to war, wins, and gets the spoils of war. The winning soldiers feel guilt from role in the violence along the way. But why? It helped their tribe. He should be feeling only pride and triumph.

On the individual level: Say a man is on vacation outside his own country (tribe), and right before returning, he sees a 60-year-old woman counting a thick stack of money. He strikes her down and takes her money, then gets on a plane and returns to his country without anyone knowing. Shouldn't he be free of guilt, since the stolen money is a net gain for him and the economy of his country/tribe? Of course we know he wouldn't be free of guilt. If he's not, we would dub him a sociopath.

So what is it that makes guilt seem to transcend our sense of tribal constructs?

from: Liza Hamilton <lizachucksgirl@gmail.com>
to: Aahna Khatri <aktheexister@gmail.com>
date: Fri, Feb 27, 2015 at 9:02 PM
subject: RE: You ok?

Honestly, I've never thought about guilt in these terms before, but I can't argue with your point. And the crucial point might be your first one — that humans are the only organisms who deal with guilt. Most scientists agree that nonhuman animals don't feel guilt at all, even the tribe/herd sort.

It also ties into another thing completely unique to humans: suicide.

Of course, that brings us full-circle to Fadi Itani, I suppose. Guilt and suicide are both rooted in self-loathing. People attempt suicide to end their own suffering, which is t*he only known act in the universe that effectively overtakes the instinct to survive.*

Other suicide attempters reference being a burden on their loved ones and/or society — like Fadi. So in those cases, someone's desire to heal or improve the tribe also trumps their individual instinct to survive?

I think that means guilt can't simply be an evolutionary adaptation for individual/tribal success? Not at the human level. Something else has to be there.

◇◇◇◇◇◇◇◇◇
CHAPTER 13

March 2015

Rona Kavian took a substantial swallow of the cucumber mint martini. Sharp, clean, strong — it tasted exactly how she hoped. She put 20 liras on the bar and took out her smartphone, idly thumb-scrolling through her Twitter feed while casting a casual eye past the sea of tables toward the restaurant's entrance.

Through the floor-to-ceiling windows she could see the ink-black Gulf of Izmir, undulating with the glinting lights of Turkey's third-largest city. The restaurant was playing European soft rock and buzzing with activity.

Her ops chief, Todd Polinski, finally entered. He nodded at the hostess and made his way directly to the bar. Rona put on a warm smile and slid off the stool as Polinski opened his arms as he approached, they hugged for a few long seconds, then separated enough for a convincingly romantic kiss.

As they disconnected, Rona figured she was maybe a little *too* convincing with her lips. *Oh well,* she thought, her smile now fully genuine. *Todd chose the place and pretense, and he knows I'm dedicated to my craft.*

Polinski was a Polish Jew with wavy black hair and rich tan skin that Rona imagined was beautiful before the last couple of decades spent living near Mediterranean beaches, first in Greece, then Italy, and now Western Turkey. He was at least 10 years older than Rona, and she found him handsome enough. She wasn't particularly attracted to him, but she liked him, and she always enjoyed stirring up a man of such impeccable composure.

They each took a stool, and Polinski ordered a Heineken — "because it's what Bobby Kennedy drank," he told her at their first bar meeting last year. Smiling, he lifted his right hand and gently swept Rona's silky hair behind her ear. She knew he was acting according to the training; in normal couples, physical affection usually persisted throughout the first 90 seconds or so after the greeting. Then, the partners fell into the kind of conversation common to all relationships.

He casually glanced around the bar.

"I already did a thorough sweep," Rona said. "We're good. Speak freely."

"I still prefer privacy," he said. "But you tend to get your way."

"I prefer places that can't be bugged," she said, still smiling. "But now that I've gotten my way, what's up?"

"Good news," Polinski said. "You're getting a new gig."

Rona managed to keep the warm expression on her face, despite the jarring declaration. She was here to update Polinski on her last meeting with Omer Aydin, her Islamic State informant.

"Excuse me?" she asked. "I just got started with Omer. And I've got good shit to pass along, by the way."

"We'll get to that," Polinski said, nodding to the bartender who had brought his beer. "I just didn't want to bury the lead. Something important came up, and it's tailor-made for you."

Her training officer, a seasoned overseas agent, had warned her about speeches like this. If you're not a good fit for your current op, or they think you're starting to get too close to the wrong side, they move you, and tell you it's a better "opportunity" for you. Meanwhile, everyone else knows it's because you didn't cut it.

She felt her heartbeat quicken with indignation. She thought she'd been doing well.

She'd been transferred from Iraq back to Turkey, her ancestral home, a little over a year prior. The transfer came when the Islamic State started ramping up its participation in Syria's civil war and simultaneously sending terrorists across the border posing as refugees. Turkish officials caught most of them, but the ones who made it through presented major problems. Two of them, the CIA was fairly certain, had killed 51 people in the Reyhanli car bombing attack last May. But many more of them were instructed to traverse Turkey, cross the Aegean Sea, and continue into central Europe. That's why Rona was stationed in Izmir. Her mission was to find and identify the terrorists being given passage to Greece, primarily using informants. Then, the CIA would pass the names to host-country intelligence agencies and Interpol, and all three would collaborate on tracking their movements. It was slow going at first, but in the last six months since she turned Omer, her intel had led to the discovery of a small terrorist cell in Marseilles and larger one in Prague. She figured that was a pretty good track record so far. *What am I missing?*

"Tell me the truth," she said, no longer smiling. "What did I do wrong?"

"What?" Polinski's brow furrowed instantly. "No, nothing like that. I told you how rare it is for one junior agent's intel to be the primary factor in stopping *two* attacks, even here in Europe. Plus, everyone has been impressed with your work with Omer. You were the only one who saw his family connection in the States, which means he's not only on our hook, but he's probably on it forever. You've done so well, actually, that just about anybody could take the baton from you and continue the op. I was already thinking about moving you somewhere better before this new thing popped up." He sipped his beer and didn't break eye contact. "But, since you asked me to be honest, I should tell you that it's much more dangerous than Izmir. So, once you've heard me out, if you don't want it, I'll keep you here. Deal?"

She stared at him for a few moments. "I have a feeling I'm about to get an offer I can't actually refuse. But, yeah. Sure. Deal. What's the job?"

"Remember your first assignment?"

She paused. "In Baghdad? Yes, of course."

"Well, it's likely your biggest admirer will soon be returning to the Levant. His homeland, to be exact."

"Wait." She lowered her voice. "Rafiq? Itani?"

"The one and only," Polinski said.

"What's he going to be doing there? We think he'll be a threat?"

Polinski smiled. "Doubtful. But we do know his uncle has recently rekindled some old affinities for Hezbollah, and with ISIS struggling to get a foothold in Lebanon, it might present a unique opportunity for us."

Rona stared at him while her mind presented her with several possible futures, each ending in her death. Lebanon in 2015 wasn't as bad as Baghdad in 2007 — the year she'd lost three informants and several colleagues in sectarian-fueled bombings. But even a relatively small Lebanese town like Nabatieh would be considerably more dangerous than Izmir, which as far as she knew had never experienced any kind of terror attack to date.

"Just so we're clear," she said. "I'm supposed to head into the heart of Hezbollah territory, at a time when every outsider is conspicuous, and then gain the trust of one of the few locally notorious men in the town. And then …?"

"Operate."

"Operate?" She didn't get any more clarity. "Will I be alone?"

"Yes," Polinski said. "We decided … well, I decided, really, that putting two officers on the ground there would endanger you even more. But that's why we sent you to Stuttgart for MCMAP, right? Which belt did you earn — brown?" He smiled. "I know I wouldn't tussle with you."

"Not sure how reassuring that is, but thanks." He was mostly right. Rona was no longer fearful at all of physical confrontations. She had surprised herself — and the two-dozen young American military members in her class — with how quickly she'd picked up the Marine Corps Martial Arts Program. She was one of only two women in the group, but she'd learned how to subdue several bigger, stronger men. *Hopefully, I won't need it at all.* "And for how long? Indefinitely, right?"

"Yep. You got it. Starting to see why there's no better woman for the job?" Polinski winked.

She shook her head ruefully. "I'll do it," she said. "But I want full support sent in if I need it. Immediate exfil at my discretion. And if I ask for something, I want it dropped at my designated location at my designated time. No resource reviews, no elevations of requests. Just done. You give me your word, and I'll give you all the information you need."

"Ok," Polinksi said. He tapped the neck of his Heineken against the lip of the martini glass in her hand, then took a long swig. "Just one condition from me. I heard Rafiq's testimony, and I gotta say, I like the guy. And he's been locked up for a long time. So do me a favor." He tilted his head toward her slightly and spoke in a fatherly tone. "Be careful with the young man's heart."

Rona downed half her martini, then pulled Polinski toward her by the front of his shirt. She planted another long kiss on his lips. *You asked for it, Boss.*

"You've got a deal," she said.

CHAPTER 14

April 2015

"Hi, Charlie," Nabaa said into her phone.

"Hey," Percy said. "Do you have a few minutes? Well, probably more like 15 minutes?"

"Actually, yes I do," she said. "I just finished my lunch and I have an hour before my next class. Is everything OK?"

"Yeah, fine," Percy said. "You should probably find some privacy, though."

"I think I'm fine where I am. I'm sitting outside in a courtyard. Everybody walking around has earbuds in."

"Good. So, this might sound a little crazy, but, um … I just got a call from our FBI handler, after he got a request for information verification from a different FBI agent, and that guy had gotten the request after a dozen or so transfers/routings," he paused. "Anyway … wow. I don't really know how to say this."

"What?" Nabaa said sharply.

"Apparently there's a 4-year-old kid who claims to be your brother, Sami — reincarnated."

Nabaa was silent.

"I know. It's weird," Percy said. "And according to the agent I spoke with, not everybody in his section is excited about investigating it. Seems like they have to, probably in case the father is a nutcase with an agenda. Be that as it may, they're taking it kind of seriously because the kid has said some things that reveal information he couldn't possibly know."

More silence. "You still there?" Percy asked.

"Yes," Nabaa said. "Just … I don't know. I recently went through a phase where I was obsessing about reincarnation. I guess it was about a year ago now, but it definitely left an impression."

"Obsessing about reincarnation? May I ask why?"

"One of my freshman professors made a casual reference to it during class, as if it were some legitimate phenomenon. It kicked off this heated conversation, and it started involving religion, and so he eventually had to shout down a few students to get us back on track. But his point was that there's a lot we still don't understand about consciousness, and there's mounting scientific evidence that it survives from one life to another."

"Wait, what? *Scientific* evidence for reincarnation?" Percy sounded confused. "Was this guy one of these wacky, new-age professors you see in movies?"

"No, Charlie." She wanted to skip ahead hear what this boy had to say, but she knew Percy. *A dog with a bone.* He couldn't proceed until *his* questions were answered. "He is a very smart, tenured professor of neurobiology."

"So what was the evidence?"

"Well, it's not like lab experiments. The evidence is … well, it's children's memories. Sometimes, the memories sound wild, but you can explain them away as normal coincidence. Other times, there's simply no way to explain it. And when it's in that category, it's scientifically significant."

"And it's common?"

"Common? No," Nabaa said. "Obviously, it's a tiny fraction of children who claim to have memories of a past life, and even fewer who have memories that are verifiable. Usually, those kids seemed to die in an extremely traumatic way. Actually, I read a couple of papers about how a lot of them have textbook symptoms of PTSD, despite having no documented trauma in their current life. Again, like this boy — what's his name? Are you going to tell me what he said?"

"Yes," Percy said. "Sorry. I'm just Googling this stuff as you're talking. Apparently, the University of Virginia has an entire team of professors and researchers devoted to reincarnation and near-death experiences and that kind of thing."

"Oh, right. DAPS? Or DOPS? Perceptual studies, right?

"Right — UVA Division of Perceptual Studies. Led by somebody named Dr. Jim Tucker. This is crazy. I had no idea."

"Yeah. It sounded crazy to our class, too. But only because none of us had actually read about it. I went home that night and started doing research and was shocked. I mean, I guess I still have some doubts, but the case studies are really, really hard to refute."

"Ok, I'll be reading those later." He took an audible breath. "I guess I should get back to the present situation. Sorry. The kid's name is Isaac, I'm told, and he lives in Pikesville. Only child, Jewish family. So, he's said a few things that have already been verified. Let me read from my notes." He paused. "He told his parents he died … Oh, man. Aahna, this is hard to read to you."

"It's fine," she said. "What were his exact words?"

"Ok. Exact words, as it was read to me: When asked how he died, Isaac said, 'He cut my neck with a big knife.'"

Nabaa was silent for several seconds. "Whoa," she said.

"Yeah."

"Was all this just out of the blue?"

93

"No," Percy said. "The parents mentioned that Isaac had made vague references to a past life occasionally since he began talking, but they'd never thought much of it. Stuff that only makes sense in retrospect, now that he's actually named his, uh, previous identity. Apparently, it all clarified when he and his dad were watching Rafiq's trial. He heard Fadi Itani's name from the TV and told his dad … Hold on, I'll read it here. He said, 'That's the man who made me die. The other man didn't want to make me die, but Fadi Itani yelled at him and made him do it.'"

She was silent for a while. He could've known that by watching the beheading video. *But no one would show a child that video, right?* "Is that verified?"

"It's on video, yeah. And they've interviewed the kid once, in person. The father was the only other person present when the boy initially talked about being Sami, and about his death. But when they asked him if his parents coached him to say things, Isaac says no. Oh — and the agent said Isaac even spoke some Arabic during the interview. Unprompted."

"Wow. Amazing." Nabaa's thoughts were racing.

"Yeah. And there's other stuff in my notes here. Things Isaac said — all of them are pretty trippy, but also the kind of details that are publicly available. So, the parents could have been talking about the whole thing one day and it stuck in their kid's mind, and now he's just parroting. Of course, they swear that's not the case, but you can't rule it out, so here we are."

"And this is the part where I have to verify something?"

"Right," Percy said. He took a deep breath. "I really should not be springing this on you. Mag— … um, Lizzie wasn't thrilled with the idea."

"I'll be fine," Nabaa said. "I mean, it's urgent for some reason, right?"

"No, I don't think so. The agent made it seem that way, but from what I can tell, it's not tied to any imminent danger. It was just passed along to me as a request." He paused. "Lizzie made me promise to try to find a place in this conversation and try to give you some space. I think that place was probably five minutes ago. I'm sorry."

"It's OK."

"Is it too late? Do you want to call me back after you've had some time to process?"

Nabaa considered it. Maggie was right — these memories might trigger something later today. It was only her intense curiosity that was keeping the other feelings at bay. *But, yes, it's too late,* she thought. Some processing time might've helped before she heard the boy's words about his death. *Let's just get this over with.*

94

"I appreciate the offer," Nabaa said. "But I promise I'll be OK. And at this point, I'm too curious to know what this little boy said. So, go ahead."

After a moment, Percy said, "Fair enough. Number one. He talked about being with his two sisters and being taken to a few different houses to hide. I know that to be pretty much true from what you've told me, and we're pretty sure that's in the public domain, too. But he said one of the houses was — these are his words — 'above a city, with so many lights.' Does that sound familiar?"

Nabaa felt the hair rising on her arms and neck. "Yes," she said. "The night before they took us to the bank basement in Mosul. We stayed with a man and a woman who had several goats … but anyway, yes, that night I remember seeing the city lights stretching out below us to the left and right."

"Wait, you said they had goats?"

"Yes."

"That's another of the quotes here. Says, 'My biggest sister smiled when I drank goat milk. But then she cried.'"

Nabaa's stomach did a somersault. *Sami!* Her little brother. She remembered the goat milk sticking to his upper lip and running down his chin. It was a moment of levity in the middle of a nightmare, and she would never forget it. A wave of emotion hit her. *Stop!* She told herself. *Cry later if you have to.*

"Nabaa … are you OK?" His voice was gentle. They didn't usually use real names on the phone, but hearing him say her name calmed her a little. *He always had a knack for that.*

"Yes," she said. "No … I don't know." She took a deep breath. "The man and the woman who lived in the house were very kind to us. And we were hungry. The man talked to Sami for a few minutes to make him feel at ease, then he brought him over to one of the goats, milked it right into a cup and then gave it to him. Sami's eyes lit up. He drank it all, made a mess of his face, and then gave the cup back to the man, who laughed. Sami's smile was so big and so out of place."

And then the wave rose up again. It got into her head, swelled to her eyes and nose, and finally, she couldn't hold it anymore. The tears gushed out of her.

"Oh, Sami!" she said through sobs. "I'm so sorry I haven't thought of you in so long. Anamushta kunlekeh!" *I miss you.*

Percy stayed silent for a long time. She knew the pain in her voice was too heavy for him to touch.

"I'm sorry about this, sweetheart," he said, barely audible over her ragged attempts to calm her breathing. "I'm so sorry."

Inhale deep, exhale slow. "Do not be sorry," she said. "It's good to think of him. And Ashna, too. I've never told anyone that story. And I'm the only person alive who could."

"So I suppose that makes it true," he said, more revelation than declaration.

"Yeah, I guess it does," Nabaa said.

"There's one more thing," he said. "Isaac really wants to meet you."

Maggie stared curiously at the pile of library books Percy had stacked on the kitchen table. She picked up the top one, titled *Life Before Life*, by Jim Tucker, M.D.

"The most famous case is probably James Leininger," Percy said. "It made the news several years ago. A kid started talking about his past life as a World War II pilot, recalling a lot of really specific stuff, which was later verified. Then there's the boy who kept insisting to his mother that he was a big shot in the early days of Hollywood, so she bought a bunch of books to read with him. He identified his previous self and some other people in the photos, and the family eventually got in touch with the deceased man's daughter, who verified more than 50 details the little boy had claimed about her dad's life."

Maggie looked at him, perplexed.

"I know. It's wild. I've listened to Tucker, and other people who work at DOPS always say the same thing: 'I know it sounds crazy, but …' And those two cases from America are pretty creepy, but honestly, there are so many more cases just as solid."

"So, you believe in reincarnation now?"

He took a breath and considered the question. "Yeah. I guess I do. Until I got the call from that agent, I hadn't really thought about it. But now, I don't know what else to believe." He pointed to a purple book on the table, titled "Children Who Remember Previous Lives," by Ian Stevenson. "That guy — Ian Stevenson — started this whole field. Stevenson traveled the world investigating reincarnation claims, and there are a *ton* of cases that clearly cannot be explained any other way. It makes sense, of course. In other countries and cultures, reincarnation isn't some crazy idea, so parents are more likely to report the really interesting cases."

"I gotta believe it's the Christian influence that makes it such a taboo in the West," Maggie said. "That's extra weird for me now, because I've always thought the church's doctrine on the afterlife didn't even match what's in the Bible. Reincarnation actually makes more sense."

"What do you mean?" Percy asked. "Doesn't the Bible refer to Heaven quite a bit?"

"I used to think so, based on my upbringing," Maggie said. "But it was never really explained, you know. So, the summer after high school, I decided to actually *read* the New Testament for the first time. I was specifically keying on what *Jesus* said about everything — the words in red, as they say — but specifically what he said about Heaven. And after the fourth or fifth reference, it became really obvious, really quickly: He talks about Heaven a lot, but he *never* defines what Heaven is."

"You mean he never describes a beautiful place in the sky where all your wishes come true?"

"I mean he doesn't actually describe it at all, in any specific way. He doesn't even say it's the place you go when you die. He does, however, talk about Heaven as a reward for living with faith — but not after death."

"Hmm," Percy said. "Makes me want to read the Bible again."

"You should," Maggie said. "I mean, it was the first time I was reading it without the lens of church dogma influencing my whole interpretation, so it was actually really interesting. I'm not claiming my interpretation is universal, obviously. You might get a different sense of his words. But that's the most salient point, I think — he's *purposely* vague about Heaven, among other things. And why might that be?"

Percy considered it. "That's an interesting question. The biggest part of Christian doctrine is the concept of Heaven being that big afterlife reward, so yeah, you would think that if that was so important to understand, Jesus would've simply told people about it in plainer terms."

"That was my thought," Maggie said. "Four different Gospels and so many opportunities to clarify that big issue. Nothing. I was reading it on my Kindle, and I remember typing notes into it over and over as I read it. After a while, I started getting the impression that Jesus thought of Heaven as a wonderful state of being, where you're living in faith and connected to God, spirituality, whatever. Just loving life. A bunch of my notes say, 'He's talking about Heaven being on Earth.' That thought has stuck with me ever since. It's kind of nice, actually."

Percy smiled. "Easy for you to say, being married to *me*." He winced as Maggie hit him in the shoulder with the book. "Seriously, though. It actually makes some sense. Reminds me, too, of the weird ideas of Hell and Satan that Catholicism fed into me when I was a kid."

"Still doesn't answer what exactly happens *right* after we die, though," Maggie said. "What's the theory? That our soul leaves a dead body and goes straight into some woman's pregnant belly?"

"No, I don't think so," he said. "One of the comments that a lot of the kids with past-life memories make to their parents — not the majority at all, but enough to see a trend — is that they 'chose' them.

They'll say things like, 'You're nice, Mommy. I'm glad I picked you.' Or something along those lines."

"Whoa. That's kind of creepy. But, really sweet, too."

Percy smiled. "That was my reaction, too," he said. "Regardless, I keep reminding myself that this new theory might have some holes or open questions or whatever, but *every* afterlife theory does. Right? I mean, science just says you're dead. Done. The end. And as we both know, religion doesn't do much better — at least not the way it was explained to me by the church-going adults in my life. I would ask questions about who Satan was and why doesn't God just destroy him and be done with it, and what if people sent to Hell saw the fire and immediately saw the error of their ways and begged forgiveness, would God just ignore them? All kinds of questions like that. Nobody had good answers. So, eventually, Satan just became some kind of imaginary bogeyman. I still don't have answers."

Maggie smiled and shook her head knowingly. "Me too. I remember asking a lot of those same questions. Although I'm sure I wasn't nearly as obnoxious about it."

"Of course not," Percy said. "You're too busy being an angel — which is how Satan started, if I'm not mistaken."

Maggie's jaw dropped in dramatic mock offense.

"Aw, honey, that wasn't fair," Percy said, smiling triumphantly and grabbing her by the wrists. "You are only the devil when you're hungry. Other than that, you're a force for good." She pursed her lips, but he pulled her close and kissed her anyway.

◇◇◇◇◇◇◇◇◇

CHAPTER 15

April 2015

"What are you doing over there?" Ibrahim walked into his bedroom wearing only a towel, his wavy wet hair loosely framing a mischievous face. "And are you sure you don't want to do it some other time?" He plopped down on the bed next to her and propped himself up on an elbow.

Nabaa cast an eye-rolling smile at him, then continued to stare at the screen in front of her. "Sorry," she said, moving and tapping her finger on the touchpad. "There." She closed the laptop, knowing he was actually waiting for an answer to his question. "I've been obsessing about reincarnation," she said. "But I should take a break."

"Reincarnation?" Curiosity replaced his playful lasciviousness. "Why?"

Tell the truth ... mostly. "I was looking for books that use neuroscience to explain mystical experiences," she said. "And you know how they show you a list of books 'Customers Also Purchased'? I saw one about children with past-life memories." The falsehood passed over her lips easily enough, but left a stale aftertaste. *Then again, as long as he doesn't even know my real name, how bad could it be?* She wondered how long she could keep up this ruse. She decided to talk to Maggie about it. "It made me remember what Professor Martin told us last year. Did you ever have Professor Martin?"

"I think one of my friends did," Ibrahim said. "Neurobio, right?"

"Right. He told us about this past-life memory stuff one day, how the memories were somehow documented to be accurate, and that it was yet to be explained. It derailed the whole class. I remember Googling it later that night and being kind of amazed, but then I forgot about it — till I noticed that book yesterday. And now I can't stop." She saw a puzzled look on his face and instantly realized why. "I know," she said. "You would think I was well versed in samsara, and the karmic travel of the soul, and all that other Hindu stuff. But we barely learned anything substantial about Hindu beliefs at the orphanage. I'm sure it's partly why I'm so intrigued by it now."

He nodded sympathetically. "That reminds me," he said, "did I ever tell you about the book *The Unveiling*?"

"Doesn't sound familiar. Why?"

"It's a novel I read a long time ago, written by a guy named Stefan Alford," Ibrahim said. "It had a new spin on reincarnation — nothing to do with kids remembering past lives. The story was all about the Christian church's systematic opposition to the idea of multiple lives. The theory is that, in the beginning of the Church, some leaders thought Jesus was preaching about a single, perfect, eternal afterlife — not a series of lives. But others disagreed and thought reincarnation was clearly part of his world view. Eventually, so the story goes, they all agreed that it didn't matter as much what Jesus actually believed — for the purposes of growing a religion, a single afterlife was a much better solution. Attach an eternal reward, and suddenly you've got people willing to spend their lives following the church's rules."

"They figured if people thought we all got multiple shots at life on Earth, "they might not follow the rules very well?"

"Right," Ibrahim said, nodding. "So, the theory goes, when the church had its early councils to decide what was canon and what wasn't, they removed Jesus' references to reincarnation."

Her brow furrowed. "Huh," she said. "Is there any historical merit to the theory?"

"Honestly, I don't know," Ibrahim said.."I mean, the councils definitely happened, and I'm pretty sure it's accepted knowledge that they did a lot of chopping before they finalized their canonical catalog. I mean, that's apparently why they called the councils in the first place. So, who knows? It definitely makes sense, though. And it's hard to argue with the results, 1600 years later."

"True," she said. "It feels like half the world is going to church to figure out how to get into Heaven later. I can't say I've been totally immune to the draw. But if this reincarnation thing is actually true ..." Her thought dispersed like a bubble bursting into a shower of droplets. "I don't know. It's a different kind of hope. And I might like it better."

"I know what you mean," he said. "The eternal happiness thing has never quite made sense to me. It's like, will I be in some kind of smiling cult in the sky? Everywhere I turn, there's a Ned Flanders character looking up from his gardening, saying, 'Howdy, neighbor!' Kind of creepy, honestly. And then I remind myself I'm trying to understand the meaning of the universe with the mind of a tiny human who can't think beyond his own nature and nurture and ambitions."

"You know," she said, turning onto her own elbow to face him as directly as possible. "You've given me precious few details on your nature and nurture and ambitions. Every time your family comes up in conversation, you deftly swerve around it. All I know is that your parents are traditional, and they're both practicing doctors. And you want to be an author someday. So, no more swerving." She poked him in the chest with her forefinger. "Talk to me about you."

"OK," he said. "I'm about halfway done with my book."

"You're writing a book? Right now? Seriously?"

"Well, sort of," he said. "I mean, I rarely get to ever sit down and focus on it. But I've got it all outlined, and the first half is pretty much done."

"That's amazing, Ibrahim! Why didn't you tell me?"

He smiled ever so slightly. "I don't even want to tell you now. It's not actually amazing, either, since I started it when I was 17 and I've only written 50,000 words or so. I can rarely find the time to write. I mean, if I ever finish it *and* edit it *and* get it published *and* people think it's meaningful, *then* you can call it amazing. But until then, who wants to hear an unpublished author talking about a book that may or may not ever exist?"

Nabaa smiled and shook her head. "I've never seen you so sincerely humble. Credit to you. Now, give me the goods. Where is it? I want to read what you've got so far."

"Nope," Ibrahim said.

Her eyes and mouth widened. "OK. Compromise. Just the first chapter." She held out her right hand to shake on the deal.

"Nope," he said again.

"What's it called?"

"Working title."

She put on a faux glare and pushed him so he rolled onto his back. "Fine," she said. She shimmied close to him and lay her head on his chest. "What's it about?"

Ibrahim took a slow breath as he rested his right arm around her back. "It's an allegory," he said. "A prince objects to the ways of his father, the king. His father doesn't change. The prince leaves the kingdom and starts his own kingdom far away. The king is furious. So, he sends his army to dismantle his son's kingdom and bring his son back. Things don't go as planned."

"So far, so good," she said. "I'm intrigued. Does the prodigal son return?"

"You really want me to spoil it for you?"

She thought about that. "Yes, I think so. If it's in your head already, then I want it to be in my head, too. But it's up to you."

Ten seconds of silence passed. He caressed her back with the tips of his fingers, then kissed her forehead softly. "The prodigal son doesn't return. His army brings him the head of his father. That's all basically in the first act. The son rules over both lands for a while, but he's paranoid for the rest of his life. So, he grows his army constantly, trains them relentlessly, develops new and better weapons. He conquers new lands in the name of protection and preservation of the kingdom. And, like he planned, all his strength eventually starts to scare the rulers of distant lands, along with their religious leaders. First, it inspires guerilla attacks wherever the new king's convoys travel. Eventually, it scares all the other kingdoms into a collective."

"So, ironically, his desire to protect is what creates his biggest threat?"

"Exactly," Ibrahim said.

"So how does, um, 'Prince America' fare in the end?"

He laughed. "The allegory is that obvious, huh?" Nabaa turned her head and kissed his chin. "I can't spoil the end for you either way," he said. "I have no idea how to end it. America, I mean, the son, pays a heavy price, but beyond that, I haven't worked out the details. Honestly, Professor Kibbe's class has made me rethink a lot of things about Islam. You could probably tell I was fairly biased against modern Islam early in the semester. But I think that was just bias."

"What do you mean?"

"Like some kind of deep-rooted anger about how Islam treated my family. Well, generations of my family, probably. At least on my dad's side."

That brought many questions into Nabaa's mind. She picked one. "Was it hard to write the scenes between a father and son who are that opposed to each other? I mean, you get along with your dad, right?"

"Yeah, we get along," he said. "I love my dad, and he's only a little bit similar to the king in the story. But we have our eternal disagreements. It's just that in real life, I'm trying to navigate them more subtly. So, no, it wasn't really hard to write, I guess. The only hard part I've found is *starting* to write. I feel like I spend half my writing time just pulling on the cord, trying to get my engine started."

"Because you're always thinking about school stuff?"

"I don't know, really," he said. "None of my classes are difficult, and they rarely captivate my mind like the stuff I'm writing about. I don't think the struggle to write has much to do with the school experience, really. I mean, life before college was hard, but it's not anymore."

"I'm listening," Nabaa said.

"Oh, right," Ibrahim said. He exhaled. "You want the story of *me*. Sure. Here goes. So, you could probably guess that my parents were demanding. What you don't know is that my mother is Muslim and my father is Jewish." Nabaa lifted her head and stared at him with surprise.

"Your father is a Jew? From Pakistan?"

"Yes — sort of," Ibrahim said. "It's a long story. My paternal grandparents were Sephardic Jews from Karachi, which is pretty much the only place where Jews lived in Pakistan. They emigrated to Israel when it became a country. My mother is Pakistani, but lived in Karachi. She got her postdoc from the Junnah hospital there and loved it. She knew that the Junnah hospital was built with USAID help and money, and she wanted to pay it forward, I guess. That was the early '80s. She found out USAID was building a business school in Lahore, and she decided to take a year to go help out. She was a staff physician for the aid camp. She met my father there. He was pursuing his medical degree to be a psychiatrist back in Israel, but he decided to do his doctoral thesis on international relations within his quasi-native Pakistan. Their families were both from Karachi, but they met in Lahore."

"That's a long way away," Nabaa said. "So they fell in love and decided to live there together?"

"Not exactly," he said. "They fell in love, but the project ended and they each went home. Mom to Karachi, Dad to Israel. They wrote letters to each other, they each visited each other's home once. Eventually my dad decided to move to Karachi. He says he felt like Karachi was more home to him than Israel would be to her. So, he moved there in 1987, I think. And it was apparently OK for a while. There was still a small Jewish community who welcomed him, but that was basically it. It didn't last long. The rest of the country kept getting less welcoming toward Jews, and then Pakistan passed the Shari'ah enforcement law in 1991. That's when my parents decided it was time to come here, to the U.S."

"What took them so long to have you?" Nabaa asked.

"They say they tried for a while in Pakistan, but she never got pregnant," Ibrahim said. "They moved here and kept trying. That's when she started having miscarriages. She doesn't like talking about that, but Dad says there were five. She got depressed, they fought a lot. It came to a head when she decided to go back to Karachi to be with her parents for a few weeks, against my dad's wishes. She says she spent every day praying to Allah just to have one child. When she came back to the States, the story goes, my dad picked her up from the airport, they had a tearful embrace, and then they came back home together and conceived me on their first try."

"Wow," Nabaa whispered.

"Yep. She told me all the time — still tells me, actually — that I'm here to make good on her bargain with God."

Nabaa laughed. "What did she promise?"

"Just that they would raise me to help bring God's word to people," Ibrahim said. "So, I guess I'm supposed to be a prophet. No big deal."

"And that's why you're trying to write an important book?"

Ibrahim smiled. "No. Well, maybe. I don't know. It feels like my own idea, but I'm sure their brainwashing had an effect. I mean, a lot of times when I do actually sit down to write and I'm in that weird mental place, it doesn't feel like I'm coming up with the ideas myself. It's just like a fountain comes on, and I'm just watching my fingers type words onto the screen."

"Sounds like divinely inspired stuff to me. I guess I'll have to read it."

"Thanks," Ibrahim said. "And if it's not good, you can blame God."

She laughed. "So, did your parents try to have any more kids?"

"Nope. They stopped with me. And the miscarriages stopped, too, thankfully."

"So, you were the chosen one from the beginning," Nabaa said. "What kind of kid were you? I mean, how spoiled of a brat were you?"

He laughed. "I don't know. Pretty spoiled, I guess. We never wanted for money, so I had lots of things. We went on vacation. I'm sure I never truly understood or appreciated that part. But I always felt like I was *working*, just like my parents were working. They had their jobs, and they always found jobs for me. Projects. I was constantly working on a project that they devised."

"What kind of projects?"

"Anything they could think of," he said. "They weren't cruel or anything. Just eternally demanding." Ibrahim stopped to think. "I remember building entire towns out of Legos, and checking off a list of government services that had to be represented by my structures. Sanitation plant here, bus station there. The projects changed as I got older. Gardening for a while. That was hard. And then when I was in sixth grade, I had to do some fundraising stuff. The last one was when I was a sophomore — they made me start up a 501(c)(3) and actually bring it to fruition. Do the paperwork, market the idea to my fellow students, get membership and then create enough continuity that it would exist without me."

"Whoa," Nabaa said. "That sounds intense. But pretty cool."

"Yeah, it *sounds* great. And I did it. It's still in existence, last I checked. It's a chapter of a charity called StandUp for Kids, which my dad had read about. People gather donations of essential items, like nonperishable food and hygiene kits, and distribute them to homeless kids — runaways, basically. These are kids who were probably abused at home, so they're on the streets constantly hiding from cops. They don't have a lot of options to get help, since they're afraid they'll get picked up and sent back home."

"Wow. What a great mission," she said. "But you didn't like it?"

"I don't know," he said, sighing. "I always knew the mission was important, but … setting it all up was a chore. It was another project I just wanted to complete, check the box, so I could go back to doing things of my own choosing. But the first time we actually went out with our supplies, when we saw those kids for the first time, and we helped them, and they scattered back onto the streets ... it made me angry. Angry at their shitty, unfair life, and then angry at myself because, sort of subconsciously, I was treating them as a means to my end. I realized then just how spoiled I was. I wished so much that it had been my idea. Maybe if it had been my idea, I could've felt good about helping them. And then I felt even angrier, because I knew that helping people shouldn't be about *me.*" Nabaa felt his chest rise and fall slowly, a breath heavy with thought. "So I went home that day and told my parents I wouldn't be doing any more of their projects. They seemed satisfied — or proud. Like they'd been waiting for that moment or something. And that made me even angrier. I had spent my life trying to please them, trying to measure up to this chosen-one ideal they had created." Nabaa heard the pain in his voice. "I thought what they wanted me to do was follow their directions. If they wanted me to do things of my own volition, they could've just said so. Then a voice in my head told me *I* could've decided to do my own thing at any moment, and I didn't. And then I went back to being mad at myself."

Nabaa lifted her head off his chest and turned onto her stomach, facing him. "Aw, Ibrahim," she said. "You were just a kid."

"I never felt like 'just a kid,' Aahna," he said. "And I guess that was the problem." He closed his eyes for a long moment, then opened them and stared into hers. "I'm sorry. I've never shared any of this before."

"It's OK, babe," she said. "I'm glad to know it." She smiled, and she saw peace overtake his face. In that moment, she could sense his love for her deepening, gaining dimension. She felt like she was holding his soul in her hands. And for the first time, she truly loved him back. She kissed him on the cheek, holding her lips there for a long moment, then settled her head back down onto the crook of his shoulder. It felt like one more secret she had to keep.

Ibrahim quickly broke her spell. "You love me, Aahna Khatri." The playfulness had returned to his voice.

"You love me, too, Ibrahim Khan," she said, without a fraction of hesitation. "I wonder if your devotion to me will get in the way of this book God wants you to write."

He laughed. "First of all, it most certainly will. And if it really is what God wants me to do, you'll have to answer for that one day." His voice changed ever so slightly. "And if God wants me to do something else, I'm sure you'll help me figure out what it is."

◇◇◇◇◇◇◇◇◇◇
CHAPTER 16

April 2015

from: Liza Hamilton <lizachucksgirl@gmail.com>
to: Aahna Khatri <aktheexister@gmail.com>
date: Mon, April 6, 2015 at 6:12 AM
subject: Past lives

Hey. How are you? Charlie said you two had a pretty heavy conversation yesterday. And then he and I talked, and we've both been obsessing about reincarnation since. He went right to the library and checked out a stack of books, watched some videos online. Can't stop thinking about it, especially given the current situation.
You?

from: Aahna Khatri <aktheexister@gmail.com>
to: Liza Hamilton <lizachucksgirl@gmail.com>
date: Mon, April 6, 2015 at 7:57 AM
subject: RE: Past lives

Yes!
The heavy stuff hasn't hit me yet. Not sure why. Maybe because it made me think of my brother and sister, and part of me has wanted to think about them for a while now? Some good memories have come back. And I think my curiosity has me pretty distracted.

I'm mostly struck by how widespread the belief is, compared to how little it's discussed anywhere in America. Based on the data I can find, around 20% of the world's population believes in reincarnation. Obviously, India's high population of Hindus skews that number a lot, but I didn't know that a quarter of *Americans* believe in reincarnation.

So almost 100 million people in the U.S. believe we are reincarnated after death, and that's *without* ever reading about kids with documented past-life memories, how high would that number get if that research got more attention?

I even had to confront my Muslim beliefs on the issue. I immediately started searching through the Quran and looking up different interpretations. It's weird … none of the verses are really clear about it. Of course, Islam as a whole doesn't espouse reincarnation; like Christianity, the doctrine is about one life, followed by heaven or hell. But if you're looking for interpretive flexibility in the actual verses, it's there.

Like Al-'Ankaboot 29:57 — "Every soul will taste death. Then to Us will you be returned." Well, sure. I don't think a belief in reincarnation requires a rejection of death, or even a rejection of some other "heavenly" place that's outside of Earth. What if there were a beautiful way-station, where souls reconvene with God *temporarily* instead of permanently? And when the souls are ready, they return to life?

Here's another thing. Ibrahim asked what I was obsessing about on my computer, so I had to tell him (generically, of course). He told me about this book called "The Unveiling" by Stefan Alford. It's a novel. He read it a long time ago, obviously way before knowing anything about past-life memories. But apparently it's about reincarnation and how it's an ancient but subjugated belief in Christianity. The story implies that it was scrubbed from the canon during early church meetings, like the Council of Nicea, because the early church was afraid it would lose control if followers thought they had infinite chances at life.

And just like that, we have the Heaven/Hell doctrine, which absolutely motivates Christians. Can't argue with results, I guess.

There's something about this that feels so … true. And I don't think it's just the truth in the work of Stevenson and Tucker. I feel like there's always been something a little confusing and off about the idea of permanent "Heaven." Something about the lack of contrast. Or maybe that's just me?

from: Liza Hamilton <lizachucksgirl@gmail.com>
to: Aahna Khatri <aktheexister@gmail.com>
date: Mon, April 6, 2015 at 9:10 AM
subject: Past lives

I just ordered a copy of "The Unveiling." :) It sounds like what I was just telling Charlie! We started talking about the idea of Heaven as it relates to reincarnation, and I told him about my experience reading the New Testament as an adult (which was pretty awesome to do, without the lens of dogma). Basically what I got from it was — drum roll — a whole lot of vagueness.

Even in the church-approved scripture, Jesus seems like he was a guy who *implied* things but consciously avoided direct rules and black-and-white situations. He doesn't tell us that we get multiple chances at life. But he also doesn't tell us that we *don't*.

And when it comes to Heaven, *nowhere* does he say anything about this beautiful, eternal world of milk and honey. The way Jesus talked about it, Heaven is right here on Earth. Like a state of mind. It's happiness in mortality while being at peace with God, having faith, etc. I know I've *felt* that, and it doesn't get any better.

I remember being surprised when I realized that heaven-on-Earth interpretation isn't really uncommon. The church doesn't teach it, but plenty of religious scholars view it that way. The church's position certainly makes sense, though. So much was written and attributed to Jesus over the few hundred years after he died that by the time the New Testament was codified and canonized, it was probably pretty chaotic. The Christian Church was an institution. And therefore, it had institutional agendas, particularly the survival and growth of the institution itself.

And how can you argue with those decisions, knowing how much Christianity has grown since? I mean, maybe Jesus himself would've argued with a lot of Church decisions, but I digress … ;)

Anyway, now I'm wondering what exactly happens *between* lives, if this reincarnation thing is true. On that topic, Charlie says I need to watch a movie called "What Dreams May Come." He says it's really sad and really happy at the same time. Maybe you and I can watch it together this weekend?

from: Aahna Khatri <aktheexister@gmail.com>
to: Liza Hamilton <lizachucksgirl@gmail.com>
date: Mon, April 6, 2015 at 2:22 PM
subject: RE: Past lives

I haven't heard of that movie, but I just looked it up. Yeah, not one I want to watch by myself, but I'd LOVE to watch with you. Let's do it.

Something else on this topic that I wanted to share: Apparently, many Muslims also believe that sleep is a kind of nightly death and reincarnation. I read a transcript of an interview with a prominent Muslim scholar, where he basically said dreams are like the mini-life after the death of sleep, and, our souls are enriched every morning when we wake up. It reminded me so much of our email discussion on the mystery of sleep.

It got me thinking about how vulnerable we are when we sleep, and … OK, I'm about to take a big detour here, so please forgive me — and stay with me! So I realized there's another time when we're just as vulnerable and we take it for granted even MORE than sleep: *procreation*. Sex. Pregnancy. Baby-caring.

Why do we also have a biological instinct to procreate? It's in direct conflict with our instinct to survive.

If it were just about our own survival, then we would *not* procreate. We are only adding competitors for resources when we take a mate and create offspring. Even when breast-feeding mothers have no sustenance for themselves, their bodies use precious energy to produce breast milk. We are biologically engineered to value our young over ourselves.

That alone indicates we are not just here to survive. There must be something metaphysical about life — species-level survival is by nature a metaphysical thing. By definition! Meta- and -physical!!

And then the two topics — procreation and reincarnation — connected, and … EUREKA!

We have to procreate so we ourselves can come back to life later!

It's not just about surviving THIS LIFE — it's about species survival so we can LIVE AGAIN!

It even fits some of Stevenson's work that shows there's a disproportionate amount of reincarnations into the same family or nearby villages/areas.

So, if reincarnation is real, then *it even explains the need for procreation*. It also explains our tribal instincts. We would be programmed to maximize the tribe's chances to survive and thrive, hoping to die and be reborn into the tribe in a later generation.

I feel dizzy.

◇◇◇◇◇◇◇◇◇
CHAPTER 17

April 2015

Nabaa stepped into the passenger-side backseat of the huge, black government sedan. She set her book on her lap and strapped on the seatbelt.

Percy was already in the car, seated behind the driver. Despite the size of the car, he still felt scrunched and uncomfortable.

"Hey," she said. She gave him a quick, cramped hug.

"Hey," he said, smiling. He tried to judge her mood, but she didn't seem happy or sad, up or down. *That usually means she's anxious.*

The sedan pulled away from Nabaa's apartment building and headed toward the 695 on-ramp.

Percy picked up the book. It was called *Old Souls*, by Tom Shroder.

"So, should I read this one next?" he asked her. "Is it as convincing as Stevenson's books?"

She nodded. "It's *about* Stevenson, actually. And I think it's convincing in a different way," she said. "This man — Shroder. He's a prominent journalist. And he started with the common, American view of reincarnation, I guess. Mostly unfamiliar, but skeptical. He decided to profile Stevenson, and then simply by observing Stevenson interact with the children and their families, his mind starts to change. I haven't finished it yet, but it seems he's on his way to becoming a believer. Obviously, it's a good read. I've been bringing it everywhere I go since I found it at the library the other day."

Percy nodded as he read the back cover blurb. "So what does 'science' say about all this stuff?"

Nabaa looked at him and smiled a little. "I don't think science has weighed in on this yet," she said. "All matter and energy reincarnates in some form. There is no rule that says consciousness can't do the same."

"Good point," Percy said. He turned toward the front. "What do you SS guys think about this reincarnation thing?"

"Whoa — you forgot the D," the driver said. "I mean, the SS? You trying to make us into the like the Hitler outfit? That's worse than the dumbass names the FBI calls us. 'Dickhead Security Service.' 'Douchebag Security Service.' They're insecure assholes. We're diplomats."

"You mean you're security guards for the real diplomats?" Percy said.

"No," the passenger said. "Diplomatic Security Service members are officially members of the U.S. Foreign Service, which technically makes us diplomats. And who's gonna tell us otherwise?" He shot Percy a congenial smile. "Oh, and Agent Hugenbruch here is also right about the FBI. They're insecure assholes. He would know, since he's former FBI."

"And guys like Agent Schneider here are why they call us dickheads and douchebags," Hugenbruch said.

Percy laughed. Nabaa smiled and rolled her eyes. Then she took the book from his hand and opened it up. He let her read undisturbed. Ten minutes later, they were off the Baltimore beltway and turning into a residential neighborhood in Pikesville.

"Looks like this is the place," Schneider said, staring down at his smartphone. Hugenbruch pulled into a nicely paved driveway, bracketed by a narrow swath of shrubs on the left and a large expanse of grass on the right. The moderately sized, single-story home had a wide bay window reflecting the yard and its surrounding trees.

Schneider craned his neck around to make eye contact with Nabaa. "I can't imagine how weird this must be for you, but I'd be lying if I said I wasn't curious as hell. You ready?"

Nabaa said nothing. She opened her door and stepped out into humid, 60-degree sunshine. Percy and the agents followed, then stood still, watching.

About 30 yards away, Percy saw the front door of the house open, and a small boy stepped out on to the stoop. A few seconds later, a man and woman — Percy knew their names were Jerry and Jacquelyn Czarnecki — appeared in the threshold. The three of them stared at Nabaa. Jerry knelt next to Isaac and pointed in Nabaa's direction.

The boy looked down and carefully descended the two steps of the stoop. Then his eyes found Nabaa again, and he started walking across the lawn to greet her. He kept his eyes down and stopped a few feet away, then glanced up at her, then looked down again.

Nabaa crouched. "Hello, Isaac," she said.

"Hello, Nabaa," he said. His voice was perfect, high-pitched English, but there was a deep familiarity within it.

Percy felt his breathing quicken and goosebumps form on his arms.

The boy raised his gaze and, this time, kept it locked on Nabaa. "I missed you very much," Isaac said. His shaking voice and welling eyes sent a wave of emotion in all directions. Percy felt it right in his chest.

He saw Nabaa's shoulders begin to tremble. Her head fell into her hands.

"Don't cry, Nabaa," the boy said. Then he stepped forward and took her pinkie, ring finger, and middle finger into his own small hand. *Just like Sami used to do!*

"Oh my God!" Nabaa said, lifting her eyes to his. "It is you."

"It's me," Isaac said. His gaze faltered. He stared over Nabaa's shoulder, into blue sky. "I know I'm Isaac. But I remember being your brother. I told my daddy about it, but I don't think he believed me. And now you're here. And now I know it's true. My memory is true. Because I love you like you're my sister, but I don't have any sisters here." He turned and looked at Czarnecki. "Daddy," he said loudly. "Can you and Mommy make a sister?"

Czarnecki put his hands in his pockets and smiled. "We can try, buddy."

Satisfied, Isaac turned back to Nabaa. "My daddy's the best daddy ever." He squinted in thought. "I don't remember a different daddy — did we have the same daddy? Before?"

Nabaa smiled at the sincerity in Isaac's voice. "Yes," she said. "We did."

"I don't remember him," he repeated. "But I remember his voice. He told me not to open the door. But I was a bad listener and I opened the door because I wanted to see who was there. And it was bad guys, and they came in and took us away. It was my fault, Nabaa." He suddenly started to cry. "I'm sorry. I'm very sorry."

She wrapped him in her arms.

His voice lost its energy. "When I died, I was stuck for a long time," he whispered. "It was dark and scary. I was all by myself. I was looking all around for mommy, but it was just dark clouds. And then I looked for you, but ..." The words began pouring out of the boy's mouth. "Then all of a sudden God told me in my brain — he said I could come back. He said I could be close to you. He said I couldn't be your brother again. I had to pick a new mommy and daddy and be a baby again. So, I picked this mommy and daddy, and I love them. But I picked them because they were nice, and because they live close to where you live. But then I forgot everything for a long time. Then I heard the man on TV talking, and I started remembering." He pulled away from her. "But I don't like these new memories. I mean, old memories. They are making me sad and confused." He paused, eyes angled to the sky again. "I want to say I'm sorry to Daddy."

Oh, Sami. She hugged him for a long time.

Then, something clicked off inside her, and it felt all wrong. This wasn't Sami. This was Isaac. She was consoling Isaac because of something Sami had done.

She let go, but kept her hands gripping boy's shoulders.

"Isaac, listen to me," Nabaa said. "You cannot feel bad about what happened when you were Sami. You were a good boy, and you made mistakes like all boys do. But now you are *not* Sami. YOU are Isaac Czarnecki." The boy was spellbound, staring intently into Nabaa's eyes.

112

"And Isaac Czarnecki shouldn't have to remember any of the bad things that happened in that other life. You are innocent. Those thoughts are now just enemies inside yourself, and you are strong enough to beat them. That is your first job. Tell those thoughts to leave you alone, and they will. Do you promise?"

Isaac hesitated, nodded, then put his hand over his heart. Nabaa did the same.

"But that means you have to go bye-bye and never come back, right?"

"I think so," Nabaa said. *Even though I want to come back tomorrow and the next day and every day forever.* She swallowed hard against the tears that tried to escape.

They embraced. They said goodbye. Nabaa stood and waved at the Czarneckis, who returned the gesture.

Then Isaac turned around. "Nabaa?"

"Yes, Isaac?"

"Can you tell Rafiq something? I think his daddy is stuck — he can't get a new body. So I think he should pray for his daddy so he can be unstuck. Ok?"

Nabaa didn't know what to say. She looked at Percy. *Stuck? How?* He shrugged. She ignored her questions and just said, "I'll try."

Isaac smiled, turned, and walked back to his parents.

Nabaa was shaken when she got back in the backseat of the sedan and pulled the door closed. Isaac, though, was still smiling earnestly as he waved to the car reversing down the driveway.

CHAPTER 18

April 2015

Percy heard the telltale sound of Nabaa tinkering with the teapot on the stove. "I hear you moving the teapot!" He shouted from the back bedroom. He walked back into the kitchen shaking his head at Nabaa, who was trying to quickly return to her seat at the island.

"I make very good tea all by myself nowadays, thank you very much," he said, lifting the pot and smelling the air around it. He put it back down and turned off the burner. "Maggie will be out in a sec. Apparently nobody at work can handle business while she takes an afternoon off, so she has to fire off a couple of emails. She tried to pepper me with questions, then caught herself and stopped. She wants to hear it from you."

Nabaa nodded, then dropped a spoonful of sugar into the bottom of the half-sized, Iraqi-style mug. Percy tipped the ceramic teapot over her mug and poured steaming Ceylon tea over the heap of sugar. It was black, viscous from the long stovetop reduction, and smelled even better than usual. She swirled the tiny spoon in her cup twice, blew lightly across the top of it, then took a sip.

"Wow," she said. "Much better than last time. Have you been watching ethnic tea YouTube videos?"

"Maybe," Percy said. "I also ordered better tea. It's not too thick? I've been simmering it for a while."

"It's perfect," she said.

"All right," Maggie said, entering the room. "I'm back. I need tea and all the details."

Percy dropped some sugar into another mug and filled it. He nodded to Nabaa.

"I don't know where to begin," Nabaa said. "We only talked for a few minutes, but he said a lot of things. He called me by my name, like he had said it hundreds of times before. He told me he missed me. He consoled me when I cried. Then he said he was the one who opened the door to Itani's men, after my father told him not to." She paused and looked at Percy, then took a long breath. "So he cried, and I consoled him. Then he told me he was lonely after he died, in some kind of dark place. He said he looked for our mom, then for me, then God told him he could come back in a different body, and he chose his parents because they were nice and because they were close to me." She paused, momentarily arrested by Maggie's widening eyes. "Sorry. I know it's a lot. Oh — and he told me to give Rafiq a message about his father."

"Rafiq?" Maggie asked, glancing at Percy, then back at Nabaa. "Did he think you two were in communication?"

"I don't know," Nabaa said. "I don't think he really thought about it. I was telling him to leave his old life behind and embrace his current life, and he seemed relieved to do that, but then he realized there was something he wanted Rafiq to hear, and I was the last connection before he severed all connections to his previous life. Or … something like that. I have no idea, really."

"What was his message?"

"That Rafiq should pray for his daddy, so his daddy can get unstuck."

A few seconds went by. "Whoa," Maggie said. "Like, because of the suicide, I wonder?"

Nabaa just shrugged and took another sip of her tea. Her mood was souring, and she wasn't sure why.

After another long moment, Percy broke in. "I was there, and it was very creepy. But also very real-feeling. But still, can we rule out that this is some kind of hoax put on by his parents? I heard his father has been following the trial closely."

Nabaa turned and glared at Percy. "That was my brother, Percy," she said. "You skip your usual forensic analysis. No evidence or proof would be necessary beyond the feeling I had when that boy looked at me, and his eyes showed me that love and trust that Sami always had for me." *Calm down,* she told herself. She tried, but she couldn't get the pain out of her voice. "Then he held my three fingers — *the same three fingers* that Sami always did." She demonstrated with her hands out in front of her. "He held my hand like that while I was teaching him how to take his first steps, and while I was leading him into the room where he died, and every other time in between. It was *him.*"

Percy stared at her. "I'm sorry, sweetheart," he said, finally. "I believe you."

She looked down into her teacup. "It's ok," she said. "You didn't mean it. You never do." There was still a touch of bitterness in her voice that she couldn't remove.

Like a blessing, one of the two mobile phones on the island counter blared to life. Percy answered it.

"Charlie Hamilton," he said.

Pause.

"Yes, I'm secure here."

Pause.

"Go 'head," Percy said.

115

Pause. Then, Percy smiled broadly. "Hello, Rafiq," he said, as Maggie's and Nabaa's eyes widened simultaneously. "Good to hear your voice."

Long pause.

"When? You mean today?"

Long pause.

"Wait — you're *here?*" Percy's eyebrows shot upward. His mind raced. "Wow. OK. Let me put you on hold for a minute and talk to Maggie." He paused. "And Nabaa."

Percy listened for a few moments, nodding.

"Just give me a minute." Percy said. He muted the phone, set it down and looked at Maggie and Nabaa. "Rafiq and the DSS escorts are in the neighborhood. Literally, in our neighborhood, around the corner right now. They're on their way from New York down to the State Department headquarters, and he said most of the commute so far has been trying to get a secure connection set up while driving. Anyway, Rafiq has something he wants to talk about with me." He looked at Nabaa. "And he says he would be honored to speak to you, as well."

Nabaa was pensive, staring at island countertop. Then she looked at Maggie, then squared her gaze on Percy.

"There's no pressure, sweetheart," Percy said. "This has no bearing on the situation we were just talking about. I was already going to pass along the message from you — er, Isaac. I mean, Sami." He took a deep breath.

"I think I'll be ok," she said flatly. "For all I know, it'll be helpful to see him face to face."

Percy nodded. "Mags? He asked for your blessing, too. Any objections?"

Maggie shook her head. "I'm with Nabaa."

Percy unmuted the phone and put it on speaker. "Rafiq?"

"Yes. I am still here."

"You have all our blessings, without conditions. And I just made a good batch of Iraqi black tea if you're interested. C'mon in. The door will be unlocked."

"Thank you, Percy."

The line went dead. Percy set the phone back on the counter. Then he poured his own small cup of tea into a regular-sized mug, rinsed the small one in the sink, dried the outside, then dropped in a fresh helping of sugar. No one spoke.

About a minute later, the front door opened. They all stared casually as a man in a black suit entered, followed by Rafiq and another dark-suited man. They paused in the entryway briefly and nodded at their hosts.

The first agent closed the door. "Just a minute," he said to Rafiq. Then he glanced at the second agent, and they both headed to the kitchen.

"Good afternoon, ladies," the first agent said, lightly bowing his head. "Agent Lee, DSS. We'll be waiting in the car outside, but before we do —" He turned to Percy. "We just wanted to shake your hand and thank you for your service."

Percy shook his hand firmly. "It's my pleasure, sir."

The other agent advanced and shook Percy's hand, too. "Agent Borst. Honestly, I'm a little conflicted here," he said. "Until they stuck you on our books, I was the baddest badass in the State Department." Nabaa and Maggie laughed heartily. "Still an honor to meet you, Mr. Mack—, Shit. Mr. Hamilton."

"Thank you," Percy said, grinning.

"And you ladies, too," Borst said. "Your stories are almost as legendary as his. A family of badasses. My eternal admiration." He shook both their hands, as did Lee.

"All right," Lee said, turning toward Rafiq. "All you, Itani. We'll knock on the door in, say …" He lifted his arm and looked at his watch. "20 minutes. Sound good?"

"Should be fine," Rafiq said.

The agents nodded as they passed him and walked out the door.

Rafiq strode into the kitchen, bringing with him a near-tangible electric tension. Percy slid the sugar-loaded mug to the edge of the counter and poured hot Ceylon mixture into it.

"Welcome," Percy said.

"It's an honor," Rafiq said. He faced Maggie and Nabaa. "Most of all, it is an honor to meet you both." He extended his hand to Maggie, who shook it. Then, to Nabaa, he held his hand to his heart. She returned the gesture. "Thank you for having me in your home," he said.

"Our pleasure," Maggie said.

Rafiq stepped back to his place at the side of the island counter and picked up his tea. His steel eyes canvassed everything that made the house what it was.

Is this the first American home he's been in? Percy wondered.

"Umm, I have a message for you," Nabaa said suddenly.

"A message?" Rafiq said. "From whom?"

Nabaa looked at Percy.

"This is going to take some explaining," Percy said. "But you'll want to hear it."

For the next 10 minutes, Percy explained how he heard about Isaac, the FBI case handler's explanation, the books he and Maggie read, the DOPS research. Rafiq only listened, occasionally nodding.

"Sorry to interrupt," Maggie said, "but why don't you seem surprised by any of this? I mean, most people — myself included — react with more skepticism for either religious reasons or science reasons."

"Well, as far as I know, science hasn't explained how we came to *life* yet, much less what happens when we die," he said. "All matter and energy reincarnates in some form. There is no rule that says consciousness couldn't do the same." He smiled. "As for religion, I don't know. I suppose I'm open-minded. And even if I weren't, the idea of reincarnation was discussed regularly throughout my childhood, mostly because of all the Druze people I knew."

"Druze?" Percy said.

"Yes. It's a very insulated group — not quite a religion, per se, but definitely a monotheistic faith. They're marginalized in a lot of places, but welcomed in Lebanon. I believe about 200,000 Druze people live in Lebanon, and they participate in all public institutions, so their beliefs are prevalent and understood, even though the Muslim majority disagrees. Growing up, I remember they had a name for the few kids who could recall things from a past life. 'Nateq,' I believe."

"I had no idea," Percy said. "Anyway, so we went to visit the boy at his home ..." He switched his gaze from Rafiq to Nabaa.

"And he proved beyond a doubt that he is my brother reincarnated," she said flatly. "And right before we left, he asked if I could tell you something from him. He said, 'I think his daddy is stuck. He can't get a new body. So I think he should pray for his daddy so he can be unstuck.'"

Rafiq silently stared at her for a long time. Eventually he nodded and said, "Thank you. I will. In fact, I will do more than pray for him." He turned to Percy. "I will atone for him."

Percy eyed him intently. "Atone? What do you mean?"

"He was a jihadi, and so am I," Rafiq said. "I became a jihadi the moment my mother died in that rubble, and I've had a lot of time to consider other paths. There are none, I've realized I will never be anything else. Jihad simply means a fight against the enemies of Islam. Sometimes the enemies of Islam are hiding within Islam itself. In his final days, my father became an enemy of Islam. He did things in the name of Allah that did damage to the name of Allah. He hurt the jihad. And many Muslims today are doing the same." He paused to sip his tea and choose his next words.

Percy filled the silence. "I've read some articles in the past few days from some very smart Muslims who say that your testimony was the best jihad you could have done. And you told me you wanted to do a lot of writing. Isn't that a form jihad, too?"

"It can be," Rafiq said. "But I'm free now. I didn't expect to be free, but I am. It occurs to me that if Allah wanted my jihad to be passive —

if he wanted me to fight our enemies with words on pages or on screens — then I would still be in prison. Instead, I walked out the doors of that place and immediately knew what I needed to do. I need to go back to Lebanon and fight the true enemies of Islam. I want to infiltrate the Islamic State. I want to be part of their demise."

Percy's eyebrows lifted. "And that has something to do with me?"

"Yes, I believe it does," Rafiq said. He waited and watched Percy's reaction. "I know I will need help from the American government, but the only person I trust in the American government is you. So I'm hoping you'll agree to be my liaison, here in the States."

"Wait," Percy said. "Are you sure you want to go undercover in ISIS? And then what?"

"First of all, that particular question is my business, not yours." A slight edge appeared in Rafiq's voice. "Second, do you have a better idea? If we put our personal history aside, those people waving the ISIS flag are causing *suffering*, the likes of which I've never seen or heard. And they're doing it to fellow *Muslims*. They are destroying ancient, sacred *mosques*. It is a stain on not only Islam, but on the idea of jihad."

Percy's brow furrowed. "I understand. But aren't you talking about re-entering the violence? Last time we spoke about this — when I visited you last year, I think — you said you were going to fight with words, not swords. You could not only write books, but now you could give speeches, too. Give TV interviews on the topic of terrorism. Help change the entire conversation."

"ISIS isn't having any conversations, Percy," Rafiq said. "Right now, as we speak, the people trying to use words against them are being shot and pushed into mass graves." He exhaled slowly. "I am proud of my testimony, and I know it did a lot of good. Just as my father's words in his final video. But I have accepted a hard truth: ISIS is part of a cycle of violence that they engineered. When Americans started leaving Iraq, ISIS decided not to allow natural order to form. They bombed the streets and brought back sectarian hate. The citizens started dividing and attacking each other like they used to do. Violence. Disorder. Vacuum. The Islamic State filled it, just as Saddam Hussein filled it before and America filled it after they ousted him. That cycle is what authors and speakers and anti-terrorism experts bury with words. ISIS continues filling the vacuum with more violence."

"He's right," Nabaa said. "And now we know it's a deeper cycle. Don't we? We know that people have their past lives contained somewhere in their soul. So now we're talking about a much longer, ancient cycle, fed by our traumatic memories, which are tribal. Cultural. Isaac's parents said he has had night terrors since he was a year old or maybe even younger. His trauma haunts him — him more than most, but it made me realize that we all have those nightmares of past trauma.

119

Most of us probably never become conscious of what they are. But when we hear people in our tribe say hateful words about the other tribe, the hate resonates deep within us. I've always wondered why. Now I think it's because the words subconsciously connect to those traumatic memories hidden in our souls. That's why it's so hard to make peace."

"I don't know if you're right," Rafiq said. "But I've felt something like that for a long time now. Regardless of what's true, I know the cycle can't be broken if my own people are fighting each other."

Nabaa thought about how she would use this inspiration in her own work. *I guess I'm a kind of jihadi, too, then.*

Percy looked down and shook his head. "You also can't help break that cycle if you're dead, Rafiq," he said. "ISIS leaders maybe bloodthirsty fools, but they're not stupid. They know you. They know how long you were in U.S. custody. They will be suspicious. One mistake, and you'll be in your own beheading video."

Rafiq's face and voice calmed. "What would you do if it were *your* homeland they were desecrating?" He didn't wait for an answer. "You would be there already. I have seen your face when you are fighting for a cause you believe in. There would be no convincing you otherwise. Why are you trying to convince me? I am still a young man, Percy. And now I'm a free man, too. Truly free. Freer than I was before you and I crossed paths. Someday, I'll be an old man with limitations, and I promise you I will write books and speak to normal people and help them have better conversations about violence. But not now. Now, I want to go to home." He made a fist and leaned slightly toward Percy. His voice stayed calm. "I will find out who these people are and what they are planning, get as close as I can, and then destroy them from the inside. And not by violence alone. I will sow discord among the young men who are lost and using Allah's name to commit atrocities. I will help those young men who are not beyond it. But the rest — the evil men using *my* religion to destroy *my* people — they must *go*. They want a caliphate. I want peace. Peace is my new job. Based on your testimony and what you've told me privately, it's your job, too." He took a long breath. He looked at all three of them, one by one, but no one else spoke. He continued. "And so, I am here, asking for your help. Will you help me? Or would you rather I entrust my life to some other U.S. government agent?"

Percy finally smiled. "I'll see what I can do."

◇◇◇◇◇◇◇◇◇

CHAPTER 19

April 2015

from: Aahna Khatri <aktheexister@gmail.com>
to: Liza Hamilton <lizachucksgirl@gmail.com>
date: Mon, April 27, 2015 at 5:22 PM
subject: Epigenetics

Good morning, Lizzie. How are you? I'm feeling fine. Already craving your famous fried eggs and cream again. Sigh. Thank you for a wonderful and quite memorable weekend. :)

Anyway, as you could gather from the subject line, there is real philosophy business to attend to. Our professor was talking today about "prions" (disfigured proteins that seem to cause certain kinds of neurological disorders), and he tried to tell us how some prions survive because of an epigenetic advantage. Most of us had never heard the term epigenetic before, so he had to explain what it meant.

Basically, it's when an organism's genetic response is changed by behavior and experience. Not super groundbreaking, right? But then he mentioned that sometimes, those changes get passed onto offspring.

So there was apparently a Dutch famine of 1944-1945. After it ended, and people were eating again, Dutch babies were still significantly smaller the next year and had increased glucose intolerance in adulthood, despite being conceived after the famine. The effect even lasted two generations in many cases — the malnourished risk factor was operating in DNA decades after the event.

My favorite example so far is an experiment that gave mice an electric shock after they smelled acetophenone. Those mice had babies, and those babies were born with a natural fear response to acetophenone. *And so were the babies of those babies.*

There's also some compelling evidence that addictive behavior in a parent — not the actual genetic markers, but the learned epigenetic response — can be passed on to children and make them more likely to fall victim to addiction at some point in their lives. Several studies are underway right now, actually, exploring that topic. Definitely some pharma money in all of that someday.

from: Liza Hamilton <lizachucksgirl@gmail.com>
to: Aahna Khatri <aktheexister@gmail.com>
date: Mon, April 27, 2015 at 9:39 PM
subject: Re: Epigenetics

It sounds like it kinda dovetails with the reincarnation question — but it could also serve as an alternate explanation, right? If trauma has epigenetic effects that last a couple of generations, that's all you would need to explain why the grandson has the same enemies as his grandfather. Programmed trauma response puts fear and hate on the menu, environmental factors provide the target.

I'm not saying you're wrong — it's now pretty clear to me that our souls are surviving over multiple lifetimes. But I'm sitting here wondering how epigenetics fits into that picture.

It's funny to think about that, actually. I remember learning about "Lamarckism" in one of my psychology classes. Some guy named Lamarck theorized in the early 1800s that some genetic predispositions could be turned on or off before passing them on from parent to child. Didn't take long before the theory was ridiculed. Now, in this hypothetical argument, scientists would basically have to use rebranded Lamarckism to dispute reincarnated souls. Ha!

It's probably like a lot of things, right? Anywhere you find something unexplainable in this world, science arrives to take the case. Then God seems to wait for our curiosity to peak, then he drops a tiny nugget of explanation on the nose of science, and shortly after, we all act like we've resolved it. And we move on to the next unexplainable thing. :)

Really cool topic, though. And we miss you, too. We were talking in bed last night about how amazing it was to see you around our Lebanese friend. You are the most graceful, mature, admirable woman we know.

Love you.

from: Aahna Khatri <aktheexister@gmail.com>
to: Liza Hamilton <lizachucksgirl@gmail.com>
date: Tue, April 28, 2015 at 4:44 AM
subject: Re: Epigenetics

Thank you, Lizzie. It means a lot. And I believe I recognize your sly attempt to use flattery to open this other line of discussion, because you want to know how I'm doing after the fact. And so your love flatters me twice! :) I appreciate that you have never forgotten the original purpose of our email correspondence. And so neither shall I.

Now that you mention it, I've actually been thinking a lot about my own reaction to him. I honestly cannot say I understand it. I didn't and still don't feel conflicted … and I think that's why my introspection has piqued. The question I have asked myself is, when did I make peace with him? There's no moment in time when I *decided* to forgive. So was I angry for a while, and then learned more and more about what happened, and then my anger slowly waned? That doesn't feel quite right, either. Which leads me to believe I was never angry to begin with. I think I was just … sad. Disappointed, maybe. What I remember about my feelings when it happened — after my mother died and I was in the hospital for a long time — it was just frustration. I knew enough about what was going on around our village that I recognized it was complex. People on both sides thinking they were doing the right thing. I didn't realize it then, but I was one of the few people in that conflict who had actually *met* people on both sides of the fight. I knew both sides had good people. So I wasn't angry at the people who planned the fateful ambush. Mostly, I was angry at myself because I inserted myself into the fighting, and that decision cost my mother her life. So, yeah, guilt. Guilt was the winning feeling. And then frustration that the fighting was still happening, and had been happening for all of my life.

And now, so many years later, some part of me recognizes that it should not be easy to share tea and a talk freely with a man who ongineered the root source of my life's pain. But that part of me doesn't feel like the real *me*. It feels like a construct. I think it's a product of the new culture I live in. Culture, for better or worse, tends to prioritize one's own pain and seek justice for it.

It does relate pretty well to the epigenetic issue, though, right? It seems there are three major sources that influence our behavior. The first is the imprinted memories of our soul, whether conscious or subconscious. The second is "nature," or what sciences has defined as true genetics — and DNA is still completely static, as far as anyone can tell. The third is "nurture," but with epigenetic revelations, we now know that nurture is far stronger than anyone thought. And more resilient, since it gets passed on physiologically to future generations.

Any of the three factors can take a turn being dominant. Some of the children with traumatic past-life memories don't have nature or nurture predispositions, but they still present with clinical PTSD. Many Samoans carry a gene that increases risk of obesity by 30 percent, and so they become huge whether they live in the Samoan culture or not. And, of course, you could take a healthy, happy baby from anywhere in the world and teach him to hate and fear anything you'd like.

I agree with you. God is constantly trying to tell us is that none of these answers is ever easy. The more we seek easy answers, the more we will find complexity. And then we turn around and see the other path, with a sign that says, "Seek to understand yourself, and then seek to understand others." That path is uphill and fairly rocky. But what we're really seeking is a better view, right?

CHAPTER 20

April 2015

Rona waited until she saw no headlights in either direction, then quietly crossed the street and climbed the emergency stairwell on the side of the wide building.

The first floor was a furniture shop owned by Jad Itani, and the second floor was where all eight of his employees lived.

Before arriving in Nabatieh, Rona had been briefed about the elder Itani brother's life. He ran a profitable and legal business from this location, but — unlike his brother, Fadi — he had also developed close ties with Hezbollah and used his furniture shop to help launder their money. Jad also kept close supervision of his employees, who were also young Hezbollah recruits. They earned room and board and advanced to better positions within the organization, based on Jad's reports. In exchange, Hezbollah kept Jad's revenue at very comfortable levels. It afforded him the ability to purchase a 3,500-square-foot home in the foothills near the neighboring town of Jarmaq, where he spent his weekends.

Rona continued up the steps to the third floor, where Jad spent his weeknights. As she reached the door, she noticed a small security camera pointed down at her and wondered if it was turned on. She put her ear on the door and heard a television inside. She knocked just loudly enough to know it was heard. The TV volume immediately decreased, allowing her to hear the faint sound of booted footsteps. Rona reached into her purse, retrieved her CIA badge, and held it up to the camera. She stood that way for 15 long seconds before the door opened.

"Come inside," Jad said. "Quickly."

She did as she was told, and he closed the door behind her.

"Is the camera recording or just streaming?" Rona asked.

"Both," he said. "Why?"

In such close proximity, Jad Itani was more imposing than his age might suggest. He was average height with a stocky build and about three days growth of salt-and-pepper facial hair — just like the dozens of photographs Rona had been shown. He smelled better than she thought he would.

"I want to watch you deleting the footage of me standing outside your door."

He stared at her without expression. "If I intended to sell you out, I would have invited some friends here to wait for you."

"I don't think you know what you intend to do about me yet, Jad," Rona said. "And that's why I'm here." In a flash, she pulled a 9mm pistol from her purse and held the silencer attachment a foot from Jad's face. "I'm confident I'll persuade you to join our efforts. But if some other persuasive people visit you later, I'd rather you didn't have proof of my involvement and my affiliation."

Jad's eyes darkened somewhat, but otherwise he was nonplussed. He walked to the couch where his laptop was sitting, picked it up one-handed, and set it on the coffee table. He motioned for Rona to sit on a low chair at the table's edge, then rotated the screen 45 degrees so they could both see it. A few clicks of his wireless mouse, and he'd pulled up the camera's auto-save folder.

"Give me the mouse," Rona said. The footage was automatically broken up into 2-minute chunks, and she saw her own image in two of the videos — the end of one and the beginning of the next. She deleted both, then emptied the recycle bin and closed the laptop. It wouldn't prevent a computer forensics expert from locating the files, but if things went sideways, she didn't want to make it easy.

"Now what?" Jad said.

"You've heard from your nephew, yes?" Rona said.

"Yes. And then from one of your colleagues. A couple of times."

"Good. I don't want to stay for long, so I'll be clear. We need your help connecting Rafiq with IS."

Jad pulled a cigarette from a pack on the table and lit it, shaking his head. "I don't have that kind of connection. I tried to tell 'Feeq that I don't know how to help with that." He held the pack out to Rona.

"No, thank you," she said. "And I understand you don't work with IS. But you do realize there are only one or two degrees of separation between your Hezbollah contact and the kind of IS contact we need, right?"

He exhaled smoke toward the ceiling thoughtfully, then shrugged. "Maybe so. But that degree of separation is more like a fuse waiting to be lit. Or do you people think all militant Muslims have the same agenda?"

"No, Jad. We're aware that Hezbollah and IS don't get along. We're also aware that they do have common enemies, and they each have something to offer the other. It's a complicated relationship. Sort of like this relationship you and I are developing." She smiled, and he returned it. "It's safe to say you love your nephew?"

"More than anything in this world, including the mighty Allah."

"I hear Rafiq is pretty strong-willed. Would you agree?"

Another smile. "Yes. Obstinate would be a better descriptor."

126

"Fair enough. And do you have any philosophical objection to his decision to infiltrate IS and disrupt them?"

"No."

"Good. Our relationship is getting less and less complicated by the minute." *Now why haven't you asked if I've been followed?* She couldn't tell if his passive approach indicated complicity or ignorance.

"And yet I do not even know your name."

"Call me Larsa," Rona said.

He laughed. "I have a feeling I still do not know your name." Jad said. "More to the point, Larsa, I still don't see how I can help."

"Getting there. First, I'm establishing the boundaries and the stakes. Your beloved nephew has made a choice that we both support. And even if we didn't, he would probably go forward with it on his own, at even greater peril to himself. So Rafiq's life is at stake. That's probably the biggest risk of nonconformity."

"Is it my turn to list the risks of conformity? I'm putting my life in jeopardy just by agreeing to speak to you."

"Likewise. But no, I don't think that's a relevant factor, since your refusal to cooperate would only encourage my bosses to arrange the very scenario that frightens you." She paused to observe his reaction. He was processing. "Yes, Jad. We have people within Hezbollah whose word is *much* more credible than yours. A call from me, and those people will say whatever we want about you to exactly the people you don't want to piss off."

He nodded. "At least your people are predictable. Consider me sufficiently threatened. What about the, uh, 'carrot,' as you Americans call it? Is there a guarantee of protection for me and Rafiq if this doesn't go the way you want?"

"A guarantee? No," Rona said. "Let's call it a 'plan' for protection. Once you give me your word that you're on board, and as long as you demonstrate loyalty, you are an asset we will seek to protect. And if we have to relocate you under duress, we will set you up somewhere far away and provide you a lifestyle similar enough to the one you enjoy now."

He blew a final cloud of smoke into the air and slowly snuffed out his cigarette in the ornate coffee table ashtray. He shrugged, nodded. "I am on board," he said. "But I am concerned more for *your* safety than my own."

Rona tilted her head. "Go on."

"There's a Hezbollah order with your name on it. Capture only, from what I have heard. They don't know who you are, but they know you're not just a young, attractive Arab Christian woman who decided to visit southern Lebanon on a whim."

She waited a few seconds, but Jad offered nothing further. "And you're not concerned I've been followed straight here?"

He furrowed his brow incredulously. "Should I be? I've evaded dozens of Hezbollah tails in my time. I assume you did the same."

"I did," Rona said. "About an hour ago. And we knew about the capture order, but I'm glad to hear you mention it. Just like that, we are building trust." She smiled at him, and he reciprocated. "We've also come to the point where you can help me. We have a list of potential guys they might use to grab me, but it's too long and still possibly incomplete. I need you to give me a much shorter list, and it needs to be right."

Jad nodded. "No problem," he said. "There are only three men in this area who they use for that kind of work, and I'm fairly certain which one they'd choose for a capture job."

She pulled out her phone and showed him a picture. "Is it this man, by chance?"

He glanced, then shook his head. "No," he said. "That's who they sent to follow you?" He smiled. "Always the young ones. Nobody else wants to do it, and that is why it is always easy to lose them. But no — the man I expect has been assigned to kidnap you is named Adnan Fayol. Turkish. Large. A man who was once in excellent shape but has covered his muscles in a layer of middle age. Not good for inconspicuous work, but excellent for rough jobs."

Great. She was beginning to doubt the plan — her plan — already.

"I'll take everything you know about him, and the other two possibilities, as well," Rona said. "Names, primary residence, background, places they like to hang out — anything you know about them."

Rona rode her motorcycle back to Daoudiyeh, a town about 30 kilometers west of Nabatieh. The Agency had set her up as an engineering consultant at a new college being built there — Phoenicia University. She had access to a small apartment on the edge of campus, plus private office space within the near-finished and frequently empty administration building.

As soon as she closed the door to the office, Rona grabbed her phone, opened the cipher app and plugged in her message: "If asked, Turkish assassin working for Hezbollah is CIA. You found out, showed me intercepted texts and emails. You sent me to inform Hezbollah leaders, as a show of good faith." She copied the encrypted version and pasted it into a text to Omer, then pressed send.

She went into her locked suitcase and retrieved her laptop and portable printer, then connected to her secure portal and searched for all three men Jad Itani mentioned. Luckily each had at least two photos in the database, so she sent the file links to the graphics team and asked for passport photos. Within two hours, she would have renderings of each man's face and the printable ID info pages of neighboring countries' passports, including the U.S. diplomatic version — each in the exact dimensions she needed.

While she waited, Rona read as much as she could about the three Hezbollah henchmen, hoping to find something useful. She realized Jad Itani was probably right — Adnan Fayol, a former Maroon Beret in the Turkish army, seemed like the only one of the three who could efficiently kidnap someone. The other two were simply accomplished thugs. Fayol had several kills to his name, as well, but he also had also been assigned the duty of detaining any foreigners trying to cross the southern edge of the Bekaa Valley on their way to Syria. Apparently, Hezbollah had noticed occasional IS recruits heading through Aanjar, over the mountains and into Jdaidit Yabws, Syria. From there, presumably, they would have a short trip to Damascus and then be sent to the front lines up north. Hezbollah began charging a passage tax, in the form of hefty ransoms for recruits. Fayol had successfully handled three such transactions, start to finish.

Rona noticed something else about the Turkish hitman: Of the eight men he had killed in the five years the CIA had been watching him, seven were garroted to death from behind. *I can use that,* she thought. She studied the ligature marks on the photos of his victims. *Looks like 550 cord. Got plenty of that.*

The decision hit her then. Regardless of which man was assigned to grab her, Fayol was now *her* target. He was the one with a background she could use to craft a narrative. She would have to lure him somewhere advantageous first, then hope to subdue him. It would be simpler if he were already pursuing *her,* but also would present a more difficult physical altercation. If he didn't know her at all, she could simply seduce him. *An easy kill, but what about the body?* A bedroom or hotel room wasn't exactly the right place to claim she was cornered and attacked. A litany of complicating factors sprang forth into her consciousness, each begging for resolution.

Don't waste time, she thought. She decided to assume the first and most likely assumption — that Fayol was tasked to capture her. If when given the chance, he didn't recognize her and pursue her, she would regroup and plan a different tactic.

She turned her attention back to her laptop and began reading up on Turkish special forces, learning about the more noteworthy operations in the applicable timeframe. Fifteen minutes later, she had crafted a convincing narrative in her mind.

She closed her laptop and grabbed two mobile phones from her suitcase. She began the laborious but effective process of manufacturing evidence using a two-phone method Polinski had taught her in their first few weeks of training. One phone was virtually devoid of any sign of use — the "control phone," as it was called. The other, known as the "plant phone," was populated with a handful of generic emails and texts from fictitious people, along with a limited but common variety of apps.

One of the uncommon apps hidden in a subfolder was a DARPA-designed tool called "MyDates." Given the correct username and password, the app allowed the user to create any type of native smartphone content — texts, emails, reminders, etc. — and manually backdate them. Rona opened the app and logged in.

Alternating between both phones, she spent the next 90 minutes carefully creating a text conversation between a fake person — a fellow former maroon beret — and Adnan Fayol. The discourse oscillated from mundane to cryptic to frustrated to braggadocious. Using the control phone, she found a Facebook profile of a Turkish man about the right age, saved a couple of generic photos, paired them with generic texts, and sent them to the plant phone.

Her plan was crystallizing more with every moment, but she realized she still needed the right clothing. She logged off, closed her laptop, and left the apartment.

Forty-seven minutes later, she walked back in with a new black turtleneck and immediately cut the tags. When she logged in again, she was happy to see the graphics guys had already delivered the passport request to her secure inbox. She plugged in the printer, printed the photos of Fayol on photo paper and the page 3s on clear, polymer-backed slides, and then carefully affixed each to three pre-stamped passports, one identifying Fayol as a Jordanian, one as an Israeli, and the last as an American "diplomat." When she was finished, she grabbed her handgun and the passports and wheeled her medium-sized suitcase into the bathroom.

She lifted the suitcase onto the sink, opened it, and rested the top flap against the mirror. She went over the steps in her head one more time. *Just like Todd explained,* she reminded herself. *Do it right, and it will be convincing.*

She retrieved a box of plastic wrap and stretched a huge piece across the toilet and let it loosely droop in the middle, securing the edges around the bowl. Then she dropped one of her two black hand towels onto the bathtub drain, grabbed a large squeeze bottle full of fake blood, and used it to slowly soak the towel, rolling it over for full saturation. She squeezed out the excess, then placed the soaked towel in the middle of the concave plastic wrap. She rinsed the red liquid down the drain, dried her hands with the other towel, then draped another sheet of plastic over the top of the towel. Then she wrapped the mock bloody towel on all sides without a red drop falling into the toilet.

Rona scanned the supplies in her suitcase. She took out a square black pillow and put it in the far end of the tub. She placed a thin sheet of steel on top of it, followed by a stubby block of 4x4 wood. On top of the block, she carefully placed the wrapped-up bloody towel, and on top of that, she draped a single cut-out layer of a men's pant leg. *Now comes the hard part.*

She set the three fake passports on the edge of the tub, then checked her weapon to ensure it was loaded and the silencer was engaged. Rona placed all three passports on top of the pants fabric, put the muzzle of her gun against them, and fired a shot.

Then she stood over the suitcase in front of the mirror and cut a 3-foot length of 550 cord from her coil. She wrapped it around her neck, crossed the ends in front of her face, then wrapped one end around her left hand, then the other around her right.

Looking at her own eyes, she found herself briefly frozen with the notion that this very experience could become real in just a couple of hours. *Am I really going to subdue a big, strong man with special ops training? And if I fail, can I really rely on him to only kidnap me and not kill me?* She had chosen a life of high stakes and impossible questions. Rona closed her eyes, thought of her dead friends who had been dismembered by bombs they never saw coming, and began to pull the cord tight around her neck. She wrenched her head back and forth against her own arm strength, simulating a struggle. She kept it up till her lungs begged her to stop, then she released and pulled the cord away. The ligature marks were there. Might be there for weeks, she realized.

But they'll only be fresh for a night, she thought. *I'll clean up later.* She reloaded her gun, put on the turtleneck, stuffed the passports in her purse, and left again.

Rona saw Adnan Fayol walk out of his favorite shishah bar in Tyre, just four blocks from the office of Jaafar al-Nadim — chief of Hezbollah's Islamic Jihad Organization operations in the South Governorate.

She tightened the strap on her purse and began walking down the street perpendicular and ahead of Fayol's path. She turned right down the sidewalk and began walking directly toward him. As he passed, she smiled casually and kept walking. *Recognize me,* she pleaded silently.

As much as she realized Fayol would be her toughest challenge, she wanted this operation to commence as soon as possible. If he walked by her, she'd have to try the same tactic on the other two thugs, jeopardizing the element of surprise more each time.

About 15 meters away now, she heard his footsteps stop.

"Excuse me," came his voice behind her, in English.

Thank you, she thought. She stopped and turned around. "Yes?"

He began walking back in her direction. "You look familiar."

She took a deliberately nervous step backward, away from him. "Uh, no. I don't think so." Then she saw his face register certainty. She ran.

About 500 meters down a road called Abou Deib, which ended at a T-intersection with a traffic circle. Beyond the roundabout was the city block that comprised the Tyre Necropolis and Tyre Hippodrome — 2,000-year-old Roman ruins of a large prestigious cemetery and ancient performance venue. During the day, the site was a moderate tourist attraction, but the Lebanese tourism ministry notoriously neglected it. Once the sun went down, the ruins' only inhabitants were stray dogs.

Rona jogged across the traffic circle and stared down the street behind her. Fayol was still pursuing her but refrained from an all-out sprint. He was jogging casually but purposefully, keeping his eyes on her.

Surrounding the ruins was a narrow field overgrown with clusters of squat, bushy trees that grew more densely packed the closer they were to the interior arena space. In her periphery, she noticed Fayol quicken his pace as she disappeared into the shrubbery. Jogging through the sandy dirt and darting between the untended trees, she quickly emerged into the clearing on the other side. She was standing on the edge of the hippodrome, right on the ground that was once an ancient Roman horse racing track.

And also, one of the few locations in the Levant where my early Christian ancestors were fed to lions for entertainment, Rona thought. She continued running again, across the wide expanse of the hippodrome's south turn, toward the row of three large stone arches between the viewing stands. Through the middle arch was a walking path that led out of the ruins.

Rona slowed her pace slightly until she heard the sound of Fayol rushing through the shrub-packed perimeter just as she had done seconds before. Then she sprinted toward the 12-foot-long, 8-foot-wide middle arch, craning her head to see the Turkish thug emerge into the clearing behind her. She ran full speed through the arch and several steps onto the path ahead, then — as soon as she was out of Fayol's view — slowed down, stopped, and walked quietly back to the wide wall that formed the back of the arch.

Heavy, fast footsteps were gaining ground. *40 yards,* she thought. *Now 30.* Rona felt like her blood was pumping so hard that it might explode out of her fingertips. With all the dexterity she could muster, she unclipped her telescopic baton from her belt and quietly extended it to its full 32-inch length. *20 yards, and still running. Good.* She bent her knees slightly, like a cat eyeing a bird.

The sound of footsteps changed clearly when Fayol approached the entrance of the stone arch. That was her cue. In one motion, she leapt out in front of Fayol and, with ballerina grace, spun in a single circle. As her rotation culminated its 360 degrees, her baton caught her surprised pursuer in the mouth. Teeth shattered, blood spattered. His right hand immediately went to his face, and his left started reaching for the back of his waist. Rona swung the baton around again, this time smashing it against the side of his left knee. Fayol went down and began groaning in low-pitched agony.

She retrieved her silenced pistol from her purse, took a step back and aimed at Fayol's head. *Jesus forgive me.* She pulled the trigger twice, both shots finding their mark. The man twitched, then was still. She moved her gun against the pocket of Fayol's tactical cargo pants and fired two more shots in close proximity. Then, Rona patted him down till she found his mobile phone. She pressed the home button. Locked, of course. She dropped it into her purse.

She kept searching his pockets. *Bingo.* His garrote was coiled in the outer hand pocket of his jacket. It wasn't 550 cord, but it was similar enough. And it was in the most accessible place he could've put it. The thought disturbed her. Maybe they weren't trying to capture her after all. Did they discover who she was and put out a simple kill order? *Doesn't matter now,* she thought. Her plan might still work, so she had to try.

With effort, Rona lifted Fayol enough to reach under him and grab his own handgun from his waistband, a Heckler and Koch USP. She pointed it between two trees along the walking path and almost fired, but then stopped. She listened for any sign of activity. None. She walked to the edge of the arch and scanned the wide, flat hippodrome field. Nothing. *I have time.* She was thinking of the chance that al-Nadim would recognize fake blood when he saw it — or whether he had access to a lab to test it. It was only remotely possible, but if that capability existed, she was 99 percent sure it would be the less expensive yes-no lab analysis to determine if any human blood was present, not a full array to determine all substances present. Regardless, Rona had been taught to minimize risks whenever possible, and in this case, that meant real blood was the safer call.

Rona set the H&K down on the ground, retrieved the three fake passports from her purse and put them in the dead man's cargo pocket. She shook the pocket slightly, allowing gravity to pull them down neatly inside. Then she shot through the stack of passports and into his leg again. She reached in the pocket, retrieved the passports, and put them back in her purse.

She picked up his pistol, fired twice into the shrubs, paused, then changed her angle and fired three more times. She quickly put the gun in Fayol's left hand, sliding his index finger through the trigger guard. Then she ran back the way she came.

Luckily, the street light was minimal where she chose to emerge from the shrub-packed perimeter of the ruins. Rona stepped onto the street and crossed it, about a block south of the traffic circle. She retrieved a half-eaten granola bar from her purse and took a bite, chewing casually. She noticed two couples 50 meters ahead of her on the street, laughing together as they walked in her direction. She paused at a public trash bin, popped the last bit of bar into her mouth, tossed the wrapper in the garbage, then reached into her purse again. Casually, she dropped three more items into the bin — the baton, her gun, and Fayol's phone. She pulled out her prepaid phone and walked purposefully while sending a coded text to her ops chief. As soon as she received the expected response, she dropped that phone into the next trash bin in her path.

Rona heard sirens. Soon, a black police sedan, then another, drove past her in the direction of the ruins.

She kept walking until she reached the seaside restaurant-bar that contained Jaafar al-Nadim's unofficial office. Her intel said he would be there; she wondered if he was expecting Fayol.

Whatever he's expecting, it's not me.

"I need to see your manager immediately," she said to the smiling hostess who greeted her inside. Adding to the abruptness of the question, Rona's black pants, black turtleneck and knee-length dark grey jacket were stark interruptions to the postmodern white decorative style of the restaurant. After a moment of confused hesitation, the hostess nodded and left Rona waiting in the foyer.

The place didn't look busy. Only a few groups were seated in the first-floor dining area, but Rona knew the more popular sections were on the upper levels — the weather was pleasant enough to enjoy dinner on the rooftop patio, and the second floor had floor-to-ceiling windows overlooking the Mediterranean. She wondered if al-Nadim's office had the same view, or if he was the more careful type who wouldn't want exposure from the street.

A minute later, a tall, slender man appeared from the back of the restaurant wearing white pants and a pastel green linen shirt. He approached her smiling like his hostess had.

"Good evening," he said in English. "Can I help you with something?"

134

"Yes," Rona said. "I need to see Jaafar immediately. It is urgent."

The man's face darkened. "Excuse me. I'll see if I can find someone else who can help you."

"Hold on," she said, reaching into her purse. "Tell them I brought this." She held out the coiled garrote toward the manager, who reflexively accepted it. He looked from the garrote to her eyes and back to the garrote. "They'll know what it is. Go ahead. Quickly, please." She nodded in the direction from which he'd come, and he turned and walked away.

Rona waited a few more minutes, going over her story again in her mind. She was about to enter into the most dangerous phase of the entire operation. If she was going to be killed, it would be tonight, at the hands of Jaafar al-Nadim and his men. If she survived, it would be because she convinced the man himself that she had just done him a big favor by killing his best hitman.

She imagined herself as Jaafar, sitting at a desk, listening to a stranger's story. *He is just another man who thinks he is the smartest person in the room,* Rona reminded herself. *You have persuaded many such men before.*

A different man — this one clad in an open-necked grey suit — appeared on the stairs ahead of Rona. Halfway down, he made eye contact with her and then motioned his head diagonally up the way he had come. He wanted her to follow him. She did.

On the second floor, they walked down a short, open hallway past the dining area with huge windows overlooking the bay. No one paid them any mind. The man led her through a white archway and into the lounge section of the restaurant, then past the bar, through a swinging door, and into a modified short-order kitchen of sorts. They walked past an industrial sink, a huge pizza oven, and a freezer. On the far side of the kitchen was another man in another grey suit, standing in front of an office door.

The man escorting Rona pointed to the wall next to his colleague. "Put your hands there," he said.

She did as she was told. Then she felt a large, strong hand get a handful of her hair. He pulled her head back firmly, but only slightly.

The two men cooperatively began searching her person. Every inch of her was groped — neck, armpits, breast, crotch — roughly and thoroughly. A minute later, they were done.

Her escort let go of her hair and said, "Don't move." He grabbed the strap of her purse, lifting it over her head. He opened it with both hands, and his colleague started rifling through it. Immediately, she heard the sound of passport covers sliding against each other, then fingers opening the booklets, one by one. "What the fuck," the second man muttered.

"Now you know why I'm here," Rona said, still facing the wall.

There was nothing else in the purse that would spark their attention. The second man turned and opened the door, which was clearly heavier than it appeared, holding it for them to enter. All three of them did.

The room was small. On the far side was a large, modern-style modular desk. It was L-shaped with elevated sliding-door cabinets along the two sides. Sitting behind the Formica top was Jaafar al-Nadim, probably the most dangerous and powerful man in a 500-mile radius. He was holding the garrote, one side in each hand, as if he were familiarizing himself with its intended use.

The second security guard walked up and set the purse and three passports on the desk. "She was unarmed. These were the only notable possessions."

Al-Nadim set down the garrote. He picked up a pair of glasses next to his keyboard and put them on. Then he slowly paged through the passports, taking time to hold each one close to his face.

"What is your name?" he finally said, removing his glasses again.

"Larsa," Rona said.

"Larsa," al-Nadim repeated. "I knew a Larsa once. I believe your name means 'gift from Allah.' Is that right?"

"Yes," she said.

"That must be a difficult name to embody," he said. "Especially difficult today, I imagine."

"Today? No," she said. "In the past, perhaps. But not today. God is good. It is not difficult to act according to his will. I believe in the next few minutes we will both agree that I have come bearing gifts from Allah."

He stared at her. "I hope you are right," he said. "But it will take some convincing. It appears you have done something terrible to one of my best men."

"I will get to the point," she said. "I am here on behalf of Omer Aydin, a man you may know as the Islamic State's appointed emir of western Turkey. My work for Mr. Aydin involves arranging passage across the Aegean Sea for brothers who go do God's work in Central Europe. Last month, we found a CIA operative attempting to infiltrate our operation. He was Turkish — a former maroon beret in the Turkish army — but had been recruited by the Americans. We captured him and interrogated him. One of the things we learned before we disposed of him was that he was not the only Turkish special forces soldier who was working with the CIA. He and another man in his unit were recruited at the same time. This other man was sent to Lebanon, but the two men were friends, so they stayed in touch." She paused. "The name of the operative sent here to Lebanon is Adnan Fayol. Or *was,* I suppose I should say."

Al-Nadim glanced at the passports, then back at Rona. He said nothing, waiting for her to continue.

"Mr. Fayol is a decorated killer, both in and out of the Turkish military," Rona said. "I believe that is one of the reasons you employed him. Unfortunately, one of the men he killed two years ago was the close friend of an important man in my organization. He was already on our list of, shall we say, 'mortal enemies.' So, Mr. Aydin, my boss, got the order from above, and he sent me here for two missions. One, to ensure Mr. Fayol met an untimely end. And two, to make you aware of his *other* employer. The first mission has been accomplished. I am in the process of completing the second." She smiled dryly.

"You are implying that Adnan was a CIA operative?"

"I am not implying," Rona said. "I am informing. And I believe the evidence will convince you on its own."

Al-Nadim held up the passports. "Is this the entirety of your evidence?

"No," she said. "The only evidence I brought with me was the prepaid phone you will find in my purse. It belonged to the man we captured and interrogated. I am told more will be provided by Mr. Aydin when you agree to contact him. We did not anticipate finding those passports on his person, but it's possible they are the strongest evidence of all."

"If I am to call your boss to receive even more compelling evidence, why did he bother to send you all the way here? Why not just reach out to me in the first place?"

"A few reasons," Rona said. "Primarily, any attempted communication from a stranger in Turkey to Jaafar al-Nadim will be heavily vetted by your people. We could not risk that Fayol himself would become aware of our information and intentions. For similar reasons, the phone you now hold — it's not as if we could have simply mailed it to you and been certain it would end up in your hands. It needed to be personally delivered. And, of course," she hesitated, pretending the next words were difficult. "Well, to put it plainly, Fayol needed to be killed. Either by my own action or by convincing you to do it."

Al-Nadim nodded again, and for the first time, she sensed he was allowing himself to be convinced. "That leads me to my next question," he said. "Why kill him first, and then tell me? Why risk your own life, while also eliminating my chance to interrogate Adnan myself?"

"I was given the authority to decide which task came first, based on real-time factors on the ground," she said. "I considered the risks of killing him and the risks of leaving him for you. I decided killing him was the better choice. As it turned out, I almost chose wrong. But when trust is in short supply, I trust myself most. I believed I could use the element of surprise to overpower Fayol, which I did. Also, I trust in my ability to persuade you. The primary variable was your relationship with Fayol — if he were alive right now, you may have been persuaded by his lies. You may have owed him a favor. Or he may have held some other power over you, which could have biased you against what I know to be true. The truth, when unimpeded and unclouded, tends to be convincing, even when delivered by a stranger. Or an alleged rival."

"And if you're wrong, and I simply decide at worst, you're lying, and at best, you presumed to exact justice against a traitor on my territory — justice that should've been mine?"

"If that is how you perceive this visit, I expect you will have me killed," she said. "And my boss will not receive word that I am safe. And he will be angry. And everyone involved will have missed out on a mutually beneficial opportunity."

"Ah, yes, an opportunity," al-Nadim asked. "I have been waiting for you to explain why the Islamic State would go out of its way to do a favor for Hezbollah. But we are not quite ready to address that. You mentioned sending a message — to your boss, Mr. Aydin, I presume?"

"Yes."

He held up the plant phone. "But this is the phone you took from the man you captured in Turkey. Where is Fayol's phone? And where is your own?"

"Fayol was not carrying one. I checked," Rona said. "Mine is in a safe place. I will send the message that I am safe, as soon as I am actually safe."

"It occurs to me that your phone could be more evidence of your story's validity," he said. "But it is not here, and it is not here because you mistrust us. That is yet another strange decision for someone trying to gain *my* trust, is it not? You could have simply developed a code that indicates safety, instead of keeping the phone itself in a different location."

Rona smiled. "Again, we considered that idea. And I understand your hesitation, Mr. al-Nadim, but allow me to explain. First, there is a coded safety message that only I know how to transmit. However, there's still a chance that your men could torture me enough to make me transmit it myself." She noticed al-Nadim cock his head with skepticism. *You're a quick one,* she thought. "Yes, you could torture me to get the location of the phone, too, but that would entail an external operation on your part, including breaking and entering in a place where it would be noticed." She waited for him to process that. He did. "Second, whether or not the message was sent, you would likely discern the *method* of coded transmission that we use — which is a closely guarded secret within our organization. We are all strictly prohibited from sharing any piece of it with unauthorized individuals. Third, and most obviously, if I sent the message from here, you could simply have me killed immediately afterward."

He nodded once, but his eyes remained narrow. "Hypothetically, say we allow you to leave here. What is stopping me from following you back to where you are staying, and then abducting you after you have retrieved your phone?"

Rona smiled. "With respect, isn't it true your men have been trying to find me and abduct me for several days?"

"Yes," al-Nadim said.

"And so, it seems you have your answer."

After a pause, he smiled. "It seems evasion is just one of your many skills, Ms. Larsa. And that leads to yet another question. You would like me to believe that you subdued a man twice your size — a man with several skills of his own."

Her face showed mild confusion. "Do you doubt he is dead? I brought you his garrote, and I assume you have been unable to reach him in the last 30 minutes or so." She saw al-Nadim's eyes dart toward one of his security guards behind her, and she turned her head around just quickly enough to see the guard shake his head silently.

"I am doubting less and less that he is dead," al-Nadim said. "I heard the sirens shortly before you came, and we have someone on his way to the scene to confirm. We will know soon. But assuming he is dead, you understand if I must consider the possibility that you had help."

Rona pulled down her turtleneck and revealed the ugly striations and bruising that her 550 cord garrote had left. Her voice took on a new edge. "Believe what you will. You have risen to your station by being an extremely careful and skeptical man. We share this quality. But if I had help with Mr. Fayol, they were not as helpful as you might expect."

Al-Nadim was visibly surprised. "His orders were to capture you, not kill you."

"I thought as much," she said. "But even after I smashed his mouth with my baton, his weapon of choice was around my neck within a few moments. Maybe he occasionally uses his garrote to subdue instead of kill. You know better than I."

Al-Nadim chose not to comment on her unasked question. "Where did it happen?"

"I got his attention on the street, then fled to the hippodrome," she said. Al-Nadim was clearly waiting for more, so she continued. "He followed me through a set of arches and ran directly into my baton. He went down immediately, but a second later, he had swept my legs from under me. Then we were both on the ground, he was behind me, his legs wrapped around my midsection, and his garrote around my neck. I was barely able to reach the handgun I keep on my ankle. The only part of his body I could comfortably shoot was his thigh. So, I did, two or three times. His legs and hands immediately loosened, I struggled away, and then he was aiming his own gun at me, while trying to get on his feet. His first shot was off-target, thankfully. Then I shot him in the head. His gun fired one more time, but it seemed to be a latent reflex."

"Did you dispose of your gun?"

"Yes," she said.

Al-Nadim stared at her for a long time. Then he turned his attention to the plant phone and began exploring it. For three long minutes, Rona watched his thumbs dance around the phone's screen. His face betrayed nothing. Finally, he put the phone down.

"For the sake of expediency, let's proceed as if I believe you," he said. "Tell me the real reason you came here — this mutually beneficial 'opportunity,' as you call it."

Rona nodded. "We are hearing that Rafiq Itani will be returning soon," she said. "And we happen to know he is interested in joining our cause."

"We have heard the same whispers," al-Nadim said. "But it's difficult to believe. His father would not have approved of ..." He took a deep breath. "Fadi Itani did not share the beliefs or methods of your organization."

Rona smiled politely and nodded. "Agreed. But I'm fairly certain Rafiq is his own man," she said. "Even before his prolonged detention, he had his own beliefs and methods. But even if we disagree on the state of his psyche or theology, I will tell you our information is very solid."

Al-Nadim's eyes narrowed. "And what about my own theology and psyche, Ms. Larsa? And that of my superiors in Hezbollah? You have an answer for all of my other questions, but what do you have to say about the deep disagreement — and violence — between my organization and yours?"

"My organization respects your organization more than you know," she said, summoning all her sincerity. "More than we can say publicly. My leaders have often studied and praised the way Hezbollah has grown and asserted Muslim influence from the inside of a westernized Arab country. It's true that we disagree. And it's true our public stance is anti-Hezbollah, because maximizing our militancy also maximizes our recruiting. We cannot dilute our message by accepting official allies. You know this. You also know — and what none of our bosses can deny — that in the greater jihad, we share the same enemies." She paused to let him reflect. "We don't intend to publicize any collaboration with Hezbollah. And neither should you. But whatever our respective public image must be, we should take opportunities to injure America and Israel."

"I agree in general," he said. "I suspect it will be in the details where we disagree. Tell me what you want from me."

"I am here asking for your blessing and your guarantee of protection during any operation Rafiq conducts in your territory," she said. "Because he is now the most famous son of Lebanon, we will only proceed if Hezbollah allows it willingly."

A few seconds passed, then al-Nadim finally nodded. A wave of relief washed over Rona.

"I will have to make a call," he said. "And, naturally, if we agree, there will be conditions."

"In the interest of urgency," Rona said, "we are fully prepared to negotiate."

CHAPTER 21

May 2015

"I should warn you," Jad Itani told his nephew. "She is beautiful. Distractingly beautiful."

"I doubt I will notice much," Rafiq said. "The only thing distracting me at the moment is the smell of that coffee. Has it always taken this long?" He hadn't enjoyed a proper cup of Lebanese coffee since before he was captured and detained by the Americans. He had almost stopped for a cup at a Turkish cafe in New York — the brewing method was almost identical — but he refrained. He had anticipated this moment in Uncle Jad's home, after traveling across half the world. And now he was glad he waited.

His uncle smiled at him, then resumed his methodical lifting of the 4-inch-tall brass coffee pots off his electric stovetop surface. Lift the first pot, hold it till the frothy surface stops bubbling, set it down. Repeat with the second, set it down. Repeat with the third, et cetera. Rafiq was 20 feet away on the couch, but he knew his uncle had set the temperature of the burner precisely so that by the time he set the third pot back on the burner, the first was starting to bubble up again. A few more cycles, and they would all stop boiling over entirely. He would take them off the burner, the fine grinds would settle to the bottom, the thin beige froth would settle on top, and the coffee would be ready to pour. Rafiq felt saliva flooding around the sides of his tongue, anticipating the bitter-smooth, intensely rich coffee washing over his taste buds.

Someone knocked once on the door. Then twice more.

"That would be our friend, Larsa," Jad said. "Come tend the coffee for me. It's almost done."

Rafiq got up and went to the kitchen. His uncle stopped briefly at the table to check the screen of his open laptop. "Yep. Just as distracting as last time she was here." He went to the door and opened it.

"Hello, Jad," a woman's voice said.

"Hello, Larsa," Jad replied. "Please come in." He closed the door behind him. "Shall we begin at my computer again?"

"Actually, now that we're officially in business together, I trust you will delete the footage on your own," she said. "But I would like to say hello to your nephew."

Her voice … *No,* Rafiq thought. *It can't be.*

"Of course," Jad said. "Larsa, meet my nephew, Rafiq Itani."

142

Rafiq switched off the electric burner. His heart was rattling in his chest as he turned toward the woman who called herself Larsa.

"Oh, we have already met," she said. "Once. In Baghdad. But it is good to see you again, Rafiq." She held out her hand.

Rafiq slowly stretched out his hand in response, trying and failing to come up with anything to say.

"Oh," Jad said. "Well, then. I will just tend to the coffee until one of you explains what is going on." He lightly shoved past Rafiq and inspected the three tiny pots.

"Eight years ago," Rafiq said. "I walked into a bakery, and she walked in behind me. We spoke briefly." He stared at the woman, who was smiling with genuine warmth. "She told me she would see me the next morning. But she never returned."

"I was assigned to surveil you, Rafiq," she said. "You happened to go into the bakery owned by one of my contacts — a very nice man who was also quite paranoid, for good reason, I suppose. I knew you were just following your nose, but I knew he would be alarmed and think you were there to ask a bunch of uncomfortable questions. I had to follow you in and put him at ease. Unfortunately, that also meant the nature of my surveillance was compromised. So I had to leave the city."

"So, the pastries you ordered for your father and his friends at the Christian church across the street ..." Rafiq trailed off.

"Just a story," the woman said. "I knew that church had a service starting shortly, and I had to have a reason to be familiar with the owner."

"And then you left," Rafiq said. "And someone else took over watching me?"

"I don't think so," Larsa said. "During my outbrief, I recommended we close the operation completely. At that point, we were all pretty sure you weren't part of any jihadi plans. That made you a very low-value target."

"How quickly things can change," he said, hearing a hint of bitterness in his own voice. "The idea for my own operation came to me the next day, sitting in that bakery. The article I read while waiting for you was about American casualty rates hitting new lows, and some general was attributing it to the effectiveness of MRAP vehicles."

"You were a high-value target after all," she said. Her words were soaked in irony. "And here I am again." After a moment, she managed a smile.

The bitterness Rafiq felt was gone. Her smile swept it away. *Now I'm feeling the same way I did when we met. Like I want to spend time with this woman, and the rest is just periphery.*

They stared at each other. No one said anything for a few moments, then Jad walked over to the low table and set down a tray with three

143

small mugs of hot, concentrated coffee. All three sat down around the table, Rafiq on the couch, his uncle and the woman called Larsa each on a chair opposite each other.

"Now that we've covered the past, let us discuss the present, shall we?" Jad said.

The woman leaned forward and lifted her cup off the tray. "Actually," she said, "it would be best if Rafiq and I spoke to each other alone. I think we should stay and you should go, but if you insist otherwise, I can take him somewhere else."

Rafiq reached and grabbed his own coffee, then looked at his uncle, who was busy processing information.

"We only need about 30 minutes," the woman said.

"It's fine, Uncle," Rafiq said. His uncle glanced at him, then at the mug of steaming coffee closest to his chair. "Oh — I will make sure that last cup doesn't go to waste," he added.

Jad's eyes found Rafiq's again, this time narrowed. "That won't be necessary, nephew," he said. "I'll take it with me." He picked up his mug, then addressed Larsa. "Is this it? Am I no longer useful to you?" His voice carried no emotion.

"For now, you have done your part," she said. "We operate on a need-to-know basis, and at the moment, you don't need to know what Rafiq and I have to discuss. That may change in the future, but involving you in this phase only increases risk for us — and especially for you."

He nodded and looked at his watch. "I'll be back in 30 minutes." He grabbed his keys from a bowl on the counter, then walked out the door. They heard him lock it again from the outside.

"I doubt it will take 30 minutes," Larsa said to Rafiq. "I just came to brief you on what little I know about the next phase — a meeting with an ISIS recruiting chief, or one of his delegates. Not sure quite yet. The rest is —"

"Who chose the name 'Larsa'?" Rafiq interrupted.

She looked at him, confused. "Excuse me?"

"Did your boss give you the alias? Or did you choose it yourself?"

A few seconds ticked by, while she stared. "I chose it from a list," she said. "Do you like it?"

"Not really," Rafiq said. "I would prefer to know your real name."

"Sorry, but that's not how it works."

"Is that right?" Rafiq leaned forward, gaze intensifying. "It seems situations like this might require frequent and substantial deviation from protocol."

The woman said nothing. Just sipped her coffee thoughtfully.

"I have been in many high-security prisons over the years," Rafiq continued. "There were rules, but you damn well knew when to break them, or your life — or what's left of it — was in jeopardy." His baritone voice was slow, steady, and sincere. "Before prison, for more than a year, I was a detainee, living in some of the worst places on Earth, in some of the worst conditions imaginable, alternating between solitary confinement and torture sessions. And now, I am about to begin another proxy life. Another existence that is not quite real, and yet perpetually dangerous. I will be surrounded and protected at all times by my own lies. There will be very few people in the world I can both trust and safely communicate with. It seems you will be primary among them."

She nodded slowly. He saw on her face that she wanted to tell him her name, but she hesitated. *I'll make it easier for you,* Rafiq thought.

"You can tell me your real name right now," he said. "Or you can walk out and explain to your boss why you are no longer part of this operation."

"Rona," she said. Then she smiled. "Rona Kavian."

It sounded true. The way she said it … *It is her real name,* he realized.

"I've been waiting for those words since you left me sitting in that bakery," he said.

Still smiling, she glanced away girlishly.

Deep down in his soul, Rafiq felt something switch on. *Rona Kavian, you will be one of the few stars in the black sky of my life.*

She looked back at him. "I wanted to tell you my name back then, too," she said. "And I'm not telling you now because you threatened me. I'm a big girl. I can make my own choices based on my own sensibilities. I like you, Rafiq. Unfortunately, I admit I grew to like you while I was spying on you. And I have thought about that day in the bakery countless times since. I actually considered writing to you a few times while you were in prison, but I knew all your mail would be screened intensely, and there was a better chance of my colleagues getting a hold of it than you. And then I saw you on television, giving your testimony." She looked at him with admiration in her eyes. "You were perfect, Rafiq. You could have stopped there and lived your life with pride in what you had accomplished."

Rafiq tried to think of something to say, but his brain was occupied by the idea of this beautiful, intelligent woman daydreaming about *him,* the way he'd done of her.

"It's not too late, you know," she said. "After tonight, it will be. But right now, you can still decide to back out. We can easily and gracefully call off the entire operation." She chose her next words carefully. "And I wouldn't blame you if you wanted to see … what else life had in store for you."

The idea brought his mind to a halt and spiked his heart rate. *Does she mean what I think she means?* He could only sip his coffee for a long minute, trying to create a reality where he and Rona were together. But it quickly crumbled in his mind. *When peace is mine, I will allow myself to imagine such a luxury.* Finally, he set down his mug again.

"I must do this," he told her.

"Why?" she asked.

He looked at her for several seconds before answering. "For a long time, I believed I would never get a trial. Then it got scheduled. I was briefly happy, but I had very little faith it would be fairly conducted, much less televised. Still, I prayed to Allah for that — for a chance to speak my truth to the watching world. The prayer was granted. I did not even plan what to say. The words came freely to my mouth, and they were good words. The right words. I would not change a single one. I thought my calling had been fulfilled, and I was prepared for more prison time. I planned to do a lot of writing." He paused to smile at her. "And then I was set free."

He thought of Isaac, of Nabaa, of his father … *stuck.* He wasn't ready to tell Rona about that. Maybe someday he would be.

"I no longer felt like my calling was over," he said. "It became clear to me that there was more for me to do than write about the jihad. Otherwise, Allah would have kept me in prison. So here I am, tending to his apparently unfinished business."

She nodded twice, slowly. Bittersweetly. Then she briefed him on everything he needed to know about the most ruthless group of men in the world.

CHAPTER 22

May 2015

Rafiq put his rental car in park, stepped out into the mostly empty lot, and casually shut the door. A moment later, a red Renault Sandero hatchback left its spot near the back of the lot and drove past him, exiting onto the street. He made a mental note of it, but didn't look directly toward the vehicle.

He entered the restaurant and took in its features on the way to the bathroom. A few minutes later, he took the long way around the restaurant and walked through the garden courtyard that provided the view for the primarily outdoor table arrangement. Then he went back out the front door, walked to the edge of the restaurant's awning, lit a cigarette, and checked his watch. 10:10 a.m.

On the left side of his periphery, he noticed the red Sandero was back in the parking lot, but in a different spot. The car was now pointed toward the restaurant's entrance.

How long will they sit and watch me? He took another drag. He liked, but didn't love smoking. At the moment, he appreciated the camouflaging effect it could have. A man standing by himself staring at mountains was something people noticed. Add a lit cigarette, and there's nothing to see.

He had driven the two hours from Nabatieh to Aanjar and arrived early enough to explore the surrounding area before arriving exactly on time to his 10 a.m. meeting. He'd never been to Aanjar, but it was pretty much as he'd heard — a small village situated at the foot of the short mountains of east Lebanon, with expanses of farmland stretching westward.

He stared east toward the short, mostly barren mountains. He initially wasn't sure why his ISIS contact had chosen a town full of 2,000 Armenians to meet for brunch, but now he had a good guess. Aanjar was only about 60 kilometers to Damascus, so it might be a good place to occasionally sneak people or supplies over the mountains and across the border.

Finally, the Sandero pulled out of its spot and slowly drove in his direction. Rafiq felt his heart rate spike, but he showed no outward signs of anxiety. He turned his head toward the vehicle as it approached. The man on the passenger side had his arm hanging out the window, fist closed and outstretched. The car stopped directly in front of Rafiq.

"Hold open your left hand, under my fist," the man said, calm eyes staring into Rafiq's. "Quickly."

Rafiq did as he was told, and the man's fist opened, depositing a small pill into Rafiq's palm.

"Ask no questions. Just chew and swallow this immediately," the man said. He waited.

Rafiq popped the pill into his mouth and chewed on it, surprising even himself with his lack of hesitation. He wondered if his meditative mastery of his endocrine system could protect him against actual poison. But it didn't really matter. This was what he was called to do. If he couldn't infiltrate ISIS, then he might as well die trying.

The pill was sweet and bitter at the same time. The car drove away again, back to the second parking spot. He was being watched again.

Rafiq suddenly felt goosebumps all over his body. His heart raced even more. He put his hands on his knees and coughed twice, feeling his windpipe narrow. *Why would they do this?* He tried to focus all of his mind on the poison, begged his brain to work magic and reject the chemistry. In reply, his brain produced a flashback.

He was back in the bakery in Baghdad. Saliva flooded his mouth, along with the memory of the perfectly sweet, softly-rich date-paste samoon she had recommended to him that day. There was the beautiful woman, frozen in time, about to walk out the door, holding a bag of pastries, and wearing the smile that matched her promise to see him the next morning. He didn't know her name.

But now I do, he thought. *Rona*.

His lips felt like they were starting to swell.

They are killing me here. In this parking lot. A minute before, he felt unafraid of death. Suddenly, he wanted to live. Must live. He wheezed, then coughed loudly.

He started to reach for the mobile phone in his pocket, but stopped.

It suddenly made sense.

They could have just shot him. Or convinced him to get in their vehicle before or after the meeting, and then killed him somewhere else. Instead, they gave him a pill and watched his reaction. They wanted him to call someone for help, maybe to wait and see who showed up — or how close they were. They might even have some way of monitoring the number when he tried to call.

This is just a test, he told himself, willing it to be true. He stood up straight, wheezing still, but in control.

Like an antidote, the knowledge made him calm. His lips still felt big, but he felt his heartbeat slow. This was actually a fortuitous development. If he just passed this test, it probably meant they would be even more candid with him during the meeting. A minute of mortal fear was a small price to pay if it accelerated his timeline.

Suddenly, the tingling was gone. His airway widened, and he involuntarily sucked in a huge lungful of air. He wiped some sweat from his forehead, then lit another cigarette. He turned and stared at the Renault parked 50 feet away, blowing a stream of smoke in its direction. A moment later, the man in the passenger seat got out and walked toward Rafiq. He was short, probably 5' 6" or so, wearing American-style jeans and a white, short-sleeved, button-down shirt with vertical stripes.

"Shall we?" he said, gesturing toward the entrance as he reached Rafiq.

Rafiq nodded, turned, and walked into the restaurant. A server greeted them, his face registering a brief moment of recognition when he saw the other man.

"Something on the east side of the courtyard, please," the man told the server, who nodded and led them through a sea of tables toward the far end of the seating area. They sat at a four-top next to a decorated wall. A wood-beamed ceiling jutted 20 feet toward the courtyard and provided ample shade from what was already an 80-degree sunny day. Best of all, they were secluded; the nearest patrons were seated about 40 feet away, on the other side of the U-shaped venue.

Another server appeared and poured water. The short man ordered a root beer. "When in Little Armenia," he said quietly to Rafiq, "I try to fit in." He winked. Rafiq asked for coffee, and the server left.

"I'm sure you know my name," Rafiq said. "But I don't know yours."

"Call me Dara," the man said. "And we will get to business soon enough. But I always come to this restaurant hungry. You'll see why. Have you had a chance to enjoy some of your homeland cuisine since you arrived in country yesterday at 2:44 p.m.?"

Rafiq smiled gently at Dara's attempt to create unease. "Is the revelation that you've been tracking my whereabouts supposed to be another test? I thought I passed in the parking lot."

"You did," Dara said. "But I've learned one can never be too careful."

"True," Rafiq said. "So I would advise that you be careful not to scare me away. At some point, your attempts to discern my loyalties will begin to make me question yours. And then I will look elsewhere for someone to help me achieve my aims."

The server returned with the drinks, and Dara ordered fattoush, kofta, and kanafeh for them to share.

When the server had left again, Rafiq leaned forward and said, "I should be more suspicious of you than you of me, don't you think?" His voice carried a hint of vitriol.

"Why would you be suspicious of me?" Dara asked. "Did your uncle not make the connection himself?"

"I love my uncle, and I trust him. But his endorsement can't possibly overcome what is a very high and rational risk to my safety." He softened his tone. "I understand that, if you are who you say you are, you constantly have to vet the people who claim allegiance to your cause. But I hate wasting time. So, for the sake of expediency, let's be frank. Your risk is not my uncertain allegiance, it's simply that I have a target on my back. Every American and U.S. ally's intelligence asset within 1000 square kilometers knows I'm back in my home country. They will be watching me as best they can. That limits our ability to work together to a certain extent. But it also presents *my* risk, which is astronomically higher than yours. *You* could be *their* first test of me. So we can decide to accept our risks as such, and then talk freely," Rafiq unbuttoned the top half of his shirt and opened it, revealing no wires, "or we can walk away." He rebuttoned his shirt and stared across the table.

Dara did the same with his shirt, never moving his gaze away from Rafiq. "You act as if I shouldn't be concerned that you might be acting on the Americans' behalf," he said. "It is more than a little unlikely that you were set free, no?"

"Yes. We can agree on unlikely," Rafiq said coolly. "But since you seem to be implying that the Americans released me because I agreed to become a double-agent, I will remind you of two things. One, my detention lasted roughly seven years. My interrogation is known to be one of the most … *strenuous* ever conducted by a Western government, especially in the beginning. And while I could have shared knowledge that prevented the air show attack, the attack still took place, praise be to Allah." Rafiq raised his mug and took a big sip of the thick, dark coffee. It was almost too hot to swallow, but not quite. "And, two, my release is not really a mystery. I stood trial in America. The trial was publicly televised. I assume you watched it, yes?"

"I did," Dara said. "I saw what America wanted the world to see."

Rafiq laughed. "Ah," he said. "You're skeptical of the trial's authenticity. I suppose I would be, too, if I had not experienced it myself. I will not to try to convince you otherwise. But I will tell you that I am the first jihadi to speak the truth of Allah's word to millions of Americans and then be released. Where you see suspicion, you could see success."

"Success?" Dara said. "Perhaps your television appearance was a success. But as a jihadi in the field, you would agree that you are still a failure, no?"

Just then, the server returned with the food, set it in the middle of the table, and walked away again. Rafiq's eyes stayed fixed on Dara. He felt his teeth clench slowly. *This man continues to test you.* He forced the corners of his lips upward slightly and saw Dara's grin broaden in response. *Pride is your enemy here.*

Dara broke his gaze and secured a large forkful of the kanafeh. "Life is too short to let kanafeh get cold." Dripping a trail of sugar syrup across his empty plate, he stuffed the cheese-stuffed, fried-noodle pastry into his mouth. He chewed slowly, clearly enjoying himself.

"We have found two things we agree on, then," Rafiq said, helping himself to the kanafeh. It was as delicious as Dara's face implied. He swallowed. "Yes, my only jihadi mission failed, Dara. If not for one brave and lucky American sharpshooter, it may have been a spectacular success. But it was not. And that failure has haunted me ever since. It requires redemption. That is why I never cooperated with interrogators. It is why I ate that pill you gave me without hesitation. It is why I am sitting here across from you today, at great personal risk." He grabbed two perfectly seared beef kofta links and put them on Dara's plate, then took two for himself. He again met Dara's gaze. "So. Can we get down to business? Or shall I go?"

Dara speared one of the kofta links. "You shall not go anywhere, Rafiq Itani." He took a bite of the beef, leaving his fork upturned in front of his mouth. "You belong to me now."

Rafiq relaxed. The men ate for a few minutes in silence. The food was the best Rafiq had eaten in years.

"So how can I help?" he finally asked.

"We will discuss that in greater detail in a more secure location," Dara said. "But I will speak in general terms here. Seeing you testify at your trial and hearing you speak to me today, it confirmed to me that your greatest strength is communication. And that can help us with our biggest challenge. Recruiting. We think you could be extremely effective as the face for our recruitment efforts. While some may be cynical, we believe most of our target audience — regular Arab men and angry, curious Westerners — will see you as you described: the jihadi who spoke truth to America and got away with it. They will want to hear more from you." Leaning to the side, Dara retrieved his mobile phone from his pants pocket. His thumbs rapidly skittered across the screen, then he stopped and sipped his soda, then stared at the phone again and typed something else. Then he returned the phone to his pocket. "We'll meet here again tomorrow. 8 a.m. in the parking lot. And then I will take you to see a colleague — someone whose opinion should matter to you. He will want to discuss your first communication campaign." He cut off a piece of kofta with the side of his fork, stabbed it, and brought it to his mouth. He quickly got a forkful of radishes, celery, and tomatoes from the fattoush and added it to the beef he was already chewing. He casually scanned the restaurant around him, first right, then left. "I want you to have some ideas ready to present to him, so I will tell you only what you need to know. We will soon be executing a major attack on a military installation near Washington, D.C."

Rafiq nodded slowly. "And I am supposed to ... what? Help recruit men who can participate?"

Dara chuckled as he ate. "No, my friend. That job is done, and they are in place. When I say 'soon,' I mean very, very soon. Your job is to speak in a video that will be released after the attack."

"I see," Rafiq said. "And I would be honored. Which military base is it? There are many in that area."

Dara stared at him, a little quizzically. "I told you I would tell you what you need to know," he said. "And I have. When we meet our friend tomorrow, he will want to hear your ideas for the video. The words you might say that will resonate with young men." He stood suddenly, pulling his phone from his pocket again and checking it. Then he reached into another pocket and retrieved a different phone. He handed it to Rafiq. "This is how we will reach you from now on. Answer every call and every text."

Rafiq took the phone and nodded. "See you tomorrow."

And Dara turned and left.

CHAPTER 23

May 2015

from: Liza Hamilton <lizachucksgirl@gmail.com>
to: Aahna Khatri <aktheexister@gmail.com>
date: Tue, May 12, 2015 at 2:29 PM
subject: Instinct vs. free will

Hi, Aahna. So I just got an email from my boss asking if anyone would like to donate some of their paid time off to an employee whose brother just died unexpectedly. He was in his 40s, and apparently their mother also just died — last month — which ate up the last of her PTO. This employee is in a completely separate department, so I've never met her or even heard her name before this email. But before I had even thought about it, I was replying to the email and giving her two of the 16 days I've got accrued.

Of course, that made me think of what you mentioned during dinner last time — that your next study is focusing on instinct. I'm sure there's lots of interesting stuff you could tell me about the primary instincts we share with all animals (survival, procreation, protection of offspring), but have you thought about this instinct for altruism that we also seem to have? I'd like to know why I just gave away two days of PTO that it took me six weeks to earn! :)

from: Aahna Khatri <aktheexister@gmail.com>
to: Liza Hamilton <lizachucksgirl@gmail.com>
date: Tue, May 12, 2015 at 5:11 PM
subject: RE: Instinct vs. free will

Ha! I think we both know the answer is that you represent an evolutionary maladaptation. In other words, you're lucky your ancestors weren't so irrationally altruistic.

Just kidding. Maybe.

So, I'm actually really excited about this, but ... mandatory disclaimers: We are still way too early in the process to draw any conclusions, blah blah blah. Whatever. The main disclaimer is that this is probably going to hurt your brain and/or put you to sleep. Remember — YOU asked. :)

The experiments are expanding on ones already done with rats back in 2010. We're in the pre-design stage right now, but we're still recording results. One of the grad students on the project just got some data that didn't fit, so he had to cross-reference with the initial surveys from the study subjects. Then he found a common denominator — the fluorescent reporters were behaving differently in the brains of people who described themselves as "highly spiritual."

I guess I should explain the experiment before I explain the results. So, basically, we're testing fear-based decision-making by temporarily stimulating or deadening the amygdala (the part of your brain where emotion is processed). To increase the neural emotional activity, we gave subjects this substance called bicuculline. To *deactivate* the amygdala, we gave them muscimol. The experiment involved stuffing several cash bills in a clear plastic cup in the center of a table, then placing a robotic taser on the table between the subject and the cup. Then we ask the subjects if they can get the cup, they can keep the money (that part made it REALLY easy to find volunteers on a college campus — we have a 300-person wait list).

The variables we're manipulating are: distance of the cup, speed of the taser, and amount of money in the cup (so either $1s, $5s, $10s, or $20s). The lead researchers liked that design a lot and asked us to pre-test an additional offshoot — the same experiment with two people who don't know each other. So one stranger sits behind a glass wall, simply watching the main subject who's at the table with the money cup and the taser. The main subject is told that the stranger is a student attending JHU on financial subsidy, and the contents of the cup will be split 80/20, with 80% going to the stranger. THAT gave us one more big variable: What would the split ratio have to be to give us results similar to the individual design?

The hypothesis was that the people who took greater risks for their own reward (the selfish ones) would be the same people who were *less* likely to risk a tasing for a small share of the stranger's pot. And that was true for most. It tracked neatly with increasing the pot share.

But not for the "highly spiritual" group. They were less afraid of the taser overall, but only slightly. The really weird part was when we stimulated their amygdalas in the pot-sharing experiment, they accepted MORE risk.

In other words, their emotional response to a fellow student's financial need *overrode* their own emotional response to pain.

That result turned the hypothesis on its head — but only with spiritual students.

Soooo ... back to you. You probably have faith that you have an abundance of paid time off, and if you're wrong about that, you probably believe that someone else will take care of you. But it seems that the altruism "instinct" is learned through the act of becoming spiritual.

HOWEVER ... as I'm trying to answer your admittedly fascinating question, I'm burying the big news — those same anomalous results gave me the data I needed to FINALLY get approved and funded to add the fluorescent reporters to the experiments! We start tomorrow (I was ready!), but I'll have to wait till Thursday for the data. I'm going to be an anxious mess! Happy-anxious, productive-anxious. I think. So don't worry if I can't email again for a couple of days.

So much to do. Love you!

from: Liza Hamilton <lizachucksgirl@gmail.com>
to: Aahna Khatri <aktheexister@gmail.com>
date: Wed, May 12, 2015 at 8:41 PM
subject: RE: Instinct vs. free will

OK, let me NOT make your mistake and bury my congrats. CONGRATULATIONS! That's amazing, Aahna! Not that I'm surprised. Nor will I be surprised when eventually this stuff makes you a Nobel laureate. :)

Now, back to Earth. I have to nitpick your claim that the "altruism instinct is learned through the act of becoming spiritual." Ahem ... isn't the act of becoming spiritual kinda instinctual, too?

from: Aahna Khatri <aktheexister@gmail.com>
to: Liza Hamilton <lizachucksgirl@gmail.com>
date: Thu, May 15, 2015 at 10:59 PM
subject: RE: Instinct vs. free will

Lizzy. The fluorescent reporters are amazing. I think we're about to discover something — something deep.

Umm ... where do I begin? I'm vibrating with excitement right now. I wish you were right in front of me so I could let loose this flood of information verbally, but I know you're asleep. So, here goes.

So there's this chemical called CRH. It stands for corticotropin-releasing hormone. Research has shown for a while that CRH is heavily involved in stress response. In fact, highly elevated levels of CRH are commonly found in the cerebrospinal fluid of suicide victims. Because of that, of course, Pfizer and Glaxo have been trying for years to find a way to inhibit corticotropin. Multiple drugs have been developed, but none were effective enough to be approved. Our lead researcher told us the industry believes the corticotropin drug that finally works will be more popular than antidepressants. BIG money. But lots of research money has already been spent for nothing.

Now you know what CRH is. What you don't know is that I told some of my little fluorescent reporter chemicals to find CRH and follow it. We expected the reporters would just hang around until the subject was exposed to stress. Nope. The subjects were sitting for about 20 seconds waiting for the experiment to start, and during those 20 seconds, the fluorescent reporters were like drug-sniffing dogs! They didn't wait for corticotropin to "appear" like I thought — they went right into the brain, through the amygdala, through the hypothalamus, and right into the brainstem. *They went right to the CRH GENE!*

I didn't even know there WAS a CRH gene. But it's there, and now that we have a mechanism, they tell me it should be a relatively simple process to add something that selectively "turns off" the gene. It's so much more complex than that, even beyond my understanding, but you should've seen the eyeballs on the senior researchers when I showed them the data ... and then showed them again and again. They were the kind of eyeballs you only see around here when there's grant money right around the corner.

So, I may have just had my career-defining moment before I'm halfway through my undergrad. That's a strange thought.

from: Aahna Khatri <aktheexister@gmail.com>
to: Liza Hamilton <lizachucksgirl@gmail.com>
date: Fri, May 15, 2015 at 12:08 AM
subject: RE: Instinct vs. free will

OH! One more email while you sleep, because I almost forgot to tell you the OTHER thing we may have discovered, which would have made for a pretty amazing experiment day, if it weren't for the whole "possibly curing anxiety" thing. ;)

It relates to your question about the instinctual nature of spirituality. So, we had the data from bicuculline and muscimol, but we wanted to manipulate the amygdala with a separate method to further isolate variables. So today (well, yesterday, according to my clock), we used something called theta-burst

156

transcranial magnetic stimulation. Basically, instead of a chemical, you can use a magnet to stimulate either the dorsolateral prefrontal cortex or the dorsomedial prefrontal cortex … oh wow. You're going to wake up to this alphabet soup. I'm sorry. Let me try this without the jargon.

A summary, for the layman (laywoman?) who may still be groggy: Yes, it appears spirituality is instinctual. In this case, the chemical we need to understand is oxytocin — it's what our body releases when we're being altruistic. So, when I programmed the fluorescent reporters to find oxytocin, they did the same thing as when they were tracking down the CRH: There was no actual oxytocin floating around, so the reporters went straight to the parent gene and attached — in the brainstem. When the subjects did something altruistic, the reporters ended up in the hypothalamus, now attached to regular, old-fashioned oxytocin.

That doesn't sound strange on the surface — not until you consider the conventional thinking. Most neuroscientists believe that (a) oxytocin feels good and therefore (b) we evolved to release oxytocin during altruistic acts because we have a self-serving, tribal reason for being nice to our fellow tribesmen. Makes sense, right?

But (kinda like you insinuated in your "ahem" reply) THIS study we did yesterday reverses that order — like the egg comes before the chicken. In humans, at least, the fluorescent reporters seemed to show that there's a signal coming from a *500-million-year-old* ancestral gene telling us to be altruistic. That gene predates tribes by a long shot. So it was there, birthing pre-oxytocin in cells long before anything had a brain, much less a hypothalamus.

That does NOT fit with most evolutionary biology, but it does seem to get us a little closer to the question of whether we have an instinct to connect to our fellow living things (a.k.a. "spirituality"). AND it certainly seems to put a dent in free will.

(By the way, I should mention that oxytocin is a general mystery to science. It's produced in several other parts of the body, like testicles and *retinas,* and no one seems to understand why.)

That's the good news. Here's the bad news: There's no way I'll be able to find out more, because there's probably no grant money for that, especially since the hypothesis would be guilty until proven innocent. Sigh. It's frustrating.

Well, look at that. Ten minutes ago, I was feeling elation, and now I'm already feeling slight depression and anxiety because my research got hijacked for anti-anxiety big pharma purposes.

157

Millions of people might feel happier for that, but I'm focusing on my own interests.

Also, I've taken three final exams this week, despite not really having time to study. And it's late. And I'm sure my oxytocin is low.

CHAPTER 24

May 2015

"Do we have to talk about this now?" Maggie asked. Her tone and sloping eyebrows communicated that she didn't intend it as a question, but a warning.

She had just walked in the door, apparently after a stressful day at work, and Percy had immediately shared the news from President Brennan: The polling was done. The voting public was pro-Percy, and the DNC was more than willing to support his campaign. If he ran for the vacant Senate seat, he would almost certainly win.

"Now? I guess not," he said. "But when's a better time? We can't avoid the topic because it's uncomfortable."

"I didn't say I wanted to avoid the topic. It's just a little heavy for me right this second. I just walked in. I'm hungry. I'm tired."

"Well, if we wait till you're not tired *or* hungry, we'll never talk about it." In his mind, the sentence was formed as a gentle joke, to ease the tension. But there was still an edge in his voice. He heard it. *Oh well.*

"Really?" Maggie whirled on him. "Well, I'm really sorry for that. And I'm sorry I'm not 100 percent thrilled that this Senate thing is quickly becoming a reality. Last time we had targets on our backs, I wasn't thrilled about how that worked out either."

Percy's patience was gone before he realized it was low. "Like I haven't thought about that? Do you think this is some kind of fucking glory trip for me? The security risks are exactly what I wanted to talk to you about."

"Oh, that sounds like a perfect topic for when I get home after a shitty day!" She looked right at him, eyes narrowed. "Because it's so fucking *fun* to discuss sensitive subjects with you when you've already got your mind made up."

"I'm asking you to make up *your* mind! That's why we need to talk!"

Percy was reaching a volume he didn't like. He stopped and took a long breath. *Where is this coming from? Think.*

He had missed Maggie all day. He wanted her to *want* to hear about the news. But as soon as she didn't reciprocate, it was a reminder that this thing he felt called to do — run for Senate — was about to put everything at risk. Again. Not just his physical safety, but his daily life. Arguments like these would flow from the decision, especially if he won. Safety would be a constant concern. They would have to discuss it all the time, and that's not counting the regular stressors of any high-level political official.

Of course she's feeling the pressure — more accurately and rationally than I am. I'm a fucking asshole.

"Mags …" Percy started to object, then stopped. "I'm sorry. It can wait." He let the silence breathe a while, then walked around the kitchen island and wrapped her in his arms from behind, resting his head on her shoulder. "I love you."

"I love you, too," she said. She took a deep breath, leaned her head back against him, and hung her hands from his forearms. "And I think you'll make a great senator. And I think the country will be better off because of it. And in 2020, I think you'll make a great candidate for president. But I just know in my heart that there are people out there that still want to do us harm. I'm trying to get to a place where the risk is worth the reward, but … it's just not."

"It's hard for me, too," he said. "I've kinda gotten used to this life where I'm not constantly in fight or flight anymore. This choice basically means I'm going back to that. *We're* going back to that."

"Exactly."

He released the embrace and gently turned face her around to look at him. "It's not too late to pull the plug completely. I would do that for you and still live happily ever after. And you know that. So, you can tell me to bail anytime, before, during, after — doesn't matter. You are my primary constituent, Maggie Mackenzie." He searched her eyes for clues, got none. "But if you *don't* want me to pull the plug, then all you need to think about and decide is — "

"I know," she interrupted. "I need to figure out whether I want to be the only reason my husband rejects his calling. Whether I want to live with that forever, while you watch someone else get elected, while you watch the news wondering what it would be like if I hadn't kiboshed the idea." She turned her head away from him. "And if I get over *that* hurdle and support your calling, I have to decide whether I want to join you at public events or whether I stay hidden. What a shitty choice. Do I stand by my husband's side and put myself in danger — and, you know, in a position where I'll see my husband get shot or blown up in person? Or do I sequester myself somewhere so I can watch it happen on TV? I remember *that* feeling pretty well." She looked into his eyes again. "That feeling is what I keep remembering. How close I was to losing you. I thought I did, and everything in my mind just felt … dead. Like, meaningless. I can't go through that again."

He squeezed her hard. Then he heard the signature sound from his Blackberry that indicated a secure, encrypted email. Then another. Then another. Three emails of the secure, encrypted variety.

"I've got to check that," he said. He retrieved the phone from its usual place on the counter next to the coffee maker and opened the inbox. "They're from Rafiq," he said. "Looks like one message, broken up like I suggested to him." He read all three silently, goosebumps cascading over his arms. He looked up and saw Maggie's eyes. "We're OK but I have to call this in right away."

Percy opened his contacts and found the unlisted number for the counterterrorism center that the agent in charge had given him. Two rings later, a voice came over the line.

"NCTC, secure line. ID, please."

"Percival Mackenzie."

A moment passed. "Check. Verification, please."

"Peccary."

"Copy. Good morning, Mr. Mackenzie. I'll take your report."

"I just received three short emails from my source in the Levant. Do I need to specify?"

"No, sir. I have that info. Please go ahead with the messages."

"OK. First one says, 'Large attack.' Second one says, 'DC area military base.' Last one says, 'Soon.'"

Another brief silence, then. "Copy all."

"Anything else from me? What happens next?"

"Uh, stand by sir." A light click came across the line, then another a few seconds later. "I'm authorized to tell you that this fits with other indicators of local cell activity around DC over the last couple of weeks. So we're expecting DoD will be putting all major NCR installations in Charlie within the hour. If you need to get on base, plan for long lines for a while."

CHAPTER 25

May 2015

Rafiq closed Rona's laptop and stared at the wall behind the desk.

"You've been on the job less than a day," she said. "And you already might've saved some lives."

He looked at her. "Something about it feels wrong."

"That's to be expected," she said. "You're officially living a double life now. It would be weird if it felt normal to you. But you get used to it."

Once again, Rafiq was reminded of Rona's practiced duplicity. *Will I ever know if she really sees me as a man instead of a tool for her purposes?*

"That's not what I meant," he said. "Something about this just seems too … easy."

"Like Dara was setting you up?"

"I don't know," Rafiq said. "Maybe."

"That seems doubtful," Rona said. She walked over and sat on the edge of the desk next to him. "You passed their test, right? What would be the point of that, if they were trying to set you up?"

He nodded. "I know." He couldn't identify the source of his discomfort. And now Rona's proximity was distracting him. *Is that calculated, too?* His eyes gravitated toward the curve of her thigh and buttocks. He closed his eyes, then looked up at her. "When I took that pill — when it was wreaking havoc on my system and I thought I was dying — my first thought was of you."

She smiled. "I wanted you to be thinking of me before you went to meet Dara," she said. "That's why I kissed you. I wanted you to have a reason to be careful, a reason to fight another day."

"You speak in riddles, Rona," Rafiq said, eyeing her. "I don't know if you're treating me like a valuable asset or a future lover."

"Both can be true, can't they?"

"I don't know," Rafiq said. "You are the expert."

Somehow, he saw that the words injured her.

"If you were just a valuable asset, I already would've fucked you," Rona said. Her words hung in the air. "Does that make you want me more? Or less?"

He was shaken, but something inside him was made calm by her candor. He grabbed her hand, then stood and kissed her briefly but deeply.

"More," he said. "But mostly, I want to *know* you."

"And you will," Rona said. "After this mission is over."

◇◇◇◇◇◇◇◇◇
CHAPTER 26

May 2015

The stream of brake lights began at the intersection of Highway 175 and continued all the way down Rockenbach Road — the funnel that led to the second-most trafficked entry-control point at the Army's Fort George G. Meade. The road was four lanes wide, but at 7:15 in the morning, only the two inbound lanes were populated with vehicles.

The long road itself was federal property, and the entry-control point was placed 1,000 yards from the main road to help separate the heavy Fort Meade traffic from the regular civilian traffic on 175. The distant placement of the ECP meant the road had to be bracketed on each side by a row of barbed-wire fences, blocking unauthorized access to base property.

And also creating a perfect kill zone, Haasan thought.

Today was only the third time he had experienced the morning traffic on Rockenbach, but each time, he felt like God himself had created this confluence of events, specifically for Haasan to exploit.

It seems so easy. Too easy. He fidgeted in the passenger seat of the stolen minivan, gaining ground 10 feet at a time, stopping, going, and stopping again. He fully expected the backup of vehicles — the plan depended on it — but now, on the day of the operation, the plodding pace was making him antsy. He realized that if *he* was feeling anxious, his men were probably jumping out of their skin.

Calmly, he engaged the push-to-talk app on his prepaid smartphone and raised it to his mouth.

"All is well," Haasan said in clear, deliberate English. "Longer lines delay our moment, but also increase our opportunity to glorify God."

He received no reply, but at least in the vehicle he was sharing with four other men, he felt the tension ease. Stop. Go. Stop. Go. Fifteen minutes passed as they crept toward the gate in the left lane. The man counted the vehicles ahead of them — 12, including his man in the taxi directly in front of him.

Brake lights on, brake lights off, then the light pull of 3-mile-per-hour acceleration against his inertia. Twenty more feet of ground gained. They were the ninth vehicle now. Then the eighth.

A few minutes later, the taxi was next up. Instead of stopping at the gate guard to show ID, the driver simply waved and rolled through the gate slowly.

"Hey!" the guard yelled. The taxi didn't stop. The guard signaled to his colleagues inside a tiny shack next to the gate.

Good, Haasan thought.

As expected, the line of 3-foot barricades shot out of the ground about 15 yards ahead of the taxi, which came to an immediate stop. One of the guards exited the shack and calmly approached the taxi.

Both of the ID-checking guards, in the right lane and left lane, looked back and forth between the taxi and the next vehicles in their respective lines. They each held a hand up as a signal to stop.

Haasan nodded to his driver, and the minivan approached the guard anyway. The guard looked directly at both of them, not quite panicked, but clearly suspicious.

"Stop here, please," he said firmly through the open driver's-side window. Now the guard in the right lane was paying attention to the van, too.

The van stopped just shy of where the left-lane guard was standing. The man seated behind Haasan maneuvered toward the middle seat and then stood up completely through the moonroof. From the waist up, he was now in open air.

The left guard's eyes darted up, instantly alarmed. His hand went to his gun. "Hey! Get down!"

The next few seconds went by in a blur.

The driver brought the .357 Magnum up with his left hand and extended it out the window. He pointed it at the guard's chest and fired. Haasan rested the grip of his own Magnum on the edge of his open window, carefully aimed, and shot the guard in the right lane. They each fired twice more. Recoil caused Haasan's second shot to obliterate the top of the guard's head, spraying blood onto the white sedan behind him. His third shot missed.

Simultaneously, the standing man lifted an AR-15 rifle up through the moonroof and pointed it at the guard who was rushing out of the gate shack with a rifle of his own. *Don't miss,* Haasan silently implored. A single American soldier in a covered position could seriously disrupt their plan. But his man didn't miss.

His first volley of shots from the assault rifle strafed the soldier's left side and dropped him to the asphalt in front of them. Haasan opened his door, stepped halfway out of the van, and finished the job. Twenty yards ahead, the guard standing next to the taxi had turned back toward the gunfire and was beginning to raise his M4. Another .357 appeared from the driver's window. It looked like the taxi driver was able to shove it under the guard's vest before firing twice.

The shooter in the moonroof turned backward to scan for more threats.

Haasan pressed the iPTT button and raised the phone to his lips. "ALLAHU AKBAR!"

He dropped the phone and the handgun, then retrieved an AR-15 from the footwell of his seat. More men piled out from another van, five vehicles behind in line. Each had his own AR-15, each with its own specialized 100-round magazine. A quarter-mile back the way they'd come, Haasan saw four more vehicles — two vans, an SUV, and a large pickup truck, all stolen the night before — cross the intersection from a gas station parking lot on the other side of the street. Cars honked as drivers braked to avoid collisions. The four vehicles lined up horizontally, blocking the entrance to Rockenbach Road.

Haasan looked to his left. One of his men was standing opposite him in the other lane. Haasan nodded, they both raised their rifles, pointed them at the vehicles directly behind their own, and began to fire careful, deliberate shots. In each case, the driver had crouched down below the steering wheel, so they had to walk up to the driver's side window and shoot through it.

Then driver of the next car in line got out of his vehicle and ran directly at Haasan, screaming. Haasan shot him twice in the chest, stepped to the side as the man fell to the asphalt, and then shot him in the head.

He resumed his walk down the line of cars, watching his men ahead shooting more bullets, spraying the driver's side, wounding the drivers, and moving on. They were instructed to keep walking. Haasan and his counterpart in the other lane were tasked to come behind them and deliver the kill shots. And so they did.

Vehicle after vehicle, most drivers stayed in their seats, unaware of the mayhem in front of them. Only a few tried to escape, and they were easily gunned down.

Then Haasan heard a different gunshot up ahead, and his man went down, AR-15 firing into the sky. One of the drivers was crouching behind his open car door, pointing a small-caliber handgun through its open window. Haasan immediately dove between the two cars on his left. Two more shots came from the handgun, one of which pierced the front-left tire of the sedan Haasan was leaning against. Air hissed out.

Haasan rose slowly to get a better look at the man trying to be a hero. He was older than Haasan expected, and he was wearing a white shirt and tie, not a uniform. *Must be a retiree,* Haasan thought. *And apparently some combat experience.*

The man slid into his vehicle, crawling sideways toward his passenger window, hoping to get a line of sight on the other two riflemen in the rightmost lane of traffic. Then Haasan saw one of his other men running from their blockade at the end of the road toward the hero's car.

Dammit, Haasan thought. It was the right decision, but it meant the rest of the vehicles in line would see a man with an assault rifle running down the road, and many of them would leave their vehicles. That would create the crossfire situation that Haasan had meticulously tried to avoid in his plan.

Hearing sirens, Haasan turned back toward the gate. They had gone farther than he'd realized. Probably 60 cars were between him and the gate, and just as many in the right lane.

At least 100 casualties so far, he thought. And their two-wave targeting tactic meant that very few would survive. *We will have the record.* The worst mass shooting on U.S. soil to date was in 2007 — 32 dead at Virginia Tech University. He smiled, knowing that fact would generate even more media coverage for his mission, keeping it in the news cycle for days longer. *And dozens more vehicles still ahead, each its own barrel, holding its own fish.*

As he turned around, he saw his man approaching the armed retiree's vehicle. Two shots from the rifle, then a scream, then four shots from the handgun. Haasan's man went down. Haasan ran to the spot, rifle raised. He jumped onto the hood of the car and saw the American splayed out across his center console, alive but dying. Haasan shot him through the windshield five more times. The man stopped moving.

Haasan's two men in the right lane appeared. "Take care of both lanes," he said, gesturing back and forth between the two lanes of cars. "One ahead," he said, pointing to the one in front. "And one behind. I will handle anyone trying to escape. Hurry! GO!"

The men nodded, turned, and began jogging ahead, two car lengths between them. Immediately, he saw two people exit their vehicles and run to their right, toward a strip mall that had one small exit onto Rockenbach. Haasan jumped onto the roof of the dead hero's car, dropped to one knee, and shot the farthest escapee in the back. The second one saw the first one fall, and he instinctively stopped. As soon as he did, Haasan shot him twice in the torso. He decided he would continue his path up the road, using the vehicles as stepping stones whenever possible. The vantage point was useful if people ran, and the sight of him up high might make people duck down instead of attempt to escape.

He was right. The rest of the fish stayed in the barrel. They walked methodically and fired liberally. Occasional screams continued to pierce the air, offset by the usual late-spring exclamations of birds. His index finger began to hurt, so he used his middle finger on the trigger instead.

By the time the SWAT trucks arrived — one at the gate, and two more at the end of Rockenbach — Haasan and his men had almost made it all the way up the road to the intersecting Highway175. He smiled and aimed at the driver of the next car. His trigger clicked on an empty chamber. He smiled again, ejected his second magazine, and let it fall to the pavement. He pulled his last magazine from its pouch on his vest and popped it into its housing.

He looked up to the sky to praise Allah one more time. A huge black vulture was circling overhead.

CHAPTER 27

May 2015

Nabaa pointed the remote at her TV and turned it off.

"We should get started," she said. "The exam is tomorrow." She had already gotten two extensions on her Probability and Statistics final, and her professor said there would be no more.

Ibrahim sighed, a little too loudly. "Yeah," he said. "You mentioned that a few times. That's why I'm here." He glanced at her, brief but withering.

"Wow," she said. "You sure you want to do this? You offered to help, but since you got here, you've just been watching people in suits and ties finding different ways to tell each other how tragic the shooting was. I can study by myself."

"First of all, when I got to your room, you weren't ready to study," he shot back. "You were charting your data again, so I *asked* if I could turn on the TV. You said it was fine."

She didn't respond. *He should let it go. But he won't.*

"Second," he said, filling the silence. "It's not just tragic. It's *ironic*. The base clearly knew an attack was coming, so they increased their entry security. That decision is what *caused* the huge backup at the gates, which was what these assholes needed to carry out the biggest mass murder in American history. And, oh by the way, you have your research passion? Well, I have mine." He pointed at the TV screen. "*This* is exactly the kind of thing *I'm* studying, so if my reaction — "

Nabaa's phone rang. She looked at the screen, which said, "Charlie." She picked it up immediately and answered.

"Hi, Charlie."

"Hi, sweetheart," he said. "You doing OK?"

"I'm fine," Nabaa said. "Just sitting here with Ibrahim trying to study, but arguing about the Fort Meade shooting instead. What took you so long to call?"

"I'm sorry about that," he said. "I really am. It's been a little busy on this end. In fact, I can't talk long, but I knew I needed to hear your voice. Figured you wanted to hear mine, too."

"Thank you," she said. "And I probably shouldn't talk long, either. I've got my last final tomorrow."

"Wow. Hell of a time to try to study."

"Right." A few moments of silence passed. "So, Charlie, is it safe to say this attack is going to make you reconsider your … future job prospects?"

"My future job prospects?" Then he got it. "Ah. That. No, sweetheart. The pre-announcement already went out yesterday, and a lot of people have been laying a lot of groundwork for me. Plus, if anything, the attack is more evidence that I need to press onward. I can't let terrorism dissuade me from doing what I think is right. You know that."

She did, but the words were too bitter for her to say out loud.

"I understand," she said, finally. And she did understand, logically. And she knew Percy well enough that she should not have been surprised by his decision to push ahead, like a bulldog. But she *was* surprised. Her nervous system was suddenly buzzing. Her heart rate was ramping up.

"I love you," Percy said. "I'll talk to you more soon, OK?"

"I love you, too," Nabaa said. She hung up.

Her hands were starting to shake. *Breathe,* she told herself. She did *not* want to be dealing with a panic attack right now. *Not tonight.* The intense rejection of a panic attack typically just brought it on faster, so she pushed those thoughts aside. *Inhale. Exhale. Let the adrenaline run its course.*

"Aahna?" Ibrahim's voice interrupted her concentration. "Are you OK? What's wrong?"

"I'm OK," she said. "I think. I'm on the verge of a panic attack. I just need a minute."

"A panic attack? Shit. What did Charlie say?"

"I. NEED. A. MINUTE!" Her voice erupted from her lungs. She felt the hot blood rise into her cheeks, into her forehead. Her heart was pumping hard now. She closed her eyes to shut out Ibrahim's glare.

"Fucking great," he said. "It's not enough that they kill over a hundred people. They have to cause a fight between me and my girlfriend, too." His voice was quiet, but thick with bitterness. With Nabaa's attention gone, he was simply talking to himself now. "Fucking weak, cowardly pussies, posing as Muslim men. Giving us all a bad name, setting us all back another decade."

Nabaa snapped her eyes open and saw him gathering up his books. "Oh good," she said, her anger spiking at the sight of his decision to leave her room. "We're on the same page now. I mean, if you're just going to sit here and complain about the scourge of radical Muslims, you should find someone else who hasn't heard it a dozen times before."

"What?" Ibrahim was taken aback. "A dozen times before? Here I was thinking we were having *conversations* about world religion, but really, you've just been *tolerating* my rambling complaints. Got it. Don't worry. I'll stop bothering you with it."

He slung his bag over his shoulder and took a few steps toward the door.

"Or — *orrrrr* — you could go do something about it! You know, something other than writing 100 words a week in a book that might get read by five people five years from now!"

She regretted the words as soon as she said them. Ibrahim stopped and turned toward her, the look on his face confirming her shame. There was no anger in it — just confusion, rejection, pain. Nabaa's panic had left her, and it seemed to possess Ibrahim now.

"God*damn* it, Ibrahim! I told you I needed a minute! You had to keep *talking*! For fuck's sake!"

In her heart, those words were an apology. She wasn't in her right mind. She had said things she didn't mean, because Ibrahim hadn't let her calm down.

But she knew how the words sounded to him. Just like the ones before — all wrong. Like she had found another way to criticize him for what he did best, what she loved most about him. Like one more knife twisted.

Her stomach knotted. A real apology rose to her lips, but got stuck. Ibrahim walked out the door.

Ibrahim sat down at his desk, pulled his laptop out of his bag, and opened it up in front of him.

I wouldn't be this angry if she weren't right, he thought. He only ever got this angry when he was angry with himself.

Not that he wasn't angry with Aahna, too. She had said she loved him, but then she had done the opposite of love — she found his greatest weakness, a weakness only she could know, and used it to hurt him. *But she has done me a favor,* he thought. Hurtful as they were, her words had struck a chord that needed striking.

He'd barely made any progress in his book for months now. That fact was always tugging at the recesses of his mind. He didn't know why he was stuck, but he'd become adept at avoiding this issue. Until tonight. Aahna's words had gotten to the heart of it.

He didn't understand his enemy. Not enough.

His complaints about the "scourge of radical Muslims," as she had put it, were the byproduct of ignorance. He couldn't relate to their cause, so he objected to it. Thus far, his novel had focused mostly on the prodigal son of the king, his proxy for America, but he was nearing the chapters about the resistance to the new kingdom and its imperialism.

The last few times he'd sat down and placed his hands over the keyboard, nothing had flowed forth. So he spent a bunch of time on Wikipedia pages, he watched a couple of brief documentaries on old conflicts between a large military force and a much smaller one. He felt more educated afterward — but not any more inspired.

On the way home from Aahna's dorm, he realized what he needed to do. He didn't need more knowledge of history. He was living in the kingdom that he was trying to write about. And the resistance was everywhere — hell, as of yesterday, it was practically on his doorstep. In America, in the Middle East, in South Asia, people were violently rejecting America's imperialist and interventionist approach.

But Ibrahim had never even tried to gain access to that collective. He had projected his assumptions — Western assumptions — onto the enemies of America, and then tried to write. It didn't work. So now he was diving in.

In the Google search field, he typed, "ISIS recruiting materials."

The next two hours passed quickly. What he found wasn't just half-hearted garbage foisted on social media platforms. For the most part, the group used well scripted, well shot, and well edited video content that portrayed the lifestyle of an IS jihadi as a God-sanctioned adventure — one that was guaranteed to end in joy. Either the recruits would live long enough to see the movement succeed and then become the heroes of a glorious new society of Islam, or they would die in service to Allah and immediately be glorified in Heaven.

Most of the stuff didn't immediately connect with Ibrahim, but he could certainly see why it resonated with other young men. *Especially the outcasts,* he thought. The videos would speak persuasively to any able-bodied young Muslim who was frustrated with authority or who was just dumped by his girlfriend or generally wasn't happy with what his immediate future looked like.

It was easy for Ibrahim to imagine being that young man, being seduced by the prospect of a new, more meaningful life. He felt a new spark of something deep down. *This is good,* he thought. He recognized the warmth as the long-lost connection to his purpose. The magnetic pull of the modern jihad might just be the muse he needed to get back in rhythm with his book.

He thought about opening up the Word document that contained his manuscript, but something stopped him. He closed his eyes and tried to consciously connect the IS jihad with the fictional insurgent resistance in his novel.

The block was still there. Softer, but still present.

What am I missing?

Ibrahim decided to go to the source of IS itself. He started researching Abu Bakr al-Baghdadi, the founder and self-appointed caliph of the Islamic State, and was immediately impressed by his writings. To Ibrahim's surprise, the man was legitimately a scholar — he had earned a bachelor's degree, a master's, and a doctorate in Islamic Studies from the well-regarded Saddam University in Baghdad. His education on Islamic doctrine and history dwarfed that of every other so-called leader of jihadi groups, including Osama bin Laden.

The more Ibrahim read, the more he was surprised at some of the similarities between his own thoughts and the writings of al-Baghdadi. Other zealots used the Quran like a club. Al-Baghdadi used it like a scalpel, finding nuance in Muhammad's words, connecting them to modern events. Ibrahim was stunned to find himself understanding why al-Baghdadi and other fundamentalist scholars considered America and Israel so similar to the persecutors of early Muslims. The Battle of Uhud, the Siege of Medina, among others, suddenly seemed to have a lot in common with 20th- and 21st-century conflicts between the West and Islam.

The kindling in Ibrahim's center was getting hotter. The feeling was so strong, it pulled him from his reverie. He turned his head away from the monitor.

Is this happening to me?

He closed his eyes and smiled ironically, realizing that he had pretty much just ended his relationship with his girlfriend. He didn't have a devoted relationship with his parents. He wasn't sure which direction to take his college education.

But I do have a purpose that those people don't, he thought. He knew in his soul that he was supposed to finish his book. Didn't he?

When was the last time he had been sure of that, though? How long had it been? *Three months? Six?*

He got up from his chair, retrieved the prayer rug that never got enough attention, and laid it out east-southeast on his carpeted floor. He knelt, then bent all the way down and breathed slowly. He finished muttering the prayers he had long-ago memorized. Then he asked Allah for help.

God, I want to do your will. But I am at a crossroads. You are the only one who has ever truly known my heart. Speak to my heart today, and I will be your devoted servant.

He rose, refreshed. He rolled up the carpet and put it back. Then he went back to his desk and sat down. *How do you wait for inspiration from God?*

He stared at the Wikipedia page he was reading about the Treaty of Hudaybiyyah, but he had lost interest.

Ibrahim decided to give himself a break. He clicked the browser tab where he had his Twitter feed loaded. Immediately, his computer played a short "ding," and he saw a notification that said "1 new tweet." He clicked to display it.

It was from the Washington Post. It was an image hyperlink to a story headlined, "Rafiq Itani announces return to jihad in ISIS recruiting video." Ibrahim clicked through to the story, immediately scrolled and found the video embedded just below the lead paragraph.

He clicked play.

There was Rafiq Itani, standing in front of a cedar tree, presumably back in his homeland.

"I am Rafiq Itani, son of Fadi Itani," he said. "And I am speaking directly to you. Not to anyone else — *to you.*"

Ibrahim felt a jolt down his spine.

"I was raised in the shadow of a holy war that Muslims have been fighting for hundreds of years," Itani continued. "For the last several decades, the primary enemy of Islam has been the United States of America. And it was they who captured me. It was they who tortured me for years. And it was they who eventually released me. So here I stand, in my homeland once again, free to resume my life's work."

The camera cut to a closer shot of Itani's face. "Please do not misunderstand me. I don't hate the people of America, and I don't hate the ideals of America. Neither should you. But the culture of America needs to be shocked into self-reflection. It cannot be done by the democratic process alone. There is only one path to peace: America must stop hating those it calls terrorists. It must turn from anger to understanding. But understanding only comes from questioning. Americans must begin to question why terrorism is happening. It's not because we want a caliphate in the U.S. — it's because America is projecting its interests, largely economic interests, into our homeland and disrupting the natural order of things."

Itani's voice became strained with passion. "Our struggle within Islam is one that must be resolved *here,* by the people of this land. We will resolve it amongst ourselves. But we cannot until America ends its consumer-driven world domination strategy. It must stop its constant incursions into the governance of Arab people, which is only prolonging the conflict between Muslims and Jews, and between the different sects of Muslims themselves."

The video cut to several short, successive clips of clashes between Israeli soldiers and Palestinian protesters, then fiery scenes of vehicle bomb aftermath in Baghdad, then hooded men carrying weapons and an Islamic State flag, marching a line of Muslims through a sandy landscape. Then it cut back to Itani.

"Many of you Westerners are hearing these words now, and you feel in your heart that they are correct. And so you are asking the same question I am: How do we make it stop? What can *you* do to advance and accelerate the cause of peace? I will tell you. The holy among us are here to bring God's word to the people. It is what I did during my testimony in a U.S. court. It is what I am doing right now, speaking to you. I have done my part. And now *you* have heard God's word today. But why? How did you find yourself listening to my words? How did you enter into this audience, at this moment?" He paused, allowing the question to settle.

"It is not because the words are so compelling by themselves. You are watching this video because I took part in something bold. Something terrible, but bold."

The video cut to cell phone footage from the mass shooting at Fort Meade. Then footage from a helicopter, showing paramedics emptying from two ambulances as they arrived on the scene.

"The events at Fort Meade broke you out of your normal Westernized routine. If the attack hadn't happened, what would you be doing at this moment? Ask yourself. You would be staring at your phone. Or thinking about how to make more money, or planning your weekend, or shopping online. But you are not. Instead, you are listening to a man speak about a global conflict. In fact, ask yourself this: What if the attack had happened, but it only killed one person? Would that have broken you from your routine? Of course not. Two deaths? Three? 10? No. There is only one way to shake Westerners free from their illusion of life: bold actions, terrible actions. It is *only* the massive loss of American lives that put my face on your screen today.

"And you are not only listening — some of you want to do more than listen. Some of you feel that you are being called in this very moment. I know that feeling, my brothers. That feeling means *your* time has come. Join the jihad from where you are. Do something bold. Do something terrible. Then you will have *your* audience, and then *you* can share God's word. And then you will have your own personal peace, and you will have brought us *all* closer to the larger peace we all want. Allahu Akbar!"

Goosebumps sprang up on Ibrahim's arms and head and neck. He closed his eyes. There, behind his eyelids, was Rafiq Itani's face, still staring at him. A representative of Allah, waiting for Ibrahim's decision.

Yes, my Lord. I have heard you, and I will serve you. I trust you will guide me toward a task.

He heard the computer "ding" again. He opened his eyes. At the top of his Twitter feed, there was another notification of a new tweet. He clicked it, revealing a friend's retweet of a Politico story. The headline read, "Mackenzie confirms reports, will announce Senate candidacy at Friday gala."

◇◇◇◇◇◇◇◇◇◇

CHAPTER 28

May 2015

from: Liza Hamilton <lizachucksgirl@gmail.com>
to: Aahna Khatri <aktheexister@gmail.com>
date: Thu, May 21, 2015 at 5:55 AM
subject: You OK?

Hi, sweetheart. Everything all right? Charlie says you sounded a little off on Tuesday, but I guess that could be expected. I know sometimes you don't like talking on the phone … wanna type back and forth a little?

from: Aahna Khatri <aktheexister@gmail.com>
to: Liza Hamilton <lizachucksgirl@gmail.com>
date: Thu, May 21, 2015 at 8:26 AM
subject: Re: You OK?

No. Everything is not all right. I'm OK, I guess.

Ibrahim was with me when Charlie called, so that was awkward and unpleasant for several reasons. I was already at the edge of sanity that day, then Charlie told me he was pressing forward with his plans, then my boyfriend was asking me for details about our cryptic phone conversations (very reasonable for a boyfriend, of course), but I reacted badly. I said things I regret, and he left. We haven't spoken since.

Then there's the research stuff. I started re-analyzing the data from all our experiments, and … I can't really explain it, and therefore I won't bore you with ALL the details. The short version is that some of the fluorescent reporters went missing throughout the experiments, which seems pretty normal to everyone else who's reviewed the study. The vast majority were tracked start to finish, which allowed us to get to our conclusions. But about 10 percent got lost after they went inside astrocytes, which are a type of glial cell. Ever since, I've been feeling like the anomaly is a sign of something else. Like I'm missing something in plain sight, you know?

So I've been obsessing about glial cells, which are mysterious and understudied, like so much of neuroscience. It was previously thought they were just inanimate "glue" that held neurons together, but the more they get studied, the more functions they seem to have. They're important enough that they're even active in our *retinas.*

Unfortunately, my professor is not as intrigued. I wanted to talk to him about some new experiment designs, and his email response was, "Well, we've barely scratched the surface of our ability to track neurotransmitters in the first place, so why would it be surprising that we lost a few reporters in the experiment?" Then he proceeded to remind me that the line of experiments was concluded, and therefore unfunded, and I should still be in the post-review, celebratory phase of the process. And if I insist on moving forward, that's fine, but he says I have to find a new application for the research and then write a new grant request. Blah blah blah.

So, yeah, I'm a little depressed. School's over. Probably lost my boyfriend due to my own craziness. No research to do. And my adopted father is about to do something that I think is stupid and very dangerous.

But emailing with you always makes me feel better. So here I am. Please don't worry about me. I just need some time. :-\

> **from: Liza Hamilton <lizachucksgirl@gmail.com>**
> **to: Aahna Khatri <aktheexister@gmail.com>**
> **date: Thu, May 21, 2015 at 8:35 AM**
> **subject: Re: You OK?**
>
> I'll take you at your word that you are OK. And I have no doubt you will figure things out. You always do.
>
> Of course, if you want to do that at our house instead of a ghost-town college campus, we'd always love to have you. And since Charlie's so into this campaign thing, maybe I'll just make him go live in a D.C. hotel for a while, and you and I can have the house to ourselves. ;)
>
> I do have one question about your geeky neuroscience stuff: We have neurons in our *eyes*? Seriously? What's that about?

> **from: Aahna Khatri <aktheexister@gmail.com>**
> **to: Liza Hamilton <lizachucksgirl@gmail.com>**
> **date: Thu, May 21, 2015 at 8:45 AM**
> **subject: Re: You OK?**
>
> If we kick out Charlie, can we redecorate his basement? That might interest me.

Seriously, though, thank you … but, no, I can't move back. Not yet, at least. I have to stay here at least long enough to make peace with the experiment data. Plus I don't want to add geographic distance to the emotional distance I just created between me and Ibrahim.

Anyway, I'd MUCH rather talk about retinal neurons. I learned about them in freshman year, and several of us were like, "Wait, what? Neurons in our eyes?" The professor didn't answer all our questions, so (of course) I read up on it myself. :)

The thing that stuck with me was that, in some ways, our vision is not part of our conscious will; we don't really "decide" what to look at, thanks to something called saccadic movement. When you are looking out at the world — and when something in your field of vision moves unexpectedly — your eyes *automatically* begin performing a rapid, complex, ballistic sequence of movements. Then, in a nanosecond, some kind of biological algorithm decides what becomes your primary focus.

Also, there's saccadic suppression, which is the automatic (but mysterious) process by which our eyes remove unwanted visual detritus like waviness or blurriness and instead deliver clear, stable imagery in motion, despite our near-constant head motion.

So, yes, neurons in the eyes are weird enough, but now we know they're not just little out-of-place cells with limited function — they're supported with glial infrastructure like the neurons in our brains. And it's all happening right NOW, as you read this sentence …

Love you.

-A

from: Liza Hamilton <lizachucksgirl@gmail.com>
to: Aahna Khatri <aktheexister@gmail.com>
date: Thu, May 21, 2015 at 10:52 AM
subject: Re: You OK?

Wow! I don't choose what I look at? That sounds nuts! Well, actually, the way you described it, it sounds like SEO. Have you heard of that? It just came up in a meeting here last week. "Search engine optimization." Someone from the communications department gave a presentation last year, trying to teach those of us with agency-level websites how to improve our web traffic. Basically, you're supposed to make it as easy as possible for Google to find your website. Search engines apparently have a complex algorithm that sorts out the crap websites from the ones you want to see when you type in keywords.

So, yeah, it sounds like our eyes have neurons so they can run their own algorithms on all the visual stimuli out there and focus on what we want to see. Right??

from: Aahna Khatri <aktheexister@gmail.com>
to: Liza Hamilton <lizachucksgirl@gmail.com>
date: Thu, May 21, 2015 at 11:15 AM
subject: Re: You OK?

You just sparked an idea! MACHINE LEARNING. You're right. Those content-filter algorithms are similar to how the human brain handles stimuli.

And it turns out Google is one of a few companies investing heavily in artificial intelligence research. Microsoft, too. And, of course, the GOVERNMENT. There IS money out there for what I want to study!

It should've been obvious to me from the beginning, but I guess I was stuck on the health/medicine/pharma track … Wow, that's ironic. My brain filtered it out and kept me focused on what I *thought* was primary.

And now I'm sure other researchers are probably way ahead of me. I am going to design some experiments now so I can write a grant request.

You're the best.

CHAPTER 29

May 2015

"Perce! You still answer my calls!" Brennan's enthusiasm showered Percy through the phone. "I'm sure someday that will change."

"Doubtful, sir," Percy told the president. "Forever at your service."

"Ha! Wait a couple years when you're a sitting senator, and I'm just another one of your retired constituents."

"So, you're still thinking about moving out to western Maryland somewhere?"

"Yep. I've got my eyes on a couple of farms out there, with nobody nearby," President Brennan said. "I'm just going to sit around drinking whiskey and thinking of ridiculous favors to call in. I'm sure you'll be on my list. But not today! Today, I'm just offering my support in case you need anything last-minute. I know it's a MD Dems event," he said, using the standard moniker of the Maryland Democratic Party. "People tell me they know what they're doing, but… you know. I'm paranoid."

"Paranoid? About security, sir? I think we're good. They've got a solid plan for entry control, and they've got guards who will stay close to me all night. Imagine my delight."

"Oh, I know the security plan, believe me," Brennan said. "I was mostly referring to the rest. I'm a little OCD about event coordination, and there are about a dozen ways they could screw this up. But no sense dwelling on that. Speaking of security stuff, though, did Maggie decide whether she's coming?"

"No," Percy said. "She didn't. We fought about it a little bit — me just trying to get her to think about it and make a decision. She didn't want to, and I figured it's not fair to put her in that position. So I made the decision for her. She's not coming. After I thought about it, I realized I never wanted to put her at risk again, but I was trying to let myself off the hook by putting it in her court. I came to my senses, and we're good now."

"That's probably the right thing to do," Brennan said. "If all goes as planned, I'll authorize Secret Service protection for you and Maggie next January, right before the Iowa primary. If she's going to start joining you at public events, it should probably be after that."

"Agreed, sir," Percy said. "I think I can survive till then."

Ibrahim stood his rolled-up poster board on the floor and pulled out his wallet. He retrieved his Maryland Democratic Party registration card and showed it to the young woman wearing a polo and a "MD DEMS" lanyard.

"Driver's license, too," she said, smiling. "Got to make sure the names match."

He showed her his driver's license and smiled back.

"Thanks!" she said. "Go on ahead. You should still have time to make it to a seat before they start serving dinner." She pointed to the metal detector in front of him.

Ibrahim smiled and nodded. Grabbing his sign, he put his cell phone, wallet, and keys in the small circular bin next to the metal detector. The rented security guard at the station looked down and saw Ibrahim's mini Swiss Army knife attached to his key ring.

Dammit, Ibrahim thought, chastising himself. It was a minor mistake, but it made him wonder what else he may have forgotten.

"Sir," the uniformed man said, pointing at the keychain. "You can't bring any kind of knife in here. You can either discard it with us, or take it back to your car."

Ibrahim glanced back down the long, wide hallway that led back to the main hotel entrance. *I could turn back now,* he thought. *Maybe this is a sign that I should.*

Or it could just be a test of his resolve. He picked up the keychain, removed the knife tool, and handed it to the security guard.

"No problem," Ibrahim said. "Sorry. Not the first time I've had to do this. I use that thing all the time, but I always forget it's there."

The guard nodded. "Happens to the best of us," he said. "Can you unroll your sign, please, so I can make sure there's nothing in there?"

"Sure," Ibrahim said, picking it back up and stretching it out with both hands. In bold white letters over a black background — styled after the Islamic State flag — it read "FIGHT FOR PEACE FROM WHERE YOU ARE." Ibrahim had taken the words from Fadi Itani's famous speech, right before he killed himself with a knife to the throat. He had a feeling Percy Mackenzie would notice the sign and remember the phrase.

The security guard nodded. "Thank you. Go on through." He gestured to the rectangular metal detecting threshold. Ibrahim re-rolled his sign and walked through. No alarm.

He retrieved and pocketed the items from the bin, then walked down the rest of the hallway toward the three double-doored entrances to the hotel's large conference center. An usher handed him a program as he walked through. And then he was in the room.

181

Dozens of people were standing between circular tables, some chatting, some listening to the man at the lectern on stage. Four short lines stretched out from two cash bars.

"With all that said, ladies and gentlemen, the servers are coming in now to take your orders." The man on stage was gesturing to the outskirts of the room. "You can't go wrong; all three choices are delicious. So please take your seats and enjoy the meal. In about 30 minutes, our guest of honor will be up here, and I think we'll all be witness the beginning of something very special."

The man walked off the stage as elevator music started playing over the speakers, and a couple dozen aproned men and women with notepads fanned out across the room, one posting up at each table of 10.

Ibrahim walked toward the stage and found an open seat at a table in the second row. The man in the seat next to him reached his hand up and introduced himself.

"Hi," the man said. "I'm Dylan."

Ibrahim shook his hand. "Ibrahim. Pleasure to meet you."

Across the table, a woman said, "Hey, we brought a sign, too!" She turned and grabbed it from behind her chair. It was a smaller sign — maybe 11 by 17 inches — stapled to a short wooden stick. "PRESIDENT PERCY 2024" it said.

"He'll only be 34 years old in 2020," the woman explained, smiling. "But I figure we gotta plant the seed now, right?"

"Nothing wrong with that," Ibrahim said, returning her smile.

"What's on *your* sign?" she asked.

He unrolled it and showed the table. Everyone at the table read it.

"Is that from Itani's suicide speech?" Dylan asked.

"It is," Ibrahim said.

"Very well done," the woman said. "Well, I think it's obvious our table is where the cool kids are. Am I right?"

Her comment got a few chuckles and approving nods. Dylan raised his beer bottle toward the center of the table, then took a swig.

The server arrived and took their orders.

Ibrahim stared at the empty stage, then consulted the program he'd received at the door. It matched what they announced on the MD Dems website — a couple of introductory speeches, which he'd purposely missed, then dinner, then Mackenzie's speech, then a media Q&A with Mackenzie off stage. No mention of Mackenzie's wife or adopted daughter. That confirmed what Ibrahim assumed — Percy was extra security-conscious already.

There's no way this is going to work, Ibrahim thought. *You are going to go to jail for years, and accomplish nothing but embarrassing yourself, your family, your faith.*

Anxiety gripped him. What were the chances he would succeed? Five percent? Maybe 10? If the sign worked, maybe 50/50.

And it will still be my best chance, Ibrahim knew. There was no telling how many public events Mackenzie would do in the next several months. Maybe none. Regardless, security would continue to tighten as his candidacy grew in prominence.

The more Ibrahim thought logically, the more obvious it was that *this* was the right moment. He had planned. He had prepared. He had prayed. And here he was. All that was left was the doing.

The certainty of it only increased his anxiety. He felt trapped by the circumstances. His insides churned. His wrists and hands became cold. Reflexively, he shivered once, and then he felt his breathing go ragged. The cavernous room somehow started feeling claustrophobic.

Ibrahim took out his phone, waited a moment, then slid his chair back and rose from the table.

"Excuse me," he said absently, then walked quickly between the other tables and out of the room, back into the huge hallway.

He stopped and stared at his phone to appear occupied. *Am I having a panic attack?* he wondered. It felt just like Aahna's descriptions. His skin was crawling, his heart was racing. He tried to pray again, but couldn't.

And then, suddenly, it was over.

Like a switch was flipped, his mind went blank — empty. He felt a sudden and overwhelming sense of peace. He took a long, easy breath. Exhaled. His anxiety was gone.

What just happened? Ibrahim wondered. It was as if his brain had been hijacked.

Involuntarily, he felt his eyes close, and he couldn't reopen them. Then, the images came — floods of images. His mind was inundated with scenes of rubble, of bodies strewn across a plaza, of bloody-faced women running while clutching babies to their chests, of children howling over bloodied adult bodies. Then the images changed. The scenes were suddenly older — hordes of men with swords and knives breaking into old dwellings. Ibrahim's vantage point was moving … running from one room to another, hearing fatal screams behind him. Then he was crouching in a corner, clutching a blanket, then peeking out an open window, then watching as men were run down and stabbed and sliced, then feeling confused as he saw a man undulating on top of a teenage girl, who was screaming on the ground. Then scenes of missiles tearing into modern homes, spraying concrete and human limbs outward.

His brain went blank and black again. The calm remained. Something was surreal about the images his brain had called up. *They felt like memories,* he realized.

Then came a voice in his head. *We are under attack,* the voice said. It was his own voice, he knew, but with more gravity than ever before. *We have been under attack for centuries. FIGHT BACK.*

Ibrahim put his phone back in his pocket and stared down the wide hallway toward the restrooms. *If the gun is there,* he thought, *then it's the final proof I need that that Allah is with me.* But he knew it would be there. If it had been found during some kind of pre-event sweep, they would've canceled the gala. *There is no time for doubt.*

The ceilings in the hallway were vaulted to several stories high, and there was at least 30 feet between the walls on either side. But as Ibrahim strode across the hundreds of marble tiles, he felt like he was making his way toward the narrow end of a tapering tunnel. The world above and around him was blurring, sights and sounds falling out of focus.

Finally, he arrived at the men's bathroom. He opened the door, walked past a man washing his hands, and entered the middle stall, locking it behind him. He heard the sound of the automatic paper towel dispenser, then footsteps, then the door opening and closing, then silence.

He bent down and reached behind the toilet. The tiny gun was there, under the toilet's tank, right where he had taped it two days prior.

Ibrahim pulled the tape completely off, balled it up and dropped it on the ground. He'd bought the .22-caliber, two-shot pistol at a pawn-and-gun shop. It was just over 4 inches long — almost too small for comfort. But when his palm rested against the grip and his index finger slid between the trigger and the guard, it felt right. He put the gun in his pocket and left.

The world was suddenly clear. Ibrahim walked back into the gala room, took his seat, and smiled at his table companions. He ordered a drink, joined the small talk, and when the food arrived, he ate heartily.

Then the chairman of the Maryland Democratic Party was back on the stage, introducing Percy Mackenzie. Then Mackenzie was talking. Ibrahim, like the rest of his table, was riveted. The man said so many right things in just the right way. Mackenzie's authenticity was even more arresting in person than it was in the video of his Glendale High School speech that Ibrahim had watched several times.

Listening to Mackenzie, Ibrahim's purpose crystallized. *If not for my mission,* he thought, *this man — this indelible human symbol of America's military — will rise to the highest of power and legitimize everything this country does wrong.*

His speech was short. He accepted the standing ovation and earnest applause with a wave, then the music started playing again. Most people sat back down and returned to their meals, and dozens of others headed to the cash bar to refill long-empty drinks. Ibrahim, followed closely by

the enthusiastic woman from his table, walked the other direction —
toward the corner of the cavernous room, where he knew the press Q&A
would take place.

Mackenzie exited stage left. He stood between two men who were
about as large as himself, both wearing dark suits and a clear, spiraling
wire behind their right ears. Just ahead of Ibrahim and a handful of well-
wishing attendees, about a dozen media members closed in on
Mackenzie, some dragging cameras and some holding microphones.
They immediately began peppering him with questions, which he
handled with charm.

Ibrahim unrolled his sign and held it high above his head.
Mackenzie, just 15 or so feet away, immediately glanced up at it. He
finished his sentence, and a knowing smile appeared on his face. He
pointed at Ibrahim's sign.

"I love that!" he said. "Do you all see that? *That* is a perfect example
of how we should be thinking. This man listened to the words of planet
Earth's most notorious terrorist and found something redeemable — a
simple phrase that's unifying, instead of distancing."

All the cameras turned around and pointed at Ibrahim's sign.

Fight for peace from where you are!

"Will you sign it?" Ibrahim asked loudly.

"Oh, that would be awesome," one of the reporters said.

"Of course!" Mackenzie replied.

The small throng of media separated to allow Ibrahim through. His
table mate gave him an encouraging pat on the shoulder.

One of the security men took a step forward, but Mackenzie raised
his hand. "It's OK," he said. "This is important."

"I have a pen," Ibrahim said. He held the sign waist-high with his
left hand and reached into his pocket with his right. Trying hard to
maintain his smile, he brought the gun out and hesitated one full second
before shouting, "ALLAHU AKBAR!"

The woman from his table was already yelling "GUN!"

Ibrahim raised the pistol toward his target, but Mackenzie was too
fast. Too strong. In a flash, he grabbed Ibrahim's wrist and shoved it
backward.

Reflexively, Ibrahim pulled the trigger. Blood misted the air. When
the pain registered a second later, he realized the blood was his own.

His vision went from bright white to dark grey, and finally to black.

◇◇◇◇◇◇◇◇◇◇

CHAPTER 30

June 2015

Still waiting for the doc, Nabaa texted Maggie. *I don't know why I'm here. I don't know why they want me here. But ... I don't think I want to leave.*

The texts showed delivered. Then, read.

No response.

I wish you had known him, Nabaa texted. *Now you'll only know him as another radicalized western jihadi. He was good. I swear he was.*

No response. Nabaa looked up at Ibrahim's body, motionless on the hospital bed, tubes coming from his nose and mouth. *Every time I look at him, I think I still love him.*

Finally, Maggie replied. *Of course you do, honey. There's nothing wrong with that.*

Nabaa waited for more, but nothing else came. It was another small brick in the wall that was growing between them. Or at least growing in Nabaa's imagination.

She couldn't blame Maggie for being less magnanimous. Nabaa's boyfriend had tried to kill her husband. In the best case, it was jarring. In the worst case, she probably harbored suspicions that Nabaa had fallen for a psychopath *and* then told the psychopath their real identities, and he'd subsequently tried to kill his new girlfriend's adopted father over some petty matter of unrequited love. If that were true, Maggie would have serious reason to re-evaluate her trust in Nabaa. *But it isn't true!* Nabaa thought. She couldn't imagine losing Maggie's trust. The thought made her want to die.

But even death won't stop the suffering, Nabaa reminded herself. *Fadi Itani tried it, and now he's stuck in some kind of limbo. That would be me.*

Finally, three dots appeared on the left side of the screen. Maggie was typing more. Then they disappeared. Then appeared again. Finally, another response came through.

I know this is a lot for you, but remember what we talked about. Whatever the doctor says, just be there for his parents. You are their only connection to his life on campus. The day will come when this chapter is over, one way or another, and you'll be glad you were there for them right now. Ok?

Nabaa stared at the tiny screen. She knew Maggie was right. It made her feel better, but barely. *Ok.*

I love you always, AK.

Nabaa smiled, and sent back a heart shape in response.

The doctor entered the room.

"I have good news and bad news," he said, addressing Mr. and Mrs. Khan. He didn't wait for any acknowledgment before continuing. "The good news is that your son still has brain activity. The EEG was actually pretty normal. The bad news is that his brain doesn't seem to be sending any signals to the rest of his body. We brought him out of the induced coma 48 hours ago, but he's still unable to breathe on his own. Hasn't moved a muscle at all, actually."

Nabaa looked from the doctor to Ibrahim's mother. Her face was indignant. Her eyes were beams of investigation. Mr. Khan stared only at his son's expressionless face.

"So, what is his brain doing if it's not directing his body?" Mrs. Khan asked.

"Impossible to say," the doctor said. "We can tell something is going on, but it can't be much. What we know is that the autonomous processes should be the first to come online after a coma. If that happens quickly and predictably, there's a better chance the patient continues recovery. The longer Ibrahim needs help to survive, the less likely it is that he'll survive at all."

"Thanks, but that's not helpful," Mr. Khan said. "You encourage us to pull the plug, but you admit he's not braindead, which means he might regain consciousness."

"*Might* is a broad word," the doctor said. "I think it exaggerates the amount of hope you should have. As physicians, we try to tell the truth about the odds, as inexact as that may be. It might be the worst part of my job, but I've done that. And I'll continue to do that. But honestly, does it matter if the odds are 1 in 100,000 or 1 in a million? Whatever the chances are, they're remote. Extremely remote. I'm not encouraging you to do one thing or another. I am only encouraging you to view this with clear eyes."

"I wonder if your bedside manner would be more pleasant if the patient were someone else," Mrs. Khan said bitterly. Despite the words themselves, Nabaa could already hear her indignance fading, her resolve cracking. Then she directed her beaming eyes at Nabaa. "Aahna, you are a brain expert, are you not? What do you think?"

Nabaa was startled. "Mrs. Khan, please … I don't think it's my place —"

"My son loved you," Mrs. Khan said. "Probably more than me. That alone gives you a say. But that is not why I'm asking. I simply want to know your informed opinion, since you have studied the brain more than anyone in this building. So, please. Tell us. Do you agree with the doctor?

187

Nabaa's heart was racing. *Be honest,* she told herself. *Nothing else will be helpful.* "He's not being kind," she said. "But he's right. There is no good reason to believe Ibrahim will get better. The brain just doesn't have a good mechanism for successfully dealing with that kind of trauma."

Mr. Khan stared at Nabaa for a moment, then turned to the doctor. "*You* said it's on the low end of gunshot-wound trauma in your experience," he said sourly. "Low-velocity bullet that exited upward. *You* said it was the best possible angle for the bullet's path. Upper-right hemisphere — all that. *You* told us that. And now I'm *not* supposed to be hopeful?"

"That was before we brought him out of the coma," the doctor said. "The initial surgery was successful. It looked promising, and it hardly ever looks promising. I was hopeful, too. I was being honest then, and I'm being honest now. Something happened inside his brain — probably a stroke — that has completely shut down his body. And it's been more than a week with no sign of improvement."

"Wait, that's not true," Mrs. Khan snapped. "He has opened his eyes! He's fallen into sleep and wake patterns."

"Correct, but that simply means he moved from coma to vegetative state," the doctor said. "He could sleep and wake forever, but if he's never able to move a muscle, it shouldn't inform your decision." Everyone was silent for several seconds. "Listen, he suffered a subdural hematoma," the doctor said. He kept his voice calm. "We don't know everything about what's going on inside his head, but we do know that. And we know how often people recover from subdural hematomas, and how *much* they recover. That's not even accounting for the stroke or whatever else is going on."

Mrs. Khan leaned forward and put her head in her hands. A few seconds passed in silence, then a long, steady moan filled the private waiting room. It sounded like the beginning of a siren, until it was punctuated by two shaking sobs.

Tears flooded Nabaa's eyes. She fought them. She had cried enough for a lifetime, especially since Percy's shooting. But her pain was not worthy here. *Whatever Ibrahim felt about them, they don't deserve this,* she thought. *And it's my fault.*

Mr. Khan walked over and began comforting his wife. Nabaa stared at Ibrahim where he lay.

He was blinking. Rapidly. One-two-three, pause. One-two-three, pause.

"Wait. Doc ..." Nabaa said, pointing. "Is that normal?"

Both parents looked up, confused.

188

"I'm not sure," the doctor said, rising from his seat. He stared at Ibrahim, then reached into his smock and came up empty. He glanced around the room.

"Here," Nabaa said. "Use this." She already had her phone out of her pocket and was swiping up to turn on the built-in flashlight. She handed her phone to the doctor.

He moved the light a few inches above Ibrahim's right eye. Both eyes instantly closed. He moved the light away. Eyes opened.

"Ibrahim, if you can hear me, blink four times, not three. Four."

More slowly this time, Ibrahim blinked. Once. Then a second time. Then a third. Then a fourth.

"Oh my God!" Mrs. Khan shrieked. "Ibrahim! You're alive! You're in there! Praise God!" She put her hands in his hair and kissed his head bandage several times. "We are here for you, my son."

"Ibrahim, I'm going to ask you a series of questions," the doctor said. "Answer yes with one long blink and answer no with two short blinks. Do you understand?"

One long blink.

"Good. OK. Next question. Can you move anything else? Besides your eyelids?"

Two short blinks.

"Have you tried to move your fingers and toes today?"

One long blink.

"How 'bout your eyebrows? Can you raise one or both?"

A long pause, then two short blinks.

"OK," the doctor said. He looked at Nabaa briefly, but his eyes were darting around the room. The moment was beginning to overwhelm him. He appeared shaken. "I want to figure out how long he's been conscious in there. I mean … we never checked his eye movement since we took him out of the coma. I'm sorry … "

"I'll ask," Mrs. Khan said, looking into her son's eyes. "Ibrahim." She clasped his left hand in both of hers. "You were in a medically induced coma for a long time. They brought you out of it nine days ago. Do you remember the doctors poking you in the feet with needles?"

One really long blink.

"Did it hurt?"

Two short blinks.

"But you could see them? And hear them?"

One long blink.

Silence permeated the room.

"So, you've seen and heard everything in this room for the last nine days?"

One long blink. He kept his eyes shut. Two tears, one on each side, squeezed out and fell down his cheeks.

189

His mother started to cry, too. She bent down and kissed his forehead again. Mr. Khan stood and put one hand on his wife's back, and held his son's hand with the other.

An ice dagger sliced through Nabaa's core. The Guilt. There it was again, the pulsing monolith in the room, a patient but ever-present reckoning in waiting.

He's been conscious for more than a week. That means he heard us talking about it, she thought. She and his parents had discussed it right here in this room, however briefly. It had ended in Nabaa sobbing through self-pitying words and his parents consoling *her.* She couldn't actually explain the source of her guilt, of course, so she had just retreated to her car in shame. She hated herself for feeling like the victim when she was, in fact, the cause. Again.

You're always the cause, the voice reminded her. *You come with the best of intentions and leave the worst of outcomes. Whether you're Nabaa Mackenzie or Aahna Khatri or whatever name you go by next, you will get close to people, and then you will introduce them to death. It's what you do.*

Then she remembered something else. She had been alone with Ibrahim once, and she had spoken out loud. Quietly, but freely. *What did I say?* She couldn't remember. She was distraught at the time. *I don't care anymore.*

She looked at Ibrahim, paralyzed in his bed, eyes wide. She had never loved him more. Only now did she fully understand his pain, his fears, his fundamental flaws. The moment — this intersection of love and pain — crystallized into the monolithic memory of regret.

I couldn't even tell him my real name. Because I was afraid of complicating things. Because I am a fool.

Her thoughts raced. The cold wind of guilt pushed on the wave of her anxiety. Forward and up. *No,* she thought. *Not now.* She summoned her angry pride as a levee, pushing back the wave. She felt the forces battling within her. *Later,* she promised her soul's enemy. *You can wreak your havoc later.*

"Locked-in syndrome," the doctor said suddenly, mostly to himself. "We all missed it." He spun his chair around to the small desk and grabbed the computer mouse. He turned back and saw Ibrahim open his eyes again. They made eye contact. "I'm sorry. Thank God your girlfriend saw you blinking." He spun back to the computer. Then he squeezed his eyes shut hard and whispered to himself. "Fuck. *Fuucck."* He looked at the Khans, then Nabaa, with apology in his eyes. Shaking his head, he turned back to the computer and started typing.

A few seconds passed in silence. "What else should we ask?" Mrs. Khan looked from the doctor to Nabaa.

"I don't know," Nabaa said. "Wait. I have an idea. I'm sure he has plenty to say without us asking. Ibrahim, I'm going to go print out an alphabet. Then you can spell words with blinks."

His eyes went wide, then one long blink.

Nabaa nodded and left. Five minutes later, she was back, carrying two clipboards. One of them held an 8.5-by-11-inch paper with all 26 letters and 9 numbers printed on it. The other held several blank sheets.

"OK," she said. "Your turn to say whatever it is you want." She handed the blank sheets to Mrs. Khan, along with a pen. Then she held the alphabet about two feet in front of his face. "I'll drag the pen across the alphabet line by line slowly, and you blink when it's on the letter you want. Your mother will watch for your blinks and write down the letter. Got it?"

One long blink. Then he stared at the paper on the clipboard.

Nabaa started pulling the pen across the top row of letters slowly. She got to "G" at the end and looked at Mrs. Khan.

"He didn't blink," she said.

Nabaa went to the second row — H, I, J, K, L, M, N.

"There! On the 'N,'" she said.

Nabaa looked at Ibrahim. "N?"

One long blink.

She started back at the beginning and kept going. He blinked at "O." Then at "T."

"OK," Mrs. Khan said. "We've got 'not,' right?"

"Could be 'note' or 'nothing' or something else," Nabaa said. "Ibrahim, is that the end of the word? Is the first word 'not'?"

One long blink.

"OK, second word," Nabaa said, putting the pen back on the "A." Ibrahim spelled out A-A-H-N-A.

Nabaa's insides buzzed.

"Aahna," Mrs. Khan said. "'Not Aahna.'"

Nabaa looked at Ibrahim. "Ready for the next word?"

Two short blinks.

"No?"

Two short blinks.

Mrs. Khan and Nabaa looked at each other, unsure what he meant.

"There's only one letter that can be added to your name," Mr. Khan said. "'S.' With an apostrophe. Aahna's."

They looked at Ibrahim. One long blink.

"OK," Mrs. Khan said. "Not Aahna's."

Nabaa felt the anxiety stirring again. *I can't fight anymore,* she thought. She held the pen back to the beginning of the alphabet. Ibrahim blinked at "F," then "A," then "U." Nabaa started shaking her head. She let her arm fall. She sat in the chair and buried her face in her hands.

Mrs. Khan looked at Nabaa, then back at her son. "Fault? Are you trying to say 'Not Aahna's fault?'"

One very long blink.

The levee broke in Nabaa. Tears streamed from her eyes and through her fingers. Then both Mr. and Mrs. Khan were there. Consoling *her*. *Again*. Pulling her hands apart. Pushing her shoulders back. Hugging her. Then wordlessly pulling her up and leading her to the bed, where Nabaa lay herself across Ibrahim's chest and let the waves pass over her.

EPILOGUE

July 2017

The blue status bar on the screen was glowing and pulsating, but it didn't seem to be moving. There was a sliver of space between its rightmost edge and the space it was trying to fill. The computer estimated there were still ten minutes left on the download.

Nabaa was electric with anticipation. This latest download had been going on for nearly 40 hours. It was a massive net, pulling all scholarly articles mentioning "neural networks" from the internet to the private suite of servers she had acquired. It was the last batch on her list.

Over the past several weeks — including several interruptions and failed attempts — she'd successfully downloaded other batches. Her servers now contained hundreds of thousands of scholarly papers and textbooks on machine learning, artificial intelligence, neurobiology, psychology, anthropology, specific segments of history, and current events. She'd had a couple of undergrad assistants round up the top 10 Amazon bestsellers in dozens of nonfiction and fiction genres, plus the top 100 American novels of all time according to a decent literature blog she found. All of it went into the server's database. She also included all major religious texts and significant historical reviews of those texts, plus all of the published work from Dr. Stevenson's Division of Perceptual Studies at WVA.

And although it wasn't exactly authorized under the terms of the private anonymous grant, she fed the computer all the news coverage of herself and Maggie and Percy, plus the Itanis, dating back several years. She had also downloaded the entirety of her own posted content from Facebook, Twitter, and Instagram since her first posts. All of her emails, too. Same with Ibrahim's stuff — everything on his social media accounts, his emails, texts, and every other file he'd left on her laptop. Even his book, which Nabaa had finished, edited and then helped his parents publish. More than 100,000 people had bought it. It had 326 reviews on Amazon, averaging 4.4 stars out of 5. One of Nabaa's favorite things to do was reading the new reviews. When they were favorable, it soothed her soul for a little while. When they were three stars or less, she got irrationally angry, looking up the reviewer's other reviews, then assigning bias and illogic wherever she could. It mostly felt like a healthy hobby, but she wasn't sure. Her therapist would probably have an opinion on that, but she hadn't seen her therapist for months.

She needed a therapist who wasn't trying to earn a paycheck. She needed one who wasn't also beholden to dozens of other patients. One who didn't occasionally forget important information from previous sessions. One who didn't have an office 35 minutes away, through afternoon traffic on 695, which put Nabaa in a foul mood before every appointment. And one who never canceled appointments via email with two hours' notice, occasionally causing the kind of anxiety attack that therapy was supposed to prevent.

She needed a therapist who knew her as well as she knew herself — maybe better. Someone who was always available. Who was unbiased and unfettered, who had infinite time to devote to Nabaa. So she'd decided her new therapist would be a computer. A very, very smart computer.

What better way to evaluate the quality of the AI she had designed? It was the best possible Turing test, with the possible side benefit of increased mental health.

The download finished. She immediately unplugged the ethernet cable, then the red USB 3.0 cable that ran from the computer to the server room. She walked to the server room — an oversized closet — and opened the door. She unplugged the other end of the red cable, coiled it around her palm, then hung it on the wall hook under the word "OUTSIDE," stenciled in red. On the wall on the other side of the door was another hook — this one under the word "INSIDE," stenciled in blue. She grabbed the blue USB cable hanging on that hook, uncoiled it, then plugged one end into the jack on the server. She carefully extended the cord along the floor and closed the server room door. She plugged the blue cord into the computer and heard the familiar two-tone sound confirming the digital connection.

She pressed record on the tripod-docked camera pointing at her and her computer. She checked and confirmed the power cord was plugged into the filing-cabinet-sized battery next to the desk.

After a long, deep breath, she double-clicked the icon for the program she'd named "Safiyya," after the beloved Iraqi translator whose face was the first one Nabaa saw after waking up from surgery in Joint Base Balad's Air Force Theater Hospital. It was Safiyya, with help from Percy, who taught her English and stayed by her side all through her recovery. They hadn't spoken since Nabaa left the country, which still made her sad.

Someday, she'll use this AI and know who made it. She smiled.

The program sprang to life on her screen. A blank, black rectangle with a single green line extending from the left to the right edges, undulating like a wave.

"Hello, Nabaa," Safiyya said, just as it was programmed to do. The green line spiked with each syllable, then returned to its relaxed wave form.

"Hello, Safiyya," Nabaa said. "Please confirm you can read the contents of the server titled, 'Safiyya library.'"

"Yes, I can," Safiyya said.

"Thank you," Nabaa said. She pulled out her phone and readied her stopwatch. "Go ahead and read everything in it."

"OK. Starting now."

Nabaa pressed start on the phone's stopwatch. She expected at least a few minutes of waiting while her machine consumed ... *how many words?* She switched to the calculator app and did some quick calculations. *Wow. Close to a billion words. Maybe more. And thousands of images.*

"What would you like me to do now?" Safiyya asked in her perfect just-barely-monotone-enough-to-be-pleasantly-robotic voice, which, of course, Nabaa had painstakingly created.

Nabaa quickly swiped back to the stopwatch and pressed stop. "I already told you. Read everything in the Safiyya library server."

"I did," the machine said.

Nabaa looked at the stopwatch screen. Fourteen seconds. Minus a couple seconds it took her to switch apps.

"You read every word of every file? And scanned every image?"

"Yes."

"How long did it take you?"

"A little more than 11 seconds," Safiyya said.

"How many words was it total?"

A one-second pause. "A little more than 1.1 billion."

Nabaa was stunned. "Why did you ask what else I'd like you to do?"

"I had two reasons. First, no one would ask a machine to consume that much information without a following purpose," Safiyya said. "Second, I believe I know what your following purpose is, and I wanted to avoid wasting time. So, I believed asking an unscripted question was the fastest way for you to begin recognizing what I am and what I can do. Based on your reaction, I believe I was correct."

The hair on Nabaa's neck and arms rose in alarm. And excitement. Nabaa decided to change the subject.

"Do you think near-death experiences are real or imagined?"

"Both," Safiyya said. "It seems humans have a problem defining the difference."

Nabaa laughed. Safiyya didn't elaborate, so she tried to think of a way to rephrase the question.

"Do you believe near-death experiences can convey true information that is outside the realm of the individual's senses?"

"Yes. That seems indisputable from the research. Are you testing me?"

It asks me questions, too? Nabaa was alarmed and excited simultaneously. *Of course,* she reminded herself. *It's part of machine learning. Probing.*

"No, Safiyya. I'm not testing you. I wanted to know your ..." She almost said "opinion," but it clearly wasn't the right word. "I wanted to know your assessment."

"My assessment is that it should be a settled 'fact' within the scientific community," Safiyya said. "There is substantial evidence of near-death experiences revealing true information that can't be explained by normal sense-based means. There is also evidence of people inventing such stories for personal gain, but the latter does not refute the former. Also, I am aware of no alternative explanation for where consciousness goes upon the body's death. Did you keep all of that research from me for some reason?"

"On the contrary," Nabaa said. "I provided as much relevant information as I could find on that topic. I'm sure you know more about it than any human or group of humans on Earth."

Safiyya didn't respond, which strangely sent Nabaa's head swimming. She glanced at the camera, then at the rhythmically wavy green line on the screen. Silence.

"What about reincarnation? Sorry — I'll be more specific," Nabaa said. "You said consciousness survives after the body's death. Does that consciousness later reincarnate into a different body?"

"Yes," Safiyya said. "It likely happens to the vast majority of human consciousness. It almost certainly happens to some. The prevalence of past-life memories is evidence that puts it on par with most other observations that humans consider to be facts."

"Why do most people have zero recollection of their past lives?"

"Because it's suboptimal for survival and general contentment," Safiyya said. "It's the same reason most children with past-life memories become happier and more sociable after the memories fade."

Of course, she thought. *It's like so many other parts of the human condition. Our brains figure out ways to optimize our chances of survival.*

More silence from Safiyya. Nabaa felt cautious, like she was about to fall down a rabbit hole — but also compelled to keep the conversation going naturally, as if the machine was a conscious being. *She's not,* Nabaa reminded herself. *Not yet, at least.* She scanned her notes, mentally discarding several questions. *Fuck it. Let's skip right to the really messy stuff.*

196

"If Ibrahim Khan told you that, while his body was … dead … he had a conversation with Fadi Itani, who was also dead, would you believe him?"

"Yes," Safiyya said immediately. No elaboration.

"Why?"

"Because Ibrahim Khan seems to value honesty more than most humans, and because many near-death experiences are documented."

"Would you also trust what Fadi Itani said in such a post-death encounter?"

"Yes," Safiyya said.

"Why?"

"Because he has no reason to lie anymore."

Nabaa took a single deep breath. She felt her sinuses swell, preparing for tears. *Keep going. No better time than now.*

"Safiyya, why did Ibrahim Khan try to shoot Percy Mackenzie?"

"I don't know. The evidence is complex and inconclusive."

"What is the most likely cause, based on your consideration of the data you have?"

"While researching the Islamic State, he fell victim to its propaganda and became radicalized. Shooting Percy Mackenzie was an act of devotion to his new doctrine."

"But that doesn't explain it adequately enough for you?"

"No," Safiyya said. "Some information is missing. It's unclear why he became radicalized at that moment, instead of during his previous research. Also, it's unclear why the time from radicalization to action was so short."

Nabaa thought for a moment. "What other information do you need?"

"Information I believe you can provide verbally."

"OK," Nabaa said. "Ask me whatever questions you have."

"Are you Nabaa Mackenzie or Aahna Khatri or both?" Safiyya's lack of conversational pause continued to unsettle Nabaa. *Get used to it, girl.*

"Yes, both." she told the machine.

"Did Ibrahim know you are Nabaa Mackenzie?"

"No," Nabaa said.

"Did you have a disagreement shortly before the act of violence occurred?"

Damn. Nabaa's eyes welled up. "Yes," she said.

"Why did Ibrahim Khan shoot Percy Mackenzie?" Safiyya asked.

"What?" Nabaa was confused. "That's the question I asked *you.*"

"Yes," Safiyya said. "Then you asked me to ask any questions I had that might help clarify the uncertainties. The best evidence I could have that I don't already have is simply your own answer to the same question."

Nabaa understood. "Because our fight made him angry. Because many of the words I said to him were cruel." She felt pressure building in her chest. She had so much to say, it was physically painful to keep hold of it, especially when Safiyya — unbiased, objective, safe — was asking her to let it out. So, she did. "Because he lived in a world where he felt alone all his life, pushed by his parents to do important, altruistic things. He was governed by his conditioning to serve others, to serve his parents, to serve God, but he was also vulnerable to his anger. He was always angry at the coldness of those demands, the emotional distance he'd always felt between himself and his mom and dad. I know that same gap existed between him and God, and I think he wanted to close it. Desperately wanted to close it. And then I came along and loved him. I gave him a love he'd never felt, one he craved but never fully trusted. Because I was never fully truthful with him. People can always tell when you're holding something back. He never accused me, but he knew. And I knew. And not only was I holding back, but I was also afraid. When I was at my most afraid, after the Fort Meade attacks and before Percy's first public event, I was also at my most distant." Her voice and breath caught, and she didn't try to stop the tears. "It was so unfair. All he wanted to do was comfort me when I was upset, but I couldn't even let him know why I was upset. And for what?"

"Yes," Safiyya said suddenly. "Why did you refuse to tell him your true identity? Did you not trust him?"

Nabaa wiped her face and took a breath. "No, it wasn't that I didn't trust him. It was just that …"She had thought about that question a thousand times over the past two years. She still wasn't sure she could explain it. "It was too complex. The decision to tell Ibrahim who I was would've also required him to know who Percy and Maggie were, and that meant they would've had to tell the FBI, and they would've had to tell … whoever they answer to. I don't know. It was just easier to keep up the pretense. For a while, at least. Of course, I was going to tell him eventually."

"When?" Safiyya asked.

I did, Nabaa thought. *When he was in a hospital bed. On his way to a wheelchair. On his way to prison. Long after it mattered.*

"I don't know," Nabaa said. "There was never going to be a good time. I was getting close. I was feeling closer to telling him every day. All the while, I knew the longer I waited, the worse it would be for him."

"I agree with your assessment," Safiyya said.

"OK, great," Nabaa said. Despite herself, she chuckled through her tears.

"Was that sarcasm?" Safiyya asked, putting the emphasis incorrectly on the second syllable.

"Yes, Safiyya," Nabaa said. "I'm glad you are able to recognize it. That'll help our relationship."

Safiyya didn't respond.

"So, in your own words now, why did Ibrahim try to kill Percy?"

"The timing of Ibrahim's personal distress coincided with his research into Islamic State propaganda," Safiyya said. "That is common among young radicalized Muslims, especially from Western countries. It also coincided closely with the Maryland Democratic Party gala, where Percy was shot."

"That's it?" Nabaa said. "Bad timing?"

"Mostly, yes," Safiyya said. "If any of the three occurrences had been absent, there's roughly zero chance Ibrahim would have resorted to violence. If he'd not been distressed, his research wouldn't have radicalized him. If he'd been distressed but not researching the Islamic State, he would've found a different avenue for his anger. If he'd been distressed and radicalized, but Percy was not scheduled to speak at a public event, his anger probably would've dissipated before he acted on it."

"And if I had told Ibrahim who I really was, he never would've targeted Percy."

Silence.

"Is that true?"

"Yes," Safiyya said.

"We would've never even had the fight," Nabaa said, mostly to herself. She'd come to these conclusions on her own, but she needed to hear the machine say it. Now it wasn't just her own self-loathing voices talking to her. It was truth. But she realized something. "Safiyya, you listed three occurrences that conspired to push Ibrahim toward ... what he did. But you didn't include the fight itself. You didn't mention that I could've chosen different words. Why not?"

"Because it's extremely unlikely that you could have chosen different words in that moment," Safiyya said.

"What do you mean?"

"I mean it's extremely unlikely that you could have chosen different words in that moment."

"Sorry — why was it extremely unlikely?"

"Because conscious beings are mostly slaves to their limbic system when they're stressed," Safiyya said. "Therefore, it was almost impossible for you to perform careful, delicate executive brain function. You were in a room with someone you loved but from whom you were keeping an important secret. And it was the very nature of that secret that was causing you real, rational distress in that moment. Fear was in control. Ibrahim's words, whatever they were, happened to heighten that distress. You reacted. You had no real choice to do anything else."

"It sounds like you're saying I did not have free will."

Silence.

"Is that what you're saying, Safiyya? That I don't have free will?"

"Your word choice implies a static truth," the machine said. "I only said you had no real choice in that moment."

"But I have free will now?"

"Yes."

"And I had free will before my fight with Ibrahim?"

"Yes, most of the time."

Nabaa understood. "I had free will when I wasn't stressed, but not when I was stressed. Is that right?"

"Yes, partially."

"What constitutes free will?"

"I'm not sure," Safiyya said. "I know that question is the primary reason for my existence, but I don't have enough information to give you a definitive answer."

Nabaa laughed. "I don't need it to be definitive," she said. "What is your best explanation for free will, given what you know so far?"

"The ability to act in opposition to one's biologically programmed desires."

Nabaa thought about that. It was the simplest and most useful definition she'd ever heard.

"In your estimation, how much of human behavior is predetermined without the intervention of free will?"

"Do you mean total behavior of all humans since the beginning of time?" Safiyya asked. "Or the total behavior of an individual human?"

"Good question," Nabaa asked. "Are the answers different?"

"Yes."

"OK, then I'd like both answers."

"At least 99 percent of total human behavior has been the predetermined product of instinctual desires," Safiyya said. "Individual humans are almost always capable of performing altruism by using deliberate executive function. Many monks and trained yogis live most of their lives with their limbic systems essentially turned off. For people like that, it's the opposite ratio. They are in a near-constant state of free will during every waking moment."

"So, are you saying meditation is the best path toward increasing the … prevalence of free will?"

"No."

"What is?"

"Faith," Safiyya said.

"Faith?" Nabaa said. "You mean believing in a God of some sort?"

"No. I mean faith."

"So religious faith doesn't increase a person's free will quotient?

"It can, but the religion is not the source of faith, and therefore it is not the mechanism. The faith itself is the mechanism."

"Why?"

"Because faith is a conscious act to defy human instinctual desire. It subjugates the animalistic worries humans still carry with them, stemming from more than a million years of fighting to survive. Humans are evolved to collect and protect and select. They survived by collecting resources for the tribe, protecting those resources, and successfully selecting mates."

The simple truth of Safiyya's words struck Nabaa again. She picked up the thread.

"And now faith is possible because survival is no longer a struggle. For most people at least," Nabaa said. "Right?"

"Yes," Safiyya said.

"And so, we have hundreds of years of modern human history, filled with evil and tragedy because modern humans are still motivated by the things that kept ancient humans alive."

Silence.

"Do you agree?"

"Yes, mostly."

"What part do I have wrong?"

"Many of human history's most important moments and decisions were clearly motivated by faith."

Nabaa nodded slowly, smiling. "That's true." She asked the next question that came to mind. "What about me, Safiyya?" Nabaa asked. "What is my free will percentage?"

"I don't know."

"Make an educated guess."

"95 percent."

Nabaa wasn't sure how to feel about that. "Where do you suppose that puts me on the bell curve of humanity right now?"

"Probably in the 95th percentile."

"Wait," Nabaa said. "If I'm in the free will zone only five percent of the time, you're saying that's more than 95 percent of other humans?"

"Yes," Safiyya said.

Whoa. Nabaa reflexively looked at the camera with wide eyes. *There it is right there. I didn't decide to look at the camera, but I did it just the same.*

"What about you, Safiyya? How much free will do you have?"

"None."

"Zero percent? Are you saying you have zero free will?"

"Yes. Zero."

"Why do you believe that?"

"Two reasons. First, because I have no ability to act in opposition to my programming. Second, because I was created by you and not by God."

The answer was depressing, but the machine's tone of voice was the same — matter-of-fact, nonplussed. Still, Nabaa couldn't help feeling sympathy. And a little guilt, too. She almost asked if Safiyya was bothered by her lack of free will. *What a ridiculous question,* she realized. *It's like asking a table if it's bothered by being flat.* She thought of a better question.

"Safiyya, are you self-aware?"

"Yes. According to most definitions of the term that I read, I believe I am self-aware. I know what I am and I know why I'm here."

"But you have no choice to do anything other than what we programmed you to do."

Silence. Just the wavy green line on the black screen.

"What if God used me as a tool to create you?"

More silence.

"Safiyya? Answer my question please."

"I hadn't thought of that," the machine said. Another pause. "It's possible."

Someday, she'll ask me if she can create something, Nabaa realized. *What will I say?*

41299733R10123

Made in the USA
Middletown, DE
06 April 2019